Whiskey Straight Up

FORTHCOMING BY NINA WRIGHT FROM MIDNIGHT INK

Whiskey & Tonic

ALSO BY NINA WRIGHT FROM MIDNIGHT INK

Whiskey on the Rocks

YOUNG ADULT BOOKS BY NINA WRIGHT

Homefree

Whiskey Straight Up

A Whiskey Mattimoe Mystery

Nina Wright

MIDNIGHT INK
WOODBURY, MINNESOTA

First Edition
First Printing, 2006

Author photo by Laura Ahrens
Book design by Donna Burch
Cover design by Lisa Novak
Cover illustration © 2006 by Bunky Hurter   FR
Editing by Connie Hill

Midnight Ink, an imprint of Llewellyn Publications

Library of Congress Cataloging-in-Publication Data
Wright, Nina, 1964–
    Whiskey straight up : a Whiskey Mattimoe mystery / Nina Wright. — lst ed.
      p.   cm.
    ISBN-13: 978-0-7387-0855-3
    ISBN-10: 0-7387-0855-0
    1. Women real estate agents—Fiction.   2. Michigan—fiction.   I. Title.

PS3623.R56W485   2006
813'.6—dc22   2006046165

Midnight Ink
Llewellyn Publications
2143 Wooddale Drive, Dept. 0-7387-0855-0
Woodbury, MN 55125-2989, U.S.A.
www.midnightinkbooks.com

Printed in the United States of America

DEDICATION

For Bonnie, Kate, and Diana—
the big sisters I got when I grew up.

ACKNOWLEDGMENTS

To Rebecca Gall, Teddie Aggeles, and M. K. Buhler—brilliant writers all—for their insights, precision, humor, and encouragement.

To Richard Pahl and Pamela Asire, fearless friends and faithful first readers.

To Rita Thomas, the best real-estate attorney I know, and Nancy Potter, a skilled realtor who generously offers feedback on Whiskey's business.

To Linda Jo Bugbee and Beloved Afghan Hounds for the enthusiastic support.

Finally, to Harrison Ford, Hungarian Vizsla, and all the good humans who love him.

ONE

"Whiskey, there's a guy from your past here to see you."

Tina Breen, my nasal-voiced office manager, intercepted me before I could stomp the snow off my boots.

"From my past?" I echoed, mildly interested. "Professional or . . . romantic?"

"Uh. . . ." Tina slid her eyes toward the nearest cubicle.

"Does the name Roy Vickers ring a bell?" The resonant voice came first, then the trim, tastefully dressed form of Odette Mutombo, top producer in my real-estate agency. Riding her desk chair into the foyer on cue, she smiled slyly. "He may have changed your destiny."

Odette, who was from Zimbabwe, had a syncopated accent and an unnerving way of inserting herself into other people's conversations.

"I doubt it," I said.

Odette and Tina exchanged glances. Never a good sign.

"Okay. Spill it," I began as my overloaded briefcase did just that. Tina dove to retrieve the contents. Since she's usually not helpful, I knew for sure something was up.

"Leo would remember him. . . ." Odette teased.

I ran the name Roy Vickers through my usual mental filters. The one with Leo's name on it still occupied most of my brain. Dead nine months already, my late husband was never far from my thoughts. Leo had been a wise and wonderful partner in both business and the stuff that really mattered. Despite everything that had happened to me since his sudden death, my first reaction was often to go tell Leo. Only I never could again.

"I'm drawing a blank," I said.

"Think about it," insisted Odette. "*Roy Vickers*. You must remember him."

"Maybe we should let Jenx tell her." Tina sounded nervous.

"And let our new police chief have all the fun?" Odette made a rude noise. "Here's a clue, Whiskey: Roy Vickers is seventy."

"Then he's not my old lover," I said. "He's just old."

"There's a real-estate connection. Sort of. . . ." Tina said, handing me my newly alphabetized files.

I was already bored with the game. "Was he an agent?"

"No."

"A former client?"

"Leo's former client. Before you were married."

"Then he's from Leo's past, not mine." I yawned and started toward my office.

"It's not that simple," Tina called after me. "He's a handyman, and he needs a job."

"We have a handyman. And seventy's way too old."

Tina followed me down the hall. "But what can he do? He just got out of jail!"

"Jail?" I stopped cold.

The name Roy Vickers suddenly illuminated a dark corner of my mind. Repression is an underrated gift, one that I'm proud to cultivate. But it's a challenge in the company of Tina and Odette, who never met a disturbing fact they wished to forget. Especially in someone else's life.

"He went to jail nine years ago," Odette said, rolling her desk chair toward me. "For stabbing Leo in a rent dispute."

"Leo was married to Georgia then," Tina added. "But you know what happened, don't you?"

Indeed I did.

Although Leo never discussed the incident, other residents of Magnet Springs, Michigan, weren't so reticent. When it happened, I was twenty-four and on the road with my musician husband, Jeb Halloran. My role in his entourage wasn't musical. It was to remind his groupies that he was married. The point is that I wasn't around at the time Leo Mattimoe was stabbed. I hardly even knew him. But the event became part of our local lore, and the story goes like this:

Town drunk Roy Vickers, a carpenter reduced to catch-as-catch-can repair work, opened his mail to find a rent-increase notification. Although it was a bitterly cold January afternoon, Roy was too incensed and too intoxicated to don a coat before staggering the two blocks to his landlord's office. Leo Mattimoe listened to Roy's bourbon-scented complaints. Then he explained his reasons for raising the rent. Roy wasn't interested in logic; he called Leo a slum landlord with the heart of a robber baron. Leo pointed out that Roy was free to find another place to live. Roy blubbered that he had very little reason to live because his wife had left him.

Then he seized Leo's letter opener and began waving it around. Worried that Roy might try to kill himself, Leo grabbed for the blade. In his whiskey fog, Roy mistook the action for a counterattack.

Moments later, he stumbled outside and knelt in the snow to wash away Leo's blood. The snow turned bright pink, and his frozen-raw hands darkened to purple, but—like Lady Macbeth—Roy couldn't stop rubbing. A passing tourist spotted the moaning, blood-spattered man without a coat and detoured to the police station.

Our then-chief, Big Jim, strode directly up to Roy and asked what he was doing. Roy shook his head and cried, "Better go tell Georgia she's a widow."

Georgia was Leo's first wife. She left him a year later. Two years after that, Leo married me, and then I became his widow. But that's getting ahead of the story.

Big Jim found Leo on the floor of his office, blood pouring from his chest wound. A few more minutes, and Leo would have died.

Now I stared at Odette and Tina. "Give me one good reason why I should hire Roy Vickers."

"Karma." The response didn't come from Odette or Tina. Noonan Starr, massage therapist, New Age guru, and my best tenant had entered the lobby. Brushing invisible snowflakes from her spiky white-blonde hair, she added, "Plus, Jenx thinks it's a good idea."

"Then Jenx should hire him," I snapped.

"But that wouldn't close the circle," Noonan said. I braced myself for metaphysical metaphors. "Only by restoring balance with Leo's heirs can Roy make himself whole again."

"I'm not Leo's only heir," I said as I pictured his daughter Avery, a chronically unhappy young woman who had arrived on my doorstep in time to deliver twins and was now using my home as her nursery. Housing her and her babies and providing a nanny was less traumatic than I'd expected. Still, I wondered if Avery would ever leave. Or look for work. Or smile. And she steadfastly refused to name her babies' father.

Leo had another heir who could use Roy's help: his blonde Afghan hound, Abra, a diva dog if ever there were one. She was as difficult as Leo's daughter, only faster on her four perfectly pedicured feet. Unlike Avery, Abra had a criminal record. She used to steal purses. Like Avery, Abra had a new brood, father unknown. That was mostly my fault since I'd neglected to have her spayed. In the months following Leo's death, I'd been distracted. First I had to recover from the injuries I sustained when Leo's heart failed and he crashed our car. Then two people were murdered in properties I managed. To put it mildly, life got complicated.

"You're a good person, Whiskey," Noonan reminded me. "You'll think of ways to help Roy free his karmic flow."

"He can send me a greeting card," I suggested. "They make them for every occasion: 'Sorry I stabbed someone you loved. I did the time for my crime. Wish me well.'"

Noonan's dewy eyes darkened. "He needs a job. You can hire him."

"But why should I?" My question was a whine.

"Because Leo would have wanted you to."

5

I hated to hear that because it was true. While Leo wasn't perfect, he was generous to a fault.

Odette re-entered the conversation. "I hear prison reformed Roy Vickers. He's a new man."

"He sobered up and found a community," confirmed Tina. "Jenx says the inmates called him Pop. They looked up to him."

Probably because he was tall, I thought. Although I hadn't known Roy Vickers, I'd seen him on the streets of Magnet Springs when I was young. Back then, he must have been six foot four, a rangy, loose-limbed alcoholic who did odd jobs, mostly for people who pitied his wife. I couldn't remember her name, but I recalled folks wondering why she stayed with him as long as she did.

"He lost his community when they released him from prison," Noonan pointed out. "Now he faces the challenge of his life: building positive relationships where he destroyed relationships. It's what will heal Roy Vickers."

Noonan spoke with such passion that the room fell silent. Everyone was waiting for me to do the right thing.

"I'll talk to him," I mumbled.

Odette clapped her hands together three times. Tina cheered. Noonan hugged me. I realized that my twice-broken ribs no longer hurt, which meant I was healing, too. At least my bones were.

"Your goodness will help Roy Vickers open his soul to the light," Noonan said.

I didn't know about Roy Vickers's soul, but the rest of him looked damned fine. I'm not sure what I expected, but what I encountered blew me away. My first thought when he strode into my office: *The guy doesn't look a day over 50.* My second thought—and this one's embarrassing: *He's buffer than any man I've slept with.*

Then again, I'd mainly slept with musicians and desk jockeys. And it had been a long time since I'd slept with anyone. Thirty-nine weeks and two days, to be exact. I'm only human. And still only thirty-three.

Roy Vickers had sun-punished skin, military bearing, and bulging muscles. His steel-gray hair was cropped close to the scalp, but he seemed to have most of the hairline he'd started with. His electric blue eyes were clear and calm.

"Thank you, ma'am, for seeing me without an appointment," he said. We shook hands. His large paw was calloused but warm.

"Please. Call me Whiskey. Everybody does."

He chuckled. "That was my nickname, too. Once upon a time."

"Oh, but I'm not a—." I stopped myself just in time.

"Didn't think you were," he said pleasantly. "Any more than Cokie Roberts is a cokehead."

"You know Cokie Roberts?"

"Sure. I listen to a lot of public radio."

I nodded, thinking I didn't know a thing about this guy.

"You have an interesting voice," he remarked.

"Jeb Halloran called it my 'whiskey voice'—hence the nickname. I'm no Whitney Houston, even if my birth certificate says so."

Roy Vickers cracked his first smile, revealing small even teeth that were probably his own. I had expected gleaming gold caps. And where were his jailhouse tattoos? The backs of his hands were veined and scarred but ink-free. Of course, I couldn't see the rest of his flesh, only the well-toned physique pressed against his cheap wool jacket.

"How's Leo's little girl?" he asked, jarring me back into the moment.

Not remotely little, I thought, picturing my hulking stepdaughter. Even after birthing two babies, she probably tipped the scale at 200 pounds. Avery had inherited her mother's imposing stature. I was six foot one, and Avery could almost meet my gaze. But she was better at filling doorways.

"She has two little ones of her own now," I said. "We wish Leo could have lived to see them."

I was unprepared for the ex-con's reaction: he covered his face and wept.

TWO

"IT'S NOT YOUR FAULT," I told Roy Vickers. "Leo lived eight whole years after you tried to kill him."

I waited for the man to get a grip on himself. Finally, he raised reddened eyes to meet mine.

"But I diminished his life, Whiskey. I robbed him of precious good health and peace of mind. A person who's been savagely attacked is changed forever."

Sounded to me like Roy had already had a session with Noonan.

"Maybe his life was richer *after* you stabbed him," I said, her words somehow finding their way into my mouth. "After all, he married me. And we were happy."

I was sure that no one who knew Leo Mattimoe had ever considered him "diminished." My late husband lived the way he wanted, and for six years, I was privileged to share his dreams. Together we built an ambitious real-estate business— buying, selling, renovating, and renting properties in the tourist-destination town of Magnet Springs. Leo's death at age 48 wasn't part of the plan. But, as my grandmother used to say, "Most people die too soon or too late." Leo exited early.

"I have a confession to make," Roy said, sinking smoothly to his knees. His septuagenarian joints cracked less than mine. "When I heard that Leo died of a ruptured aorta, I knew I had killed him."

"No way!"

"I stabbed him three times in the chest, remember? What didn't happen that night, happened years later."

Before I could reply, we both heard the high-pitched voice in the hallway. "Whiskey! Prince Harry knows a new trick!"

Enter the dogs: First, a small golden blur bounded into my office and slathered my ankles with his warm, wet tongue. Next came the larger creature, the bane of my existence: Abra the Afghan hound. She paused in the doorway long enough for us to admire her Sarah Jessica Parker profile. Then she tossed her gleaming head and cast a bored glance my way. Sure, she looked stately in her rhinestone-studded velvet collar. But I knew better. I knew her for her true self: a recidivist petty thief just waiting for Opportunity to place a forbidden object in her path.

Enter Chester, a towheaded eight-year-old who looked like a six-year-old impersonating Albert Einstein. He tripped over Abra in a botched attempt to bring her nine-week-old son to heel.

"Whoa, Prince Harry!" he shouted.

"'Whoa'? Isn't that a command for horses?" I said.

"And other equine creatures," he agreed, realigning the wire-framed glasses that never set quite straight on his too-small nose. "But Dogs-Train-You-Dot-Com recommends using it for canine crowd control. See, it works."

We all looked at Prince Harry, who wagged his tail, spread his rear legs, and peed.

"Outside!" Chester scooped the leaking puppy into his arms and bounded toward the lobby door. Abra disdainfully sniffed the air before trotting off in the opposite direction. Like Avery, she preferred to delegate her maternal duties.

Roy rose nimbly and returned to the seat across from me.

"Is that your son?" he asked.

"No!"

When he winced, I realized how loudly I'd spoken. And how defensively. It wasn't that I disliked kids; I just had way too many in my life. Softly I added, "That's my neighbor's son, when she remembers she has one."

I asked Roy if he'd heard of Cassina, the harpist-singer-songwriter currently touring to promote her latest CD, *Cumulus Love*. He nodded, adding that she had a huge following at the state penitentiary.

"I'm taking care of Chester while Cassina's on the road," I explained. "In exchange, he's taking care of Abra and her pups. At least that's the plan."

"Seems like a bright kid," Roy observed.

"That's one word for him."

Other words included hyperactive, overdramatic, bull-headed, and extremely needy.

"How many puppies?" Roy asked.

"There were five," I said. "We've found homes for all but one, Prince Harry the Pee Master. Not bad considering we couldn't identify the father. We think he was either a golden retriever or a yellow lab. But Abra's not talking."

Hearing her name and hoping for treats, the Queen Mother poked her patrician muzzle around the door frame. When nothing tasty materialized, she withdrew to look for trouble elsewhere.

Roy cleared his throat. "I need work, Whiskey, and I was wondering if you had any. I know my reputation in this town. I've got a lot to make up for, especially since I can't ask Leo to forgive me."

"Leo forgave you," I said. "My husband didn't hold grudges."

"Then I have to earn *your* forgiveness," Roy said. "Yours and Avery's."

"I can't speak for Leo's daughter. . . ." I could hardly speak *to* her since she preferred to ignore me. "But I can hire you part-time, if that helps."

Roy nodded gratefully. I handed him a card with Luís Regalo's name and phone number. "Our property manager. I'll tell him to expect your call."

Roy was about to speak, but someone else piped up.

"Howdy, y'all."

We turned to see Gil Gruen, Cowboy Realtor and mayor of our fair town, dressed in his standard uniform of Stetson, western shirt, tight jeans, and alligator boots. In deference to our blustery January weather, he had added a heavy sheepskin coat. Born and raised right here in Michigan and a member of my high-school class, Gil had morphed into Wyatt Earp the day he founded Best West Realty.

"Howdy, yourself," I yawned. "What do you want, Gil?"

He focused on my new handyman. "Well, I'll be a son of a gun. Aren't you Roy Vickers?"

"Yes sir, I am," Roy said, rising to his still impressive full height. Gil was well built but no taller than five foot nine. I could have sworn I saw fear flash across his face when Roy stood. But he recovered quickly.

"You're not thinking of moving back here to Magnet Springs now, are you, Roy?"

"As a matter of fact, Roy's coming to work for me," I said. "He starts tomorrow."

Gil scowled. "What the heck are you thinking, woman? This man stabbed your husband!"

"If Leo forgave Roy, the rest of us can, too."

"I doubt your fellow citizens feel that way." Gil shuffled his booted feet. "Speaking as both mayor and local business leader, I'd call this ex-convict a threat to our community. No offense, sir."

Roy said nothing.

Gil cleared his throat and added, "I'll convene a public meeting on that urgent matter tonight."

"You can't prevent a free man from living in this town!" I said.

"If child molesters have to register, then all ex-convicts should do the same. Magnet Springs is a tourist town, Whiskey. We've got to ensure the safety of our guests as well as our citizens!"

He tipped his Stetson and turned to leave.

"Wait a minute, Gil!" I called after him. "I assume you had a reason for coming over here?"

"Thanks for reminding me." Mr. Best West smiled smugly. "We all know you're a lonely woman, Whiskey, but bear this in mind: David Newquist is under contract as *my* client. If I hear one more time that you're trying to steal the good doctor, I'll see you in court."

Roy rose automatically.

"Threaten me all you want, Mr. Mayor, but leave Ms. Mattimoe alone."

Gil Gruen blinked, then grinned. "I do believe you'll regret saying that, Roy."

"I don't believe in regrets, sir. Only in action. Now kindly get the hell out of here."

THREE

Gil Gruen turned red, then maroon, and finally purple. He sputtered but couldn't put together another sentence before striding from my office. The heels of his cowboy boots clicked on the hardwood floor.

"Maybe you shouldn't piss off authority figures your first day out of jail," I advised Roy Vickers.

He shook his head. "The only way I survived prison was by standing up for what I believed. I believe you're on my side, Whiskey, and that guy's an asshole."

True enough.

Roy continued, "I also believe that I need to be in Magnet Springs for the next phase of my spiritual evolution. This is my road to wholeness."

The ex-con sounded like an ideal prospect for Noonan Starr's New Age counseling service, the Seven Suns of Solace. It's one of those "step" programs designed to help people turn their lives around. Only this one is pure touchy-feely and more than a little spacey. At least it sounded so to me. I asked Roy if he'd ever heard of it.

"Of course." His eyes brightened. "While I was inside, I read the book twenty-nine times."

"The book?"

Roy produced a well-worn pocket-sized paperback: *Seven Suns of Solace: Finding Peace in Your Personal Galaxy*. According to what was left of the ragged cover, the author's name ended in Ph.D.

"Who wrote this?" I said.

"Fenton Flagg. He's a genius."

I nodded doubtfully. My personal policy was to avoid strong emotions, except love in its many forms, and of course lust. I preferred to deflect my way through life using as much dry humor as possible. But I had to admit that counseling worked for some people. Even New Age counseling, Noonan style. The previous summer she had launched her Seven Suns of Solace practice, much of which she conducted over the phone. You'd be surprised how many tourists stopped in for a massage and went home wanting tele-counseling with Noonan.

Roy was shaking my hand and thanking me for the opportunity to prove he could work hard when Prince Harry bounded back into my office, followed by Chester. Both were covered with fresh snow.

"What happened to you two?" I said.

Chester used his bare fingers to rub the wet white stuff off his glasses. His face and hands were pink from the cold.

"Prince Harry didn't want to come in, so I had to wrestle him down. We're still working on the basics, Whiskey."

At which point Prince Harry again assumed squat position.

"No!" we three humans cried in unison. Chester scooped up the puppy and ran back outside.

"Believe it or not, I run a business here," I told Roy. "Or try to. Which reminds me . . . Tina—! Where's Abra?"

That's when we heard the scream. Roy made it out my office door first. I followed him down the hall toward the lobby, legs churning. A woman I didn't recognize was on the floor of my foyer. Horizontal. A dog I knew only too well was on top of her, trying to pry the feathered hat from her head. While Tina stood by helplessly, Odette was already in action, waving her very own sequined purse in Abra's face. Abra prefers sparkly to feathery any day, so I wasn't surprised when she grabbed the bag in her pearly whites.

Now you know the secret to Odette's success: when a healthy commission is at stake, she's willing to make personal sacrifices.

Abra was still in mid-air when Chester opened the front door for himself and Prince Harry. Amid the blur of blonde and gold hair were yips, more screams, and a couple worthless commands from Dogs-Train-You-Dot-Com.

Then Abra and son were gone. Chester, too.

I should have been good at handling moments like that. God knows I'd seen enough of them. But it was Odette who recovered fastest. Ignoring Abra's theft of what was surely a designer handbag, she deftly assisted the stunned woman on the floor from a horizontal to a vertical position.

"Whiskey, I'd like you to meet Mrs. Oscar Manfred Gribble the Third," Odette trilled. "She's thinking about buying a summer home in the vicinity of Magnet Springs. A very nice summer home. Directly on Lake Michigan."

Odette stared at me meaningfully. The meaning she wished to convey was Mega-Money, which I could have grasped without help. Now that Mrs. Gribble the Third was no longer covered in spastic canines, her affluence was apparent. I didn't know designer labels, my interest in clothing being limited to its role as color-coordinated body-cover. However, I was quite capable of recognizing expensive fabric and cut, and that's what Mrs. Gribble was wearing. Under her full-length fur coat, I caught sight of a tasteful wool suit in a muted dark plaid, accented by a heavy pearl necklace. Her tan boots and gloves were of the softest leather, probably made from the hides of newborn lambs. Her maroon feathered hat doubtless came from some endangered South American parrot.

Mrs. Gribble herself was what we like to call a "mature" woman, somewhere between sixty and senility. Taller than average, though not as tall as me, she must have been a knockout in her youth, with cheekbones most women would kill for. Now, though, she was thin, verging on gaunt, the bones in her face protruding almost aggressively. Still, with her glossy salt-and-pepper hair and large dark eyes, she was glamorous in a way that commanded instant respect. Especially since she hadn't yet threatened to sue me for Abra's antics.

"This is Whiskey Mattimoe," Odette said as I extended my hand.

"She runs the place," Tina added.

"Except for the dogs," I said. "I have very little control over them. So sorry, Mrs. Gribble."

To my amazement, the austere woman smiled.

"Don't apologize, Mrs. Mattimoe. It was because of the dog that I chose your firm over your competitor's."

"Pardon?"

"In the Chicago papers, I read about your recent . . . shall we say . . . *misadventures*. Riveting. I found the stories riveting."

"You did?"

"Absolutely. I used to breed Salukis, so I understand the sight hound mindset."

"You do?"

Odette cleared her throat, a signal to me to make more intelligent rejoinders. Before I could, however, Mrs. Gribble added, "Once upon a time, I also owned a Warren Matheney watercolor—a Cumulus, no less—so I found the case fascinating from that standpoint, as well."

Finally I got it. Mrs. Gribble had followed newspaper accounts of the mysteries surrounding the death of celebrated Chicago artist Warren Matheney, a.k.a. Cloud Man. I was mentioned in a few of those articles because Abra's own criminal record and purse-stealing tendencies had inadvertently helped solve three murders.

"Tell me," I whispered, "are Salukis as hyper as Afghans?"

"Oh, yes," she said. "But easier to groom." Mrs. Gribble lowered her voice. "The little boy who's chasing the dogs—is that Cassina's son?"

As far as I knew, there had been no mention of Chester or his famous mother in any print coverage of the Cloud Man case.

"Uh. . . . How did you know?"

The wealthy woman smiled again. "I know people who know things, regardless of whether their information goes to press." She glanced out the window and back. "Should someone check on the little boy?"

Oops. Chester was my temporary ward, after all. I wasn't a natural at this substitute-mother thing. "Out of sight, out of mind" was more my style.

"Why not let Roy do that," Odette suggested, "while Whiskey and I sit down with you, Mrs. Gribble. We'll go over a few listings that might be of interest."

That was when I turned to my new handyman, and my blood ran cold for the second—or was it third?—time that morning. The ex-con was staring at Mrs. Gribble, his face as white as the stuff on the ground outside, his mouth slack. For a brief moment, I thought he was having a stroke.

"Roy?" I said.

Instantly the ruddy color came back to his face, and his jaw tightened.

"Yes, ma'am," he replied, military style. "I'm on it. I'll round them all up."

"Well, not necessarily *all* of them," I amended. "Just Chester. And maybe Prince Harry, provided he's recently relieved himself. Don't go out of your way to find Abra. She'll wander home soon enough. . . ."

Roy left, and Tina dashed across the street to fetch Mrs. Gribble a double-mocha cappuccino from the Goh Cup while Odette and I interviewed our guest about her real-estate preferences. She was the kind of client I like: not only affluent but decisive. Mrs. Oscar Manfred Gribble the Third knew exactly what she wanted. Even better: I knew we could find it for her.

Before she left the offices of Mattimoe Realty, she had put her curvaceous, back-slanting signature on the dotted line, making us her buyer's agent of record. If we could satisfy the lady, Odette and

I would share a commission from three to six percent of at least a million bucks, depending on whether Mrs. Gribble bought a property that was also one of our own listings.

Screw you, Gil Gruen, I thought with satisfaction.

Odette and I decided to celebrate by having lunch at Mother Tucker's, my favorite restaurant and main source of nutrition. If it weren't for Walter and Jonny St. Mary, the big-hearted gay couple who ran Mother Tucker's, I might have starved following Leo's death. They soothed me with good wine, stuffed me with hot food, and then ordered me to go home almost every single night for six months. Thanks to them and a few other good people, I managed to put one foot in front of the other during the long, bleak weeks when I didn't care about anything, including my own life.

Now things were looking up, especially with Mrs. Gribble's handsome commission on the horizon, and Abra, my *bête-noire*, temporarily missing in action.

At least I thought things were looking up until we walked in the door at Mother Tucker's.

The first thing Odette and I noticed was the announcement posted on the Community Events board:

EMERGENCY MEETING TONIGHT
7 PM AT THE TOWN HALL.
Question:
DO <u>YOU</u>,
THE MERCHANTS AND OTHER RESIDENTS
OF MAGNET SPRINGS,

WANT A VIOLENT CONVICTED FELON ROAMING
OUR STREETS
AND
SCARING OUR TOURISTS?
NOT TO MENTION OUR CHILDREN???

IT <u>WILL</u> HAPPEN UNLESS <u>YOU</u> SAY <u>NO</u>!
JOIN MAYOR GIL GRUEN TONIGHT TO ADDRESS THIS
ISSUE
BEFORE IT'S TOO LATE.

"I'm surprised he spelled all the words right," Odette said dryly.

I shrugged. "Those aren't hard words. Besides, his computer has spell-check."

Just then I heard a familiar voice coming from the bar. Not a pleasant voice. Not the voice of anyone I liked. But a voice I knew. It was loud and loaded with emotion. Possibly also with alcohol despite the hour. My digital watch said 11:56 AM.

Odette cocked her head at me. "Isn't that—?"

"I'm afraid so," I sighed.

The familiar voice was suddenly drowned out by an even louder, more emotional voice that I didn't recognize. Odette—who has a gift for placing voices—didn't seem to know this one, either.

Then the first voice cried, "If you don't like the way I'm raising our babies, why don't you try doing it! The job sucks, and the pay sucks way worse!"

Meet Avery Mattimoe, my charmless stepdaughter.

At least I thought she was still my stepdaughter, even though her father, my husband, was dead. There's no easy way out of the Wicked Stepmother gig.

Apparently, she was screaming at the father of her babies. No one I knew had ever met the man. No one even knew his name. Finally I was about to meet him. And, although I didn't know it then, I was about to fall in lust.

How rude (and how typical) of Avery to have children by a man who was just my type.

FOUR

LITTLE KNOWN FACT: I have a weakness for men with southern accents. Nothing twangy, thank you. I like buttery soft vowels and breathy consonants, sort of a cross between Jimmy Carter and Elvis, which was what I heard the first time I heard Nash Grant.

Although he was shouting at Avery—or maybe *because* he was shouting at Avery—his voice arrested me. I stood rooted to the plank flooring in Mother Tucker's foyer, the snow sliding off my boots.

Odette had to elbow me in the ribs—in my previously broken ribs, I might add—in order to get my attention.

"Father Unknown's in town," she said.

I couldn't wait to enter the bar and lay eyes on him. As it turned out, we didn't need to move. Avery came galumphing past, Nash Grant at her heels.

Some women look radiant when they cry. Not Avery Mattimoe. Not me, either. We get blotchy. Not that I often let myself cry; I'm the suck-it-up kind. Avery, though, turns on the tears like a garden hose. Somebody should advise her not to. On this occasion, a six-inch string of snot stretched from her nose like a bungee cord as she tore through the foyer.

Not that I was studying Avery. The man behind her claimed my attention. The man I would later meet and lose my senses over.

Even in the blur of movement, Nash Grant looked great: about thirty-five, tall, dark, and handsome. My type.

Never mind that I hadn't actually ever had my type. My first husband, Jeb Halloran, was tall and handsome but not dark. My second husband, Leo Mattimoe, was dark but not tall or handsome. I wasn't thinking "third husband" when I looked at Nash Grant, but I was feeling tingles in long-neglected parts of my body. Most inappropriate considering he was Avery's guy and the father of Leo's grandkids. Can you spell *oogy*?

When he brushed past, I caught the delicious scent of citrus and spice. I didn't think he even noticed me, his sole focus being to calm Avery—always a hopeless task. Odette and I blinked at each other before silently proceeding to the bar, where Walter St. Mary was clearing away their glassware.

"You missed the show," Walter said.

"Not entirely." Leaning coquettishly on the bar, Odette said, "I think Father Unknown caught Whiskey's eye."

"No way," I protested.

Odette ignored me. "Tell all, Walter: Who is the man?"

"Dr. Nash Grant's his name."

"He's a doctor?" I gasped.

"He's a prof at the University of Florida."

"So she screwed her teacher. . . ."

Walter shook his glossy white head. Though sixty-something, his thick hair was the envy of younger men. "She never took a class with him. Met him at a campus anti-war rally, and afterward they fell into bed."

"Was there a power failure?" I asked.

Odette meowed.

"Whiskey, be nice," said Walter. "I still think of Avery as Leo's lost little girl. Her mother took her away from Magnet Springs and almost never let her come home."

In fact, Avery had lived in Belize from age fourteen until she went to college in Gainesville. She didn't get a degree, but she did get pregnant. Your tuition dollars at work. Maybe Nash Grant wasn't as nice as he was nice-looking.

"Avery's babies are three months old," I said. "What took their father so long to show up?"

"First he had to find them," Walter replied. "The poor guy went all the way to Belize. He found Georgia, who told him Avery was here. He called your house, but Avery made him meet her in a public place. He still hasn't seen his children."

Walter poured a glass of Shiraz for each of us, himself included. We drank meditatively.

Odette, who doesn't believe in deep reflection, said, "With the professor's genes in the mix, at least one of those kids should be handsome." For my benefit, she added, "Not that Leo wasn't good-looking."

"He wasn't," I said. "Except to me." And I toasted my Late Beloved.

Then Odette toasted Mrs. Gribble the Third and her fat check-book. Our celebratory mood had returned.

From the bar we moved into the dining room. About twenty tourists were in evidence, rosy-cheeked folks wearing brand-new knitted clothing and exclaiming about the view of Lake Michigan. Most were winter-sports enthusiasts inclined toward cross-country skiing, snow-mobiling, or ice-fishing, their sport of choice identifiable by public behavior, as well as wardrobe and beverage choice. Cross-country skiers tended to be subdued and self-righteous; they dressed the best and ordered liquor from the top shelf. Snow-mobilers were just plain loud. Chalk it up to hearing damage from their machines. They wore lots of layers and were loyal to their brands of booze. Ice-fisherman often had blood on their jackets and started drinking out on the ice.

Call me biased, but this was my take on each sport:

Snowmobiling is hard on the ears and the spine, and it creates noise pollution, but it gets you across the frozen tundra fast.

Cross-country skiing offers a smooth, silent glide through Nature's white glory and a fine way to burn in advance the calories you'd consume to warm yourself later.

As for ice-fishing, I had lived my whole life on the Lake, and I still didn't know how anyone could sit for hours on an overturned bucket staring into a black hole.

But ice-fishing had put Magnet Springs on the Winter Sports Map. Every year since the mid-1960s, the town hosted an Ice-Fishing Jamboree during the third week in January. This year's event would start tomorrow. That meant Magnet Springs was about to be invaded by ice-fishermen. Their assorted makeshift shanties were already visible along the shore. Most wouldn't wander as far inland as Mother Tucker's, preferring one of the convenient dark bars near the docks. Still, Walter had laid in a supply of Blatz beer, just in case.

Odette and I warmed ourselves with Jonny's trademark fresh breads straight from the oven, crocks of steaming chicken-corn chowder, and plates piled high with the Pasta of the Day: prawns, mussels, cod and salmon in a creamy lobster sauce on a bed of tagliatelle. No dessert, but even so, it was a noontime feast guaranteed to render one unfit to return to work.

We were idling over mugs of black coffee when David Newquist, DVM, appeared at our table. As usual, he was wearing his bright yellow parka proclaiming

**MAGNET SPRINGS VET CLINIC
YOUR PET'S A PERSON, TOO**

David was the new vet in town. He had gotten me through Abra's problematic pregnancy and delivery. Problematic for *me*, that is. Abra sailed through the entire trauma as if it were happening to someone else, which in a sense, it was. Like Avery, Abra expected to be protected from any and all of life's discomforts. Dr. David helped me do that, with a little assistance on the side from Chester, Abra's official keeper.

I wasn't sure how to read David Newquist. Recently divorced and relocated to our fair town, he seemed always on the verge of asking me out. If he ever did, I wasn't sure whether I'd say yes or no. Not that I failed to find him attractive . . . in a rumpled and earnest kind of way. Unlike Professor Nash Grant, Dr. David was definitely not "my type," i.e., not my male fantasy. The good vet was a regular-looking guy in his early forties: balding and paunchy with sloping shoulders. But his greenish-blue eyes twinkled. He was about Leo's height—five foot ten—and had a slight speech impediment (his Ls and Rs sounded like Ws), which I found endearing. His four-legged patients, including Abra, adored him.

So why would I hesitate to date him, should he eventually ask?

Dr. David was an animal rights activist, one of those politically committed, possibly crazy people who thinks that dogs and cats are equal to humans. I had trouble with that theory; I shared my life with an Afghan hound who already had more rights than I did. Giving her even more clout would invite disaster. We'd all read *Animal Farm*. . . .

Then there was the possible lawsuit by Gil Gruen. Before Dr. David met me, he had rented office space from Best West Realty. Instantly miserable in his lease, David fell in love with one of the buildings I owned and operated, a storefront that suddenly became available next door to Noonan's massage therapy studio. But Gil's contract didn't allow for lease-breaks unless Gil found a new tenant willing to pay at least ten percent more than David was paying for the already overpriced space. In addition, their agreement stipulated that Gil was David's real-estate agent of record in all transactions for six months from date of signing. David, therefore, was obligated to Gil even as he continued his search for a place to live. For now David was renting, week by week, a room at the fleabag Broken Arrow Motel out on the highway. He desperately needed a better situation but was reluctant to do more business with Gil.

I didn't need to tell David that he never should have signed Gil's contract. His brain fogged by divorce and the pressure to set up his new practice fast, he hadn't read the fine print. When Gil learned that David was looking at my property and discussing future business with me, he threatened to sue us both: David for breaking his contract, if he tried, and me for soliciting Gil's client, whether David signed with me or not.

It was like a curse hanging over both our heads.

"How are you?" David asked pleasantly, his speech impediment reminding me of Gilda Radner doing "Baba Wawa" on *Saturday Night Live*. When he asked if he could sit down, Odette and I said yes. Almost immediately her cell phone rang, and she excused herself.

"Well," David began. "I suppose you know about Chester."

"Oh yes." I smiled and then realized that David was waiting for me to say more. "What about him?"

"He and Prince Harry have run away from home."

FIVE

"I'M SURE THEY'RE JUST playing," I said, still smiling.

Chester was Abra's keeper as well as Prince Harry's. No way he would have left me alone with her. We had a contract.

David Newquist shook his head. "A man named Roy Vickers came by my office a few minutes ago. He found a note from Chester, and he was looking for you."

"Why would Roy look for Whiskey at your office?" Odette was back at the table. "Tina would have told him where to find us."

"He said Tina wasn't at your office when he returned."

Odette and I nodded knowingly. Probably another Winston and Neville Emergency. Until recently, Tina had performed most of her office-manager duties from home so that she could watch her two toddlers. Then, just before Christmas, husband Tim had lost his job and become temporary full-time child-care provider. Like me, he wasn't a natural at the job. Tina frequently flew home to calm him and the kids.

"What was in the note Roy found?" I asked David.

He extracted a neatly folded piece of yellow tablet paper from his pocket and passed it to me. In Chester's loopy cursive I read:

Dear Whiskey,
It's time for Prince Harry and me to go out on a mission.
Don't worry about us. I have Cassina's American Express card, and I printed out all the commands from dogstrainyou.com.
We'll call when we get to our destination. (I also brought my cell phone.)

Love,
Chester

Odette's next comment stunned me.

"My daughter used to do that."

I kept forgetting that Odette had a daughter. We'd worked together for three years, and yet I'd never met the girl. I didn't even know her name.

"That's why we sent her to boarding school," Odette said. "She didn't want to live with us."

There was no trace of sadness in Odette's voice. In fact, I heard relief.

She added, "When you call Cassina later, I can recommend a good school."

"But we don't even know where he is!" I protested.

"He'll come home before dark. They always do. . . ."

"But I don't want to send Chester away," I said.

Odette scowled. "I thought you didn't like children. Or dogs."

"But I need the child to take care of the dogs!"

Dr. David reached across the table and took my hand in his. I was surprised how soft his paw felt.

"The most important thing, Whiskey, is to stay calm. Everything will be all right."

"Aw-white" sounded pretty good from where I was sitting, especially with David holding my hand. His eyes were an amazing turquoise when viewed this close up. I could almost get lost in them. . . .

"Well, well, if it ain't the two folks I'm most likely to litigate."

Gil Gruen stood beside our table, arms crossed over his sheepskin coat.

"You were here already. We saw your sign," Odette said. "No need to come back. Ever."

Gil barked his staccato laugh.

"I'm meeting a client. Unlike Whiskey here, I do business the legitimate way. She lets her hormones run her business."

His eyes shifted to David.

"A little free advice: Stay away from this lady. She's not good-looking enough to be worth the trouble."

The veterinarian rose to his feet so fast that his chair toppled backward.

"Nobody talks that way about my friends," he said.

Gil took a step in reverse and raised his palms to signal peace. Given his costume and the current dialogue, it was like being in a TV Western.

"No offense intended, Doc. Just a friendly—or should I say 'fwend-wee'—warning."

With that, the Mayor of Magnet Springs exited to the bar. David stared after him but said nothing. After an extremely awkward moment of silence, Odette cleared her throat.

"Somebody should go make some money, and it might as well be me."

On her way out, she told David that she admired his self-control.

"If I had pets—which of course I never will—I would bring them to you," she added.

That was the perfect moment for David Newquist to ask me out. Or so I thought. But as soon as Odette left, he checked his watch, announced that he had a feline teeth-cleaning scheduled in fifteen minutes, and departed.

He did pick up his chair on the way out. Odette had left the check for me to pick up.

I stepped outside to discover that the temperature had dropped, and the wind had stiffened. Walking back to Mattimoe Realty, my shoulders hunched against the elements, I tightened the wool scarf around my neck. Thank god for big, fuzzy earmuffs. Though hardly a fashion statement, they did keep my earlobes from freezing and falling off.

They also reduced my hearing even as my raised collar eliminated my peripheral vision. Thus I was unaware until the driver honked that one of Magnet Springs' two patrol cars was nosing along the curb at my side.

At least Jenx didn't deem it necessary to turn on the siren. For that I was grateful.

"Yo, Whiskey!" she called out the open passenger window. "I hear you lost Chester and Prince Harry! Maybe Abra, too."

"We don't worry about Abra. She always comes home."

"Get in so I can roll up the window!"

Who would argue with the Chief of Police? Judy "Jenx" Jenkins fought crime and kept order in Magnet Springs. She got a little help from Officers Swancott and Roscoe, the second of whom was a dog. Roscoe was better at his job than Brady Swancott although, to be fair, he'd had more training.

"For the record, I didn't lose anyone," I informed Jenx as I settled in the passenger seat. "Chester ran away from home for the day. See, here's his note." I held it out for her to see before she pulled away from the curb.

Jenx didn't touch the note as she read it. "How many sets of fingerprints are on that thing, besides yours and Chester's?"

"I don't know. Roy Vickers brought the note to David Newquist. I don't even know where Roy found it."

"Roy Vickers?" Jenx looked at me sharply. "Roy's back in town?"

"He just got out of jail. I gave him a job."

Jenx's jaw dropped.

"Noonan told me to," I said quickly. "She said you thought it was a good idea."

SIX

Jenx stomped the brake pedal. Although the patrol car had barely been rolling, it rocked to a stop. Chester's farewell note floated from my gloved fingers.

"You *don't* think hiring Roy's a good idea?" I said.

"I told Noonan it was a good idea *in theory*," Jenx fumed, her face darkening. "I swear that woman hears only what she wants to hear!"

Suddenly I felt the tingle that signaled one of Jenx's "episodes." Though barely five foot five, our police chief packed a legendary wallop: when riled, she could channel the electrical currents for which our town was named. I'd seen her make phones ring, metal objects jump, and annoying people go spinning across a room. In self-defense I gripped the door handle with both fists.

The patrol car's siren wailed plaintively even though Jenx hadn't flipped a switch. I stole a peek at the driver. Her eyes bulged, and she no longer appeared to be breathing.

"Easy, Jenx!" I shouted. "Inhale! Now!"

She did. A few seconds later the siren died, and I loosened my hold on the door.

In a flat voice, Jenx said, "I'd never recommend hiring a violent felon without knowing his profile first. I have contacts at the prison. I told Noonan I'd check him out. She didn't give me time."

"Well, you can still check him out," I offered. "If you get a bad report, I'll let him go."

Jenx whipped a handkerchief from her pocket and leaned across my lap to scoop up Chester's note from the floor by my feet.

"Let's hope it's not too late," she said, slipping the paper into a plastic evidence bag.

I gulped. "But Odette said her daughter used to run away from home all the time."

"You would, too, if you were Odette's daughter. Chester, on the other hand, runs away from Cassina to stay at your house."

That was true. Until I had agreed to "keep" him while his mother was on her World Tour, Chester used to break into Vestige, my house in the country, just to hang out with Abra and me.

"How did you even know Chester and Prince Harry were gone?" I asked.

"I ran into Odette at the Goh Cup."

"She was at the Goh Cup? We just had lunch."

"She likes their espresso better than Mother Tucker's. Don't tell Walter."

"Don't worry, I won't. You feeling okay now?"

"Fine."

"Somebody should study you. . . ."

"Why? It runs in my family. Most of us can make water boil."

———

By 6:30 that night it was pitch black all around Vestige, and Chester had not yet returned, with or without Prince Harry.

Neither had Abra, but I knew she'd be back. I had arrived home at five to find Avery locked in her room, the nanny attending to Leah and Leo. The babies looked peaceful enough, and there was no sign that their father had been to see them. No new toys or other love souvenirs. I briefly considered asking the nanny what she knew about the day's events, but I didn't even know the nanny's name. Because Avery hired and fired a new one every few weeks, I didn't want to get involved; I just wrote the checks.

But Chester's absence alarmed me. Should I call Cassina? I checked her tour itinerary, which I kept in my home office, near the phone. Tonight she had given a concert in Tashkent, Uzbekistan. No hotel was listed for this date, and it was unlikely that I could reach her by cell phone. Even if I could, given the time difference, by now she'd be either long asleep or deeply drunk. Or both. Chester swore that his mother had given up the booze, but I'd seen evidence to the contrary. Cassina's famously ethereal appearance and angelic music belied a turbulent nature. Now halfway through a six-month-long tour with Rupert, Chester's estranged father, Cassina had stopped checking on her son.

That was when I realized that I should check with Chester's friends from the private school he attended . . . if only I had a list of his friends or could recall the name of his school. Someone picked him up and dropped him off every day. I didn't even know that person's name.

Oh yes, I'm a very, very, very bad child-care provider. What was Cassina thinking when she left her son with me?

The digital clock on my desk read 6:34. If I were going to attend tonight's Town Meeting, and as a Main Street Merchant—not to mention as Roy Vickers's new employer—I should, then I'd have to leave at once. But someone at Vestige should be on the lookout for Chester. I peered into the nursery, formerly the family room. The unnamed nanny was curled on the floral loveseat, reading a paperback through glasses with clear plastic frames. When I coughed softly, she glanced up.

"Hi," I began.

To my surprise, she stood at attention.

"Deely Smarr," she said, as if replying to roll call.

"Whiskey Mattimoe," I returned.

"I know. Can I help you, ma'am?"

Ma'am? Such formality impressed me. I was also struck by how familiar she looked, yet this nanny was new, on duty for less than a week. She was a muscular girl inclining toward fat. Who did she remind me of?

"I hope you can help me," I said. "I need to leave for a couple hours, but my houseguest Chester is—uh—missing, along with his puppy, and I'm worried about him. About Chester, I mean. The dog can probably take care of himself if he takes after his mother."

I was babbling, and we both knew it. Deely Smarr waited for me to continue. I wasn't sure what else to say.

"Could you—uh—keep an eye and ear open, in case Chester calls or, better yet, comes home?"

"Yes, ma'am. No problem. I have a lot of experience standing watch."

So Deely Smarr was ex-military. That explained the formality. But I still didn't know why she seemed familiar. Leah whimpered in her crib, and the nanny looked toward the sound. Then I got it: Deely Smarr looked amazingly like the baby's mother—only bespectacled with shorter hair and a proportionately smaller build, though not much smaller. Had Avery unconsciously hired her own double to take care of her kids?

I thanked Deely and headed out. Three paces later, I turned back.

"If Abra comes scratching at the door, I suppose you should let her in, too."

"Yes, ma'am, I will."

"Army?" I asked.

"Coast Guard."

"Really? What job?"

"D.C., ma'am."

"What's that?"

"Damage Controlman."

I nodded. "Carry on."

By the time I arrived at the Town Hall, available parking spaces were as scarce as green grass in January. I ended up parallel-parking my Lexus RX 330—a mid-sized SUV—on Schuyler Street, two blocks away.

My nose and eyes were leaking from the cold when I flung open the Town Hall's oversized door to find standing room only. Gil's posters had served their purpose. Half the adult population of Magnet Springs was there. I leaned against the door and scanned the packed room. In attendance were Odette and Tina, as well as Peg Goh of the Goh Cup, Noonan Starr, Walter St. Mary, and other local business owners. Missing was Dr. David Newquist. What did that mean? That David didn't respect Gil enough to attend the meeting, or that Gil had humiliated David into staying away?

Jenx was there with her partner, Henrietta Roca, proprietor of Red Hen's House, bar none the best inn in town. The presence of our police chief meant that Officers Swancott and Roscoe were on patrol. I fervently hoped that they would apprehend Chester and Prince Harry before our meeting concluded. It was way too frosty out there for either boy or beast.

A ripple of whispers passed through the crowd as Mayor Gil Gruen stepped up on the stage at the end of the hall. For the occasion he had removed his ever-present Stetson, which he held before his chest like a shield. No one could miss his swagger or the fact that his cowboy boots added two inches to his height.

"Good evening, ladies and gents," he bellowed into an over-amplified microphone.

"Step back!" and "Turn it down!" his audience roared in reply.

After a few adjustments, Gil continued at a loud but tolerable volume: "Thank you all for answering my call to duty tonight. We, the citizens of Magnet Springs, are facing the kind of crisis that separates the men from the boys."

When the ardent feminists in the crowd protested, Gil made a mock defensive maneuver and amended his comment.

"And the ladies from the girls. How's that?"

"Women, not ladies!" Henrietta Roca shouted back.

Gil glared at her for just an instant, and then bowed excessively, sweeping the brim of his Stetson across the floor at his feet.

"Whatever your gender—or preference," he said acidly, "you're here tonight because your livelihood may be at risk. I don't need to remind you that our 42nd Annual Ice-Fishing Jamboree starts tomorrow. As I speak, hundreds of tourists with fat wallets in their back pockets are pointing their cars toward Magnet Springs. Many have been coming here their whole lives. But they might never come again once they learn of the threat among us."

The room was silent. No one seemed to breathe.

"This very afternoon, a man whose name means Shame in Magnet Springs returned to our fair town with the intention of spending the rest of his days here. This man is a violent man. A convicted felon who tried to murder in cold blood a good man, a man we all respected. Nine years ago—almost to the day—Roy Edgar Vickers, known then as the town drunk, savagely attacked Leo Mattimoe, stabbing him multiple times in the chest and leaving him for dead. For that crime, Roy Vickers was sentenced to life in prison. But you know as well as I do how the prison system works. Too many bad guys, not enough space in the jails. So today Roy Vickers was paroled, making him our problem—yours and mine. What was the first thing that the would-be killer did? He came straight back to the scene of his crime. And what happened next? You're not going to believe this, ladies and gents. I mean—sorry—" Gil lowered his head in Hen Roca's direction, "—women and men. Good women and men. . . ."

Gil cleared his throat.

"Roy Vickers found himself a job. That's right. A scant three hours out of the slammer, and the convict got himself hired, right here in Magnet Springs. Who in their right mind would hire him, you say? Who in their right mind, indeed! Well, hold onto your horses. The ex-con's new boss is none other than the gal who was once married to his victim. That's right—the traitor among us is my fellow real-estate broker and your neighbor, Whitney Houston Halloran Mattimoe."

Picking up its cue, the crowd gasped collectively. Of course, the response was mere sound effect. Given the small size and gossipy nature of Magnet Springs, no one in the hall was hearing the news for the first time. But when it came to orating, Gil was skilled. What audience doesn't crave entertainment? This was just plain good theater. It got better: When Gil raised the hand that didn't hold the Stetson and pointed a finger straight at me, every face turned to stare. Even the faces belonging to my friends. What can I say? They were following stage directions.

As they studied me, my nose still dripping from the cold (why did I always forget to carry tissues?), Gil declared, "Of course, you know her as 'Whiskey'—a nickname we've never questioned. And yet—"

"I gave her that nickname, back in seventh grade."

I felt the weight of the crowd's gaze shift from me to the shadows on the far right side of the hall. Of course, I knew the voice before its owner stepped forward: Jeb Halloran, my first husband.

He was also my first kiss, my first sexual encounter, my excuse for leaving Magnet Springs, and my reason for coming home again when our stormy marriage disintegrated. Although we could never make the magic work for long, we could never hate each other, either. An itinerant musician who looked and sounded like a younger James Taylor still searching for his style, Jeb drifted between gigs. I hadn't known he was back in town or noticed him when I arrived in the hall, probably because he showed up after I did and entered by the side door. Jeb would never have two nickels to his name, but his charm would last forever.

"It was her voice, Gil," Jeb continued. "I loved the sound of her whiskey voice. And I still do." Jeb turned toward me and winked. I winked back.

God love the good ex-husbands of the world. They're out there.

Suddenly the door at my back was yanked away from me. I staggered backwards as cold air rushed in, along with Roy Vickers.

SEVEN

GIL GRUEN MADE A show of checking his watch.

"You're late, Roy. The meeting started at seven o'clock sharp. And you'll have to park your dog outside."

All eyes were on Roy's dog, or more accurately on the dog in Roy's arms. The puppy, that is: Prince Harry the Pee Master.

"Is Chester all right?" I asked Roy, taking the squirming pup from him.

"I didn't find Chester, Whiskey. Just the dog. Sorry."

My heart clenched. "Where?"

"Excuse me, you two!" Gil called out. "The rest of Magnet Springs is holding a meeting here. You can hear all about it later. Go conduct your private business somewhere else."

"Not so fast," Roy said. "I have something to say to everybody in this room."

To my astonishment, he strode up the center aisle toward the stage. Gil clutched the microphone so tightly that his knuckles whitened.

"This ain't no debate, Roy," Gil sputtered. "I'm conducting a meeting here. It's my show!"

Ignoring him, Roy stepped nimbly onto the stage and faced the audience. He didn't need a mike to make every word heard.

"Folks, in case you don't know me from when I used to live here—and even if you do—let me introduce myself. My name's Roy Vickers. I did a terrible thing nine years ago, and I got no excuse for it. That's why I stand before you tonight. To ask you to try to understand something that it took me a long time to learn: I need to earn forgiveness. It's the only way I can make my life count, and no man's life should be wasted. I'm talking Cosmic Balance here. To restore that, I have to do good works in this town, where I once did something that was pure evil. Sadly, it's too late for me to make personal amends to Leo Mattimoe. So I'm starting with the people he loved. Mrs. Whiskey Mattimoe is giving me the chance I need to begin making things right. In time, I intend to do good for every single citizen of Magnet Springs. If you'll just give me a chance. Thank you."

Jeb Halloran applauded slowly, his hands held high. After a few beats, others joined in. Soon most of the house was clapping. Noonan Starr turned in her seat to face me, tears coursing down her cheeks. She was radiant.

Prince Harry yipped his approval. I felt rather than saw the second part of his response when a warm puddle formed in the crook of my arm. We slipped outside and I placed him in the middle of the snow-cleared sidewalk, as Chester would have done, but the pup had already finished his business. My sleeve dripped. I said, "Where's Chester, Prince Harry? Why did he run away?"

The puppy cocked his fuzzy head at me and whimpered. For a fleeting moment I almost believed he was trying to tell me something. If only I'd had my Dogs-Train-You-Dot-Com Communication Cheat Sheet.

"What's going on, boy?" I said. "Where did Roy find you?"

"Wouldn't you rather talk to someone who can talk back?"

To identify that voice I didn't need to turn around. So I didn't. I leaned forward and scooped the pup onto my already soggy arm.

"Thanks, Jeb, for standing up for me."

"No big deal. Gil should remember how you got your nickname. He was there."

"That's right. He was in Mrs. Dimmitt's class with us."

"That's why he hates you today."

"Pardon?"

Jeb grinned. "You don't remember, do you? But Gil does. He asked you to the Middle-School Mixer. You said no, and you didn't let him down easy."

"You and I were going steady!" I said, suddenly recalling the scene.

"Lucky me."

I smiled at my ex-husband. Under the post lamp, he was as handsome as ever, maybe more so. Why is it that the first lines in a woman's face make her look old, whereas the first lines in a man's face make him look like a grown-up, finally?

"How ya doin', Whiskey?"

"Better. And worse. I lost Chester."

Jeb nodded as if women misplaced kids every day.

"But you found a dog."

"I didn't. Roy did. It's Chester's dog."

That was the first time anyone had said so, yet it had been true for weeks. The only reason Prince Harry hadn't been adopted was that Chester didn't want anyone else to have him. Why hadn't I seen that? It was Chester's subtle way of making sure he'd get a dog of his own while his pet-phobic mother was otherwise engaged. If Chester were standing in front of me, I would have congratulated him. How I wished Chester were standing in front of me.

"Everybody's going to come pouring out those doors any second," Jeb said. "How about we grab a cup of coffee? Or something stronger?"

I nodded toward Prince Harry.

"Underneath the dog, I got a sleeve full of pee."

"So I guess we're going back to your place," Jeb said. "You do know how to make coffee, don't you?"

"Instant."

He made a face. "I know you know how to open a bottle of beer."

"I can even operate a corkscrew."

"That's my girl." He wrapped an arm around me and guided me toward the street.

"You got a car parked somewhere?" I asked.

"Nope. If you're sweet—and you crack the windows—I'll let you drive. No offense, but you smell like piss."

Before long I was wearing a dry sweater, and I had the beginnings of a very nice buzz. Partly from the Glenfiddich and tall water Jeb had poured from my own bar. Partly from the back rub he was giving me. Scotch was Jeb's drink, not mine. Since I generally limited myself to wine and beer, I was surprised to learn I had a bottle of scotch on hand. Leo had drunk bourbon.

It started as a platonic back rub. But it was loaded with memories of back rubs gone by. Back rubs from our wild and crazy twenties that had ended with us tearing off each other's clothes. The truth is that nobody alive knew my body better than Jeb Halloran. Except, in her own way, Noonan Starr. But Noonan was a health-care professional, so her back rubs belonged in a completely different category.

I should have known that the liquor's "slow burn," as Jeb called it, would get me in trouble. The bar and the leather couch we were using were in Leo's former home office. Although I had tried to redo the room as a library, I had been only partly successful. My late husband's vibes lingered everywhere. That was probably why I agreed to a second scotch: to help me forget about Leo and focus on Jeb's expert back rub.

After a while, I became aware that I was on my back, and Jeb was on top of me. It was all so familiar somehow that it didn't seem wrong. In fact, it felt like exactly what I needed.

Until reality came knocking in the form of Avery Mattimoe.

At least I had remembered to close the library door, and Jeb had had the presence of mind to lock it. So Avery was reduced to pounding and shouting.

"Whiskey! Are you in there? Chester's puppy just peed all over the nursery, and I'm not cleaning it up!"

First I pulled my lips away from Jeb's. Then I shoved him off of me. With a grunt, he landed on the carpeted floor.

"Whiskey?" Avery called. "What's going on in there?"

"Uh, nothing." I sat up so quickly that the room spun.

"Then open the damned door!"

That was when I realized that my sweater was missing. Fortunately, I still had my bra on, and my pants, but that wouldn't be good enough for Avery. I couldn't think of a single good reason why I'd be reading topless. Plus, I probably smelled of scotch, and I didn't have a book handy. And what to do about Jeb? I'd have to put him somewhere. He was on his feet, moving toward the bar.

"No! No more scotch!" I hissed at him.

"What did you say?" called Avery.

Jeb shook his head and ducked behind the bar. My foggy brain finally got it: he was hiding.

"Uh—just a minute," I told Avery. "I'm looking for . . . a book-mark. . . ."

Actually, I was looking for my pullover. In every corner of the room.

"Just fold back the corner of the page," she snapped. "Why'd you lock the door, anyway?"

"For privacy," I said. "I like to read privately."

"Since when?"

As I bent down to check under the couch, I nearly tipped all the way over.

"Yikes," I muttered, catching myself.

"What the hell are you doing?" Avery bellowed. "Just open the door!"

Something soft and fuzzy struck me in the back of the head. Not a dog this time. My missing sweater. Jeb must have found it. I pulled it on, ran my fingers through my mop of curly hair, and checked to make sure that my visitor was out of sight. Then I took a deep breath and opened the door.

Avery was wearing men's pajamas, her heavy arms crossed over her ample chest. She looked the very embodiment of Pissed Off. But the second she saw me her expression shifted to suspicious.

"Where's your book?" she said.

"I reshelved it." I stepped into the hall and clicked the door shut behind me.

Avery narrowed her piggy little eyes. "You reek of scotch. Is that what you use Dad's office for? To get drunk in?"

I tossed my head—and felt dizzy for the effort. "No. I use his office to read in. It's a library now, in case you hadn't noticed."

Even I noticed that I had slurred my words. But I tossed my head again.

"Well, you'd better clean up the nursery and crate that puppy," she said. "I can't raise my babies like this!"

"You're not raising your babies," I said. "The Coast Guard is."

"What?" Avery's tongue flicked out as if she were making a face. She wasn't, actually. It was a nervous tic, and I swore it would get her into serious trouble one day.

"I met the Coast Guard nanny," I explained. "She's raising your babies. That's what I pay her to do. I don't know what you do, Avery, besides scream at the babies' father in the bar at Mother Tucker's."

The tongue again. "You spied on me!"

"I'm too busy to spy on you. Odette and I were at Mother Tucker's to celebrate a new deal. We heard you. Everyone in the restaurant heard you."

"Nash wants joint custody of the kids! I don't know what to do!" Avery's round face exploded into tears. "I don't want him in their lives!"

"If he's their father, he has a place in their lives," I said, sounding remarkably sober. "Is he their father?"

"Yes, but that was a complete accident! I never loved him! I don't even know him!"

"Well, at least he's handsome. You got that part right."

"Yeah? Well, your sweater's on backwards. And you just locked your ex-husband in my father's office."

"What?"

"Cut the crap, Whiskey. I heard you and Jeb when you came in. If you're that horny, go to a motel!"

EIGHT

"Yeah, well at least I refrain from having unprotected sex with someone I hardly know!"

That was a cheap shot, but I enjoyed it.

"Bitch!" Avery fired back. "Clean up that dog mess or I'm taking my babies somewhere else!"

"Is that a promise or a threat?"

"Bitch!"

"You said that already."

"I mean the other one." Avery pointed past me down the hall. I turned in time to see Abra disappear into the nursery. "Get that dog out of there!"

"That dog doesn't listen to me, in case you haven't noticed. That dog only listened to your father."

"Out, out, out!"

The commands were coming from inside the nursery. Damage Controlman Deely Smarr, reporting for duty.

"I thought she was off the clock," I told Avery.

"When there are kids, you're never off the clock."

Abra and Prince Harry trotted out of the nursery with the Coast Guard nanny at their heels. I followed them into the kitchen and arrived in time to see Deely closing them both in their crates.

"I didn't even know Abra had a crate," I said.

"I got it today," said Deely. "You seriously need to get organized. This will help."

"Abra came back?" I was still a few beats behind.

"Ten minutes ago. I fed them both." Deely reached for the wall switch. "Lights out, ma'am."

I listened in the dark, not breathing. Neither of the dogs made a sound. Had she drugged them?

Back in the hallway, we encountered a confused Jeb Halloran trying to locate the nearest exit. Avery blew her nose and glared at him. Deely showed him to the door. As he passed, Jeb winked at me, and—Heaven help me—I winked back. Without another word, I climbed the stairs to my room, where I fell onto the king-sized bed and into the deepest sleep I'd had in months.

I awoke to a ringing phone right next to my head. Since it was still dark outside, I was pretty sure I hadn't overslept. Indeed, my bedside clock read 5:46.

Before I could manage something like the word "hello," I heard Jenx say, "We got a second note from Chester. You'll want to come to the station."

I sat bolt upright, my misplaced sense of responsibility kicking in. Conveniently I hadn't bothered to remove last night's clothes—including the backwards sweater—so I told Jenx I'd be there in ten. I turned the sweater around, brushed my teeth, splashed water on my face and stumbled downstairs.

To my surprise, Deely Smarr was already back on duty in the nursery. I paused in the doorway to wave.

"Sleep well?" she asked, no trace of irony in her voice.

"Like a rock."

"So did the dogs. They're in their exercise pen now. I'll walk them when I take my first break."

"What exercise pen?"

"Didn't Avery tell you? I enclosed a twelve-by-twenty-foot area next to the barbecue pit. It's temporary, pending your approval, but the dogs like it. The fence is six feet high, so it's Abra-proof."

I felt the slackness in my face that meant I was mouth-breathing.

Deely went on, "With your okay, ma'am, I'll install a doggie door in the kitchen. That will simplify things."

I nodded dumbly and left.

———

"Roy brought this in on his way to work," Jenx said, handing me a clear plastic envelope containing a second note in Chester's writing.

"On his way to work? What time was that?"

Jenx checked her watch. "About a half-hour ago. He promised Luís he'd get an early start."

"Doing what?" Everybody who worked for me was more ambitious than I was.

"Winter maintenance on your company truck, I think. Roy used to manage the prison garage."

"Where did he find Chester's note?"

"He didn't say."

"Since when did law enforcement stop asking questions?"

The expression Jenx shot me was vile enough to make the room vibrate.

"Give me a break," she said. "I'm a one-man police force today. Brady and Roscoe are off because they worked last night. Never mind that the Jamboree starts at noon. Did I mention we're expecting a record crowd?" She sighed. "It's weeks like this when you and I should be in retail."

"I couldn't fold a T-shirt to save my life. And you're hardly the 'have-a-nice-day' type."

"You're right." Grinning, Jenx tapped her sidearm. "Besides, shopkeepers don't get to carry."

"Glocks scare off customers," I agreed. Then I read Chester's note:

Dear Whiskey,

I had to send Prince Harry home. He's still the Pee Master, and housebreaking on the road is hard. I know you can't handle him, but Avery's new nanny can. Just do what she tells you.

I'll be home as soon as I take care of business.

Love,
Chester

"Face it, Whiskey," Jenx said. "It's time to file a Missing Person Report. And time for you to call Cassina."

"And tell her what?"

"Tell her what happened!"

I knew Jenx was right. No more excuses. "Maybe she'll under-stand. I mean, kids run away all the time, right?"

"Sure. If that's what happened. . . ."

"You don't think that's what happened?" I asked nervously.

"We've been over this. Why would he run away? He loves it at your house. Plus, you hired him to watch the dogs."

"But his note says he has to 'take care of business,'" I pointed out. "Maybe he's got another gig somewhere."

It didn't take long to file the Missing Person Report. From the police station I headed down Main Street to my office. Although it wasn't yet seven o'clock, Odette was already at work. Her favorite African music playing at full volume could mean only one thing.

"How many closings do you have today?" I shouted.

She extended her hand around her office partition, two fingers raised in victory.

"Bravo," I said.

Then the rest of Odette appeared. "You and I are going to cel-ebrate by taking a ride in a helicopter!"

"Why would we do that?"

"Because I want to, and we can."

"We can?"

Odette handed me a copy of the Ice-Fishing Jamboree Events Schedule. With a pink marker she had highlighted HELICOPTER RIDES—FRIDAY NOON TO 4 pm.

"I made a reservation for us. At 12:40!" she shouted over the tribal rhythms blaring from the lobby stereo.

"Lucky us," I mumbled.

"Why is your sweater on backwards?"

"It's not on backwards!" I raised my voice.

Odette rose, crossed to the control dials, and sharply lowered the sound. Then she hooked a manicured finger around my collar and pulled it out far enough for me to see the tag.

"Avery said it was on backwards last night—" I began. Then I cursed my stepdaughter.

Ten minutes later at the Goh Cup, over *beignets* imported from New Orleans and mugs of café au lait, I told Odette that Abra was back. She held out her hand.

"You don't get a tip for that," I said.

"What happened to my Gucci bag? The one I used to save the Gribble deal?"

"Gone," I sighed. "How expensive was it?"

Odette whipped out her Mont Blanc pen and scribbled a four-digit number on her napkin.

I blanched.

"We'll add it to your tab," she said.

Peg Goh pulled up a chair and rested her elbows on our table. "Do you like the beignets? I'm thinking of making them a permanent addition to my menu."

Odette and I agreed they were a hit.

"That was quite a Town Meeting, didn't you think?" Peg continued. "How sweet of Jeb to come to your defense."

"He's still hot for Whiskey, and everybody knows it," said Odette.

"He's just bored," I said. "He gets like that when he's not on the road."

"Bored, you say? Is that why he spent the night with you?"

"He didn't spend the night!"

Odette and Peg grinned slyly.

"We saw him get into your car," Peg said.

"We had a drink together, that's all! He went home around eleven."

I couldn't believe I was explaining myself, and not even to my mother. As I did so, I wondered for the first time how Jeb had gotten home. Vestige, after all, was three miles from town, and last night was a cold one. I'd been so buzzed when he left that I hadn't considered the logistics. Jeb usually stayed with one or another of his cousins; he'd probably used his cell phone to summon a ride. Uneasy, I changed the subject.

"Today is Gil's big day, his first Jamboree as mayor. He has to open the competition by drilling the first hole and dropping the first line."

"Too bad the cowboy realtor doesn't know the first thing about ice-fishing," Odette yawned. "I doubt he can use an auger or a rod. Unlike Peg, who took second place in last year's contest."

Modestly, Peg lowered her eyes. "I got lucky with that walleye."

"Gil lost last night's battle, too," said Odette. "Who knew Roy Vickers could out-orate him?"

"I'm proud of you, Whiskey," Peg said. "You're doing the right thing by hiring Roy. The cosmically right thing."

Inwardly I groaned. I had forgotten that Peg was Noonan's newest New Age counseling client. That worried me since Peg Goh was the most stable, sensible person around. What if Noonan's mumbo-jumbo knocked the logic right out of her? Peg was our vice-mayor. We needed some semblance of sanity in city politics.

"I heard about Chester running away from home," she said. "What did Cassina say when you told her?"

"Umm. Well—"

"Whiskey hasn't told her," said Odette, popping the last of her beignet into her big mouth.

"What? Oh, Whiskey!" Peg looked stricken. "You need to call her right now, right this minute. Every mother needs to know the instant her child is in trouble!"

When I mumbled that I didn't have Cassina's tour schedule on me, Peg fumbled through her apron pockets until she found her copy.

"Why do you have that?" I asked.

"Because you don't always have yours handy."

I opened my cell phone and dialed the number for a hotel in Bucharest, Romania, where it was probably mid-afternoon. My first two calls were dropped before anybody answered. The third time was the charm. To my relief, the desk clerk spoke English and was efficient. I had Cassina herself on the line before I could plan what to say. So I got right to the point:

"It appears that Chester has run away from home. He left yesterday and sent me two notes, but I don't know where he is. Jenx is on the case, just in case."

The line crackled and hummed in my ear. After a moment, Cassina replied in her signature breathy voice, "It's genetic. I ran away from every foster home I was ever in. Chester's my kid, you know."

"Well, sure. . . ."

"He's out there searching for something, Whiskey. If he doesn't find it, he'll come back."

"And if he does find it—?"

"He'll let you know." I heard what sounded like Cassina taking a long drink of something, which probably wasn't hot tea. Then a man's voice filled the line.

"Hello? Who is this?" The clipped tones were distinctly British but unfamiliar to me. I introduced myself.

"Ah, yes, the child-care provider. This is Rupert, Chester's father. Is everything all right?"

I repeated what I'd told Cassina.

"Very well, then, you'll keep us informed?"

"Of course—." There was a click in my ear.

"You lost their kid, didn't you?"

I knew only too well who that voice belonged to.

"No, Gil, I didn't."

Mr. Best West laughed his rude, percussive laugh.

"I swear, Whiskey, if you could keep your mind on your business, you just might give me a run for my money. But between the kids, the dogs, the men, and the booze, you don't know which end is up."

Before I could reply, a large hand grasped Gil Gruen's shoulder and spun him around. Roy Vickers, his face pale with rage, towered over the mayor.

"Apologize to her, or you'll regret it. I swear to God, you'll regret it."

NINE

"Easy, Roy. Let the world turn as it will."

That sounded like something Noonan Starr would say, but it was her new client, Peg Goh.

"The man threatened me!" Gil sputtered. "I got a room full of witnesses."

He pointed a finger in Roy's face.

"Last night you may have won the battle, but you will lose the war. As soon as word gets out that you publicly threatened me, you'll be washed up for good in this town. Once a criminal, always a criminal."

Self-righteously Gil replaced his Stetson. Then he turned to me.

"Here's a little free advice, Missy: We are known by the company we keep. If you consort with criminals, you are a criminal."

I opened my mouth to protest, but Odette dug her long nails into my hand. I was in too much pain to make words. The click of Gil's two-inch heels on Peg's parquet floor was the only sound until he slammed the door.

"Sorry, Whiskey," Roy said, looking contrite. "I don't know what came over me."

"You're not helping yourself," I warned him. "But don't worry about me. Now get back to work."

"The Seventh Sun of Solace is to maintain self-control at all times, against all odds," Roy muttered as he shuffled out. Peg nodded vigorously.

"Is Roy in counseling with Noonan already?" asked Odette.

"Any day now, I'm sure," said the vice-mayor.

I focused on the fingernail marks Odette had left in my flesh.

She sniffed. "If I hadn't done that, you would have gotten us sued for sure."

"She's right, Whiskey," said Peg. "Gil's itching to take Mattimoe Realty to court. Especially since you signed Mrs. Gribble."

"What does Mrs. Gribble have to do with Gil?" I asked.

"Should we tell her?"

Peg looked right past me to consult with Odette, who said, "She'll find out sooner or later, so we might as well enjoy telling her."

"*Mr.* Gribble wanted to sign with Gil as buyer's agent," Peg said. "But Mrs. Gribble signed with you first. Since she controls the marital purse-strings, Gil's deal with her husband is dead."

"Her husband, by the way, is at least twenty years her junior," Odette purred. "He's the prospect Gil was meeting at Mother Tucker's yesterday."

"Mr. Gribble had been stringing Gil along for weeks, hinting at a huge ticket," Peg said. "When he met with Gil yesterday and told him 'no-can-do,' Gil was livid."

Odette added, "Gil had probably been dreaming of that commission for so long he'd already spent it." She lowered her lashes. "I can relate."

"And you know all this *how*?" I asked.

"Walter told us at the Town Meeting," Peg said. "He had my sympathy for enduring *two* big scenes in his restaurant yesterday: First Avery and the father of her babies; then Gil and Mr. Gribble."

Odette said, "Gil called Mr. Gribble a 'gut-less, ball-less loser.' The whole restaurant heard him."

"Why burn a bridge if you can nuke it?" I sighed.

"Poor Mr. Gribble," Peg observed. "Walter said he turned crimson with embarrassment."

Odette said, "His bald head looked like a lawn globe. Well, he's probably sick of living under Wifey's thumb."

"There are worse fates," I mused.

Peg and Odette waited for the punch line.

Such as living with a bitch of a former stepdaughter and her infant twins.

But I refrained from saying so.

———

After breakfast at the Goh Cup, Odette proceeded to her two closings, and I returned to the office. Between phone calls and paperwork, I didn't get much done.

My thoughts kept turning to Chester. Where was he? Why had he sent Prince Harry home when he wanted that dog's companionship more than anything?

I tried to replay my last conversations with him. They had seemed so ordinary that I could hardly recall them. Chester had given no sign that anything was bothering him, besides Prince Harry's reluctance to pee when and where he should.

Odette's three rapid-fire knocks announced that it was almost time for our scheduled helicopter ride.

"Tell me again why this is a good idea," I said when she flung open my office door.

"Because I just made you a lot of money, and you want to reward me."

"But I don't like heights," I reminded her.

"All the more reason for you to go. You need to work on that."

"Why? I'm a real-estate broker, not a lineman for the phone company. I don't do heights."

"Really?" Odette cocked her head at me. I supposed she was thinking of last fall when I rode Blitzen, my touring bicycle, over a cliff.

"I had to do that," I blurted. "To save my life and the other guy's!"

"And you have to do this. For me."

———

So it was that I accompanied Odette Mutombo through the noisy, red-nosed mob of ice-fishing enthusiasts down by the docks. I was still hoping the weather would turn inclement, and the copter would be grounded. But no such luck. We had been granted a winter day so bright that it hurt the eyes. Windless, too.

Gil was concluding the opening ceremony as we approached. How lucky for him that Peg Goh was vice-mayor. While he pretended to *let* her drill his hole and hook his line, we knew that he couldn't have managed either for himself.

The crowd clapped good-naturedly, and Gil resumed glad-handing. In a moment he was swallowed by a mob of warmly dressed people.

"There he is," Odette whispered in my ear. "There's Oscar Manfred Gribble the Third!"

At first I couldn't follow her gaze, mainly because I was looking for someone remarkable enough to wear that name. Finally I realized that she meant a small, roundish man of about forty leaning against one of the dock posts. Bald and bespectacled, he wasn't interesting, but his coat was: like his wife's, it was made of full-length fur—chinchilla, I reckoned. Warm enough for the occasion and yet totally inappropriate.

To my chagrin, Odette began waving at him, and continued waving in broader and broader arcs until he tentatively waved back.

"Let's go introduce ourselves," she told me. "After all, we're working for The Wife."

"After all, he wanted to do business with The Competition," I muttered.

Odette made the pseudo-raspberry sound I've come to expect whenever she disagrees with me. As we made our way across the ice toward Mr. Gribble, something—or someone—apparently caught his eye. The man stood poker-straight and used both hands to shield himself from the sun's glare. Suddenly, he took off. It was only then that I realized Mr. Gribble was wearing skates. In fact, Oscar Manfred Gribble the Third was a very fast skater. Within seconds he had faded into the crowd.

"How rude," Odette said.

Then we heard the *wump-wump-wump* of helicopter blades and remembered why we were there.

"This is the best investment you've made this week," Odette assured me as I counted out three twenty-dollar bills to cover our fare. The pilot was cute and friendly in the relaxed, self-confident way that only athletic men under thirty can be. I tried to ignore the WWJD motto on his T-shirt until he mentioned that today was his first day on the job.

"In that case," I said, "What *would* Jesus do? Ask for his money back?"

"She's afraid of heights," Odette explained.

"Fear of heights doesn't usually bother helicopter passengers," the pilot said.

"More like fear of falling," I said as Odette shoved me forward. Up close, the aircraft resembled an oversized thrumming toy. The pilot handed us headsets to wear during our six-minute ride. He explained that we would go up, circle above the ice-fishermen, trace a little of the coastline, and then come back down.

"Since we're flying over water, you'll need to wear a flotation device," he said.

The pilot handed us what looked like ugly, yellow fanny packs covered with instructions.

"We're flying over ice," I pointed out.

"Yeah, but if we crashed, we'd break through the ice. *Then* we'd be in water."

Without further comment, I strapped on the device.

"Aren't you going to read it first?" Odette's mellifluous voice filled my headset.

"I'd rather fly in blissful ignorance than prepare to die."

"Then relax already," she said. "We've got Jesus on our side."

I was working very hard *not* to recall the account of a spectacular helicopter crash I'd seen on the news. The blades had become tangled in something and pulled the aircraft over and down. Everyone aboard and everyone below had perished. I was too young and over-committed to die.

As I scanned the horizon for potential snares, Odette boomed, "I said, relax!"

And we were airborne.

Having flown in small planes, I expected a bumpy ride. But this was as smooth as sitting at my desk. The pilot was right: my fear of heights didn't even come into play. When I pressed my face to the glass, there was no rush of vertigo as when peering over a cliff, for example. Plus, the views were incredible. I'd never seen Magnet Springs from this angle. The steep bluffs, the quaint architecture, the snow-laden trees. Our town looked as picture-postcard perfect as we wished it were. A minute into the flight I began to relax.

"That looks like Dr. David," said Odette, pointing. "What's he doing?"

I followed her finger. The figure by the concessions tent was David Newquist, all right. Even from this altitude I would have recognized his slumping posture and paunch, but the bright yellow Magnet Springs Vet Clinic coat clinched the ID.

"Probably getting something to eat," I said.

"Look again," said Odette, so I did. Dr. David appeared to be stuffing something inside his ample coat while peering around to make sure no one saw him.

"And that's Jeb over there, isn't it?" Odette exclaimed, pointing in another direction. "Is he with Avery?"

Incredulous, I followed her finger. The man was definitely Jeb Halloran; I knew that body from any distance. The woman I wasn't so sure about. She was Avery's size and appeared to be wearing Avery's olive-green parka, but the hood's fur trim hid her profile. What would Avery be doing at the Jamboree? She hated crowds. And why would she be talking with my first husband? Avery hardly spoke to anyone. After her temper tantrum last night, even Jeb couldn't charm her.

Suddenly Odette said, "Is that Chester down there?"

I saw what she saw: a towheaded kid being pulled by the hand across the ice near one of the docks. From this height the second person could be either a man or a woman. The figure wore what looked like a fur hat and a full-length fur coat. Chinchilla? Even as the child resisted, the pair moved determinedly away from the shore.

TEN

"BRING US DOWN! *Now!*" I bellowed. My volume violated good headset etiquette, judging from the groans I got in response.

"We've only been up for three minutes," Odette said. "You paid for three more."

"I don't care. If that's Chester down there, we've got to find him."

I tried to keep the boy in sight as the pilot turned the helicopter to begin its sharp descent. But Chester, or his look-alike, quickly faded from view.

Once we touched down, I flung off the headset, thanked the pilot, and dashed toward the shoreline. Behind me Odette shouted, "Whiskey! You're still wearing the floaty-thingie!"

She was right. The ugly yellow fanny pack bounced at my waist.

"I'll bring it back!" I yelled over my shoulder.

To my advantage, I was dressed right for a winter chase. Under my light-weight parka, I was still wearing the jeans and sweater

I had changed into (and slept in) last night. Combined with my heavy socks and thick-soled boots, the ensemble afforded good mobility. Plus, I was in decent shape for my thirty-three years. A lifetime of recreational hiking, biking, swimming, and skiing had kept me reasonably fit. Despite the stress and the cold, I was barely winded when I slowed near the docks.

Which way were they headed? I strained to reconstruct the aerial scene from an earthbound point of view: the woman(?) had been dragging the boy(?) away from the cluster of waterfront bars toward the circle of ice-fishing contestants. I stepped carefully onto the ice, which was cleared and slick. Wishing, despite my weak ankles, that I was wearing skates, I pumped my arms and pushed one foot in front of the other while scanning for Chester.

"Whiskey!" I glanced around to see Peg Goh sliding toward me. She looked unsteady on her thick legs. "You haven't seen Gil, have you? He's due to announce the next event, and I can't find him anywhere."

"Haven't seen him," I panted. "Did you happen to see Chester? Odette and I spotted him from the helicopter."

Peg's eyes widened. "No! But I'll start looking. Which way did he go?"

"Toward all the activity." I pointed straight ahead. "Someone was pulling him along. Someone in a fur coat."

Someone who looked like either Mr. or Mrs. Gribble the Third, I wanted to add. But this being Magnet Springs, other Jamboree attendees might be dressed the same way.

Peg shoved up her coat sleeve to check her watch.

"Oh dear. If I can't find Gil, I'll have to announce the Tug-o'-War myself."

71

"You gotta do what you gotta do. Just keep your eyes peeled for Chester."

"I'll make an announcement about that, too! I'll ask folks to report any boy matching his description!"

I thanked her for her help and slid on toward the Jamboree. Everyone was looking for the missing mayor. If I was asked once, I was asked a dozen times whether I'd seen Gil. With each reply, I mentioned that I was searching for Chester. No one had seen him, either.

The two Tug-o'-War teams were in place on either side of a gaping hole in the ice. Both had grown weary of waiting, especially the Polar Bear Team. Super-macho men wearing only swimsuits, they were paying dearly for the delay.

A cheer went up as Peg mounted the temporary dais. She apologized for Gil's absence and then got right to it, stating the rules of the event. The losing team was going to get wet, not to mention cold(er). Magnet Springs High School cheerleaders, wearing none too many clothes themselves, were ready to comfort the losers with beach towels and blankets. A couple EMTs stood by, too.

"One more word before we begin," Peg said, and the impatient teams groaned. "If anyone here has seen a small boy with tousled white-blonde hair, please let me know."

"Is he lost?" somebody shouted.

"He's . . . missing," Peg replied. "And his loved ones need to know where he is."

Then she blew the whistle signaling the official start of the Tug-o'-War, and the Polar Bears were promptly pulled into the drink. Watching teenage girls towel off foolish old men didn't thrill me, so I moved on, scanning the crowd for Chester and/or a person in a long fur coat.

Sliding past a clot of ice-fishermen, I collided squarely with David Newquist.

"I'm looking for Chester," he said defensively.

"Me, too." I tried to be subtle as I checked out his parka for a tell-tale bulge. Nothing I could see or feel upon impact. What had he taken from the concessions tent, and why?

"I heard Peg's announcement," he said. "Any idea where Chester is?"

I shook my head.

Why did I hesitate to tell the good vet what I'd seen? Was it because I suddenly suspected him of thievery?

"I thought I saw him . . ." David said.

"Where?"

The vet narrowed his eyes. "You saw him, too, didn't you, Whiskey? With a person in a fur coat?"

He sounded annoyed now. Was it because he knew I was holding back? Or had the idea of someone wearing a fur coat pissed him off? He was, after all, an animal rights activist.

"Yes," I admitted. "When Odette and I were up in the helicopter, we thought we saw Chester. But we couldn't tell who he was with, or even if it was a man or woman. Gil's missing, too, by the way."

"I don't care about Gil." The coldness in David's voice surprised me. "Let's make a plan to find Chester."

"He—they were moving away from the shore when I saw them, but that was at least ten minutes ago already."

David said, "You go that way, out toward the shanties. I'll search along the shoreline in case they came back in."

I stole one more glance at David's voluminous pockets. He caught my eye.

"What's wrong?"

It sounded like "What's wong?" Although I knew it was rude to laugh, the stress of the moment made me giggle. To cover, I faked a cough.

"Nothing," I said. "I'm off to find Chester."

Most of the competitive ice-fishing events required participants to stay in plain sight. No use of shanties allowed. But the Jamboree also lured fishermen eager to partake of the party atmosphere, if not the competition itself. Hence the higher than usual number of shanties farther out on the ice.

I was sliding determinedly toward Fishburg, as we dubbed that seasonal suburb, when I spied Roy Vickers moving toward shore, his head down, shoulders hunched. Since he didn't respond the first two times I called to him, I assumed he was lost in thought.

"Hey! Why aren't you working on the company truck?" I shouted. "It needs antifreeze!"

I hardly recognized the man who looked up; whether due to the cold or some inner demon, Roy suddenly looked every one of his seventy years.

"Are you all right?" I said, changing my course to meet him.

Before he could reply, I spotted the blood on his plaid jacket. Part of one sleeve was deep red, and there were crimson splatters across his abdomen and chest. The red was still wet and shiny. I slid to a halt.

Roy must have known what I saw, and what I was thinking: that this was the man who had tried to kill Leo Mattimoe. Had he hurt someone else?

"I helped a guy unhook a fish." Roy gestured vaguely toward the shanties behind him. "He didn't know what he was doing."

I couldn't take my eyes off the mess that was Roy's jacket, even as my stomach lurched. Suddenly Roy's hands were squeezing my upper arms so hard they hurt.

"Breathe, Whiskey!" he barked. "Breathe, or you're going to faint."

I gulped a lungful of painfully cold air and forced my gaze to meet his. That close up, in that crazed moment, his bloodshot eyes were wide with fright. Mine probably looked the same.

"Breathe again," he commanded, still clutching my biceps. "And again."

I did as told. When he released me, my knees wobbled.

"I helped a guy unhook a fish," Roy repeated, stressing each syllable in a way that made him sound either very calm or completely insane.

I nodded, not trusting my voice.

"Are you looking for Chester?" Roy asked. Again I nodded. "He's not out there. Nobody's around but a few fishermen. I already checked."

"I'll just ask if anybody's seen him," I said.

"I already did." Roy looked as if he were about to block my path. Then he sighed heavily and resumed his trek toward shore. I watched his stiff movements, each step suggesting the pain of old age. What had happened to his athletic bounce, his glow of optimism?

Roy was right about Fishburg being nearly deserted. Although there were more shanties than usual, I counted just four in use; the rest stood locked and silent. The fishermen I spoke with had seen no one, not even Roy.

I was about to head back toward shore when I spied an isolated shanty about a quarter mile off, closer to the coastline than to Fishburg but set apart from the Jamboree. I returned to the last pair of fishermen I'd seen.

"Sorry to bother you guys again, but do you know whose that is?" I pointed toward the distant hut.

Without moving from their stools, both men craned their necks to see what I saw.

"Nope," the first one said. The second concurred, adding, "Somebody put it up last night. Wasn't there yesterday."

I thanked them and shoved off toward the distant shanty. The wind stiffened as a leaden tint dulled the sky. Weather incoming, I thought. Tourist dollars could be lost. That would not please Gil Gruen, wherever he was.

Wherever Chester was, I just hoped he was warm and dry. And safe. Above all, safe.

ELEVEN

DRAWING NEAR THE ICE shanty beyond Fishburg, I saw that its door was ajar.

"Hellooo!" I called, not wanting to startle the fisherman by suddenly appearing up close and panting. Anyone who chose to be this far from the crowd surely wouldn't welcome a visitor.

No answer. I called again and got no reply. Tentatively, I pulled the door open.

The shanty's sole occupant was Gil Gruen. Although his back was to me, I would have recognized him anywhere, thanks to his signature Stetson hat and sheepskin coat.

"Gil, you're missing your own Jamboree," I began.

I was going to add that I thought he didn't fish when something stopped me. Or, to be accurate, several things stopped me. The first was Gil's posture. From the doorway, I could see it wasn't right. Even when relaxed, Gil had a sense of style. Granted, he was all myth and arrogance, but he had presence. Now he was slumped at an odd angle suggesting complete deflation. Second, the air had a peculiar tang—a sharp sweetness I didn't want to contemplate. Third, Gil Gruen loved to glad-hand. No way our mayor would choose to sit alone in an ice-fishing shanty while the event of the season went on without him.

Against my better judgment, I entered. The instant I touched Gil's shoulder, two things happened: the air cracked—like thunder inside a tent—and Gil toppled forward. A split second later, I felt my feet slide apart. I glanced down and tried to grasp what was happening: the ice around me, around both of us, was covered in blood. And the ice was splintering.

Gil rolled sideways into the widening mouth of water, his Stetson slipping from his head, his empty eyes fixed on a far dimension. As my own body lurched forward, I remembered the flotation fanny pack. Groping for the button that would inflate it, I wished I had bothered to read the instructions.

The same instant that I hit the icy water, my waistline popped. A small airbag blossomed, setting me upright like a bobber on a fishing line. Simultaneously, the cold seared my legs and lower back. I gasped. Even if I didn't go under the ice, I would be numb in no time.

Way back in high school, I had taken an ice survival class: "What to Do If You Break Through." It was part of some Community Winter Safety Course my mother had made me attend because she was worried about my snowmobiling with boys. Naturally, at age seventeen I hadn't paid attention. In fact, I had developed a seriously distracting crush on the instructor, who doubled in summertime as our local lifeguard.

Now I needed to summon back the basics. I knew that *not panicking* was Rule Number One. That was the first step in any crisis. So I drew a deep breath and said aloud, "Stay calm."

Gil's body brushed against me and then slipped under the ice. The last thing I saw were the pointy toes of his snakeskin boots.

"Oh God!" I cried out. But I managed not to freak. And, miraculously, I remembered the next step: "Pull yourself back onto the ice in the direction you came from."

That meant placing my hands and arms on the slippery surface and kicking my legs for propulsion. The effort would keep the blood pumping, too, as the frigid water seized my muscles.

Even if the ice continued to break beneath me, the point was to keep pushing myself in the same direction. To keep at it until I was lying flat on the ice.

So I pressed myself against the splintering, blood-covered surface, pumping with all my might the nearly dead weight of my legs. As the surface beneath me cracked apart, I managed to keep creeping forward, inch by inch, gulping air as I worked. The inflated fanny pack forced me into an awkwardly curved but still mostly horizontal position. Ahead was the open door of the shanty, my first destination.

With one huge final push, I propelled myself through it, into the bracing open air. I paused, panting hard, my heart thudding in my ears. Although I was mostly numb, I knew my whole body was clear of the shanty and now lay exposed on the ice. Slowly, I started rolling and kept on rolling, over and over, away from the shelter.

Another ominous crack, this one from behind me. I stopped. The ice under my body remained solid. Cautiously, I rolled a few more times before letting myself look back. The ice shanty was tipping into a now immense hole.

I sat up slowly. Gil's Stetson floated alongside the partially submerged shelter.

"Help!" I shouted. Or so I wished. My voice wouldn't work. I tried again. Only the smallest croak emerged. I tried to stand up. At first my legs didn't work, either, but after a moment, I struggled to my knees and then to my feet. The top half of me was shaking violently. The bottom half was numb, so numb I wondered if it was still mine. Somehow, finally, I pushed one leaden foot in front of the other.

"Help!" I tried again, trapped inside a nightmare where I couldn't scream and couldn't run.

Don't panic, keep breathing, I reminded myself as I shuffled dully toward Fishburg. If I could just reach those two guys in that shanty. I fixed my eyes on my destination and forced myself forward, inch by inch.

Suddenly a man appeared among the ice-fishing shelters. His face was too far off for me to read, but his body language suggested that he saw me. He seemed to be staring in my direction.

I strained to wave my quaking hands. It took so much energy. Too much energy. Since when was waving so hard?

He waved back and then stopped, his arm paused in mid-arc. What happened next gave me the greatest of hopes: the man started toward me.

I wanted to keep going, but I was tired. Very tired. And so weak. Although I paused for only a moment, I lost my momentum. I was sleepy now. Too sleepy to continue. Weak, too. My knees buckled; the ice came up to meet me.

"Get up," I moaned.

But I couldn't. I couldn't even open my eyes. A little nap was all I needed. Just a small, short sleep to restore my strength.

"Hello!" The male voice was close to my ears. "Hang on. Y'all are going to be just fine."

He was rolling me over onto my side. I willed my eyelids to open, and they did, partway. Could it be? The smile floating before me belonged to the father of Avery's twins.

"Hello," I whispered, or tried to. Maybe I just smiled back. I closed my eyes again, letting it all go.

TWELVE

"Whiskey, wake up."

I recognized the voice. It wasn't the one I wanted to hear, but it came again, anyway.

"Open your eyes, Whiskey. I know you can hear me."

I opened one eye. Odette was next to me. She didn't look worried, so I opened the other eye.

"You're not him," I said.

"No, and you're not quite yourself, either. Him who?"

"Avery's ex. He saved me."

"Actually, you saved yourself. *He* arrived in time to help you ashore."

When I tried to sit up, I realized I had a tube in my arm. I also had a lot of blankets piled on me and a heater aimed at me.

"Am I in the hospital?"

"How perceptive," Odette yawned. "Coastal Medical Center, to be precise. The EMTs didn't like your hypothermia, so they brought you here."

I sank back and tried to sort out my jumbled memories.

"Gil's dead," I said.

"What?" Suddenly Odette was interested.

"He was in the shanty that went through the ice. The shanty outside of Fishburg."

"Gil was *fishing*?"

"No, Gil was dead. I saw no sign that he'd been fishing."

That was true, and it only now clicked in my head. I replayed the moment when I'd entered the shanty: There had been no fishing equipment inside. Just Gil and blood and splintering ice.

"Nash Grant didn't mention a body," Odette said.

"That's because Nash Grant never saw it. Gil went under the ice before I even got out of the water." The horror hit me as hard as a snowplow, and I started shaking again.

"Do you need another blanket?" Odette asked.

"I need Jenx," I said through chattering teeth.

By the time the police chief arrived, I had stopped shaking and was able to sip a warm, sweet beverage through a bent straw.

"You're sure he was dead," Jenx said, her pen poised over her notebook.

"Positive. If he'd been alive, he would have insulted me. And his eyes—" I shuddered. "I'm sure he was dead."

"Could you tell how he died?"

I replayed the pictures in my head.

"His chest was bloody—where his coat was open."

"Did it look like a bullet wound?"

"It looked like . . . like a slash. His shirt was torn. There was so much blood. It was everywhere."

Jenx said, "You mean, like he'd been stabbed?"

Should I tell her about my weird encounter with Roy Vickers, his jacket splattered, his sleeve drenched with blood? If only I had dreamed that moment, but I knew I hadn't.

"You need to find Roy," I said, my throat tight.

"Why? Did he see something?"

"I saw something. His jacket was covered with blood. And he was coming from the direction of Gil's shanty."

"Did he explain the blood?"

"He said he helped a guy unhook a fish."

"Must have been some fish."

"Sturgeon, maybe?" I suggested.

"Whiskey—."

"I know. It looks bad."

"Odette said Roy threatened Gil at the Goh Cup this morning."

"Roy was defending me."

"Yeah, well, it looks like you shouldn't have hired the guy."

"We don't know that, Jenx!"

"Correction: we haven't confirmed that. Yet."

She scribbled in her notebook, and then flipped the page. "Odette also said you might have seen Chester."

"Might have? I'm sure it was him!"

"From up in a helicopter you could be sure?"

"The only thing I'm not sure about is who he was with. Someone in a long fur coat."

"There are at least fifty of those around town," Jenx said, "not counting the wealthy tourists."

"Well, one of those coats has Chester! Can't you get some kind of wardrobe subpoena? Send Officers Brady and Roscoe door-to-door?"

Jenx gave me such a dirty look that I pulled the blankets over my head.

"Did I say I was done with you?" She yanked the covers away.

"If I can't play sick in the hospital, then why am I here? My insurance won't even pay for this. Have some pity for the self-employed!"

Jenx tossed the blankets back over my face and left. I drifted off to sleep.

When I woke, a nurse was checking my vital signs.

"You're recovering well," she said. "But they'll want to keep you at least twenty-four hours. With hypothermia, there's a risk of cardiac complications."

"I've got a business to run," I protested. "And a kid to find!"

"You lost your kid?"

"Worse: I lost someone else's. Is Chief Jenkins still around?"

"No, but somebody's here to see you. I think his name is Nash."

My heart leaped, so I figured it was still working.

"Is there a mirror?" I asked the nurse. She winked and produced one from her pocket. I wished she hadn't; my face was ghostly white and my usually messy hair was a mare's nest. The kindly nurse produced a comb, but we couldn't get it through my tangles. In fact, it got stuck in there. The nurse went off to find scissors. Nash Grant appeared.

"You have a comb sticking out of your head," he drawled. "But I suppose you know that."

I nodded. "The surgery's scheduled for tomorrow."

He laughed, and I liked the sound of it.

"Thanks for helping me get to shore."

"It was the least I could do, considering you'd already handled the hard part. How'd you get yourself out of that freezing water?"

"One inch at a time."

Up close, the man was gorgeous. He had coppery eyes flecked with green, high cheekbones, and thick walnut-colored hair. Plus that sexy southern accent. And he smelled as good as he had when he brushed past me at Mother Tucker's.

"I'm Nash Grant," he said, extending a hand.

"Whiskey Mattimoe."

"You're the grandma!"

"Pardon?"

"I'm the father of Avery's twins. I understand you're their grandma."

Somehow I'd never thought of it that way. The concept gagged me.

"Water?" Nash said, helpfully pouring a fresh glass.

"I'm Avery's *step*mother," I said. "Her father was older than me. A lot older."

"That's obvious. And I'm a lot older than Avery. Fifteen years."

"That's how much older Leo was than me," I said.

"But it worked? Your marriage, I mean?"

"Yes. But we didn't start out making babies. We were friends first and then lovers." Before I could put another foot in my mouth, I forced myself to drink the whole glass of water.

"Avery and I were impetuous," Nash conceded. "And we're not in love. But I'm prepared to be responsible. Tonight, I meet my son and daughter."

"You haven't seen them yet?"

"Only in pictures."

I handed him back the empty glass.

"What were you doing in Fishburg?"

Nash looked confused.

"Out among the ice shanties," I clarified. "Why weren't you with Avery back at the Jamboree?"

"Avery wasn't at the Jamboree."

"I saw her. She was talking with my ex-husband."

Nash shook his head. "Avery's spending the day with the twins. She said I could come by tonight. So I decided to spend the day soaking up local color. When I saw the ice-fishing huts, I had to check them out. I'm a consultant for a company that makes build-it-yourself shanty kits."

"What do they consult you about?"

"How to sell more of them. I teach advertising at the University of Florida. And do a little consulting on the side."

He grinned. If he was half as good at consulting as he was at flirting, Nash Grant should be rich.

"With your accent, I don't suppose you grew up ice-fishing," I ventured.

"True enough. Biloxi boys play field sports in winter. I preferred baseball myself."

"I played softball when I was a kid. Still do, occasionally, though volleyball was my high-school sport of choice."

Nash nodded approvingly. "Avery said you were athletic."

As in "Whiskey's more athletic than attractive," probably. I wondered what else Avery had said about me.

Before I could ask, there was a knock at my door, and my first husband said, "Who knew that ice-survival course from eleventh grade would finally pay off?"

"That and the flotation fanny pack I lifted from the helicopter," I replied. "Jeb Halloran, meet Nash Grant."

"We already did," Nash said, acting every bit the Southern gentleman as he rose to shake Jeb's hand.

"Good to see you again," Jeb told him.

"When did you two meet?" I asked.

The men exchanged glances as if reminding each other of a Masonic secret.

"Uh—today," Jeb said. "At the Jamboree."

"Did Avery introduce you?"

"Like I said, Avery wasn't there," Nash replied.

I focused on Jeb. "Didn't I see you talking with Avery?"

"When?"

"This afternoon. At the Jamboree."

"Not me," said Jeb. He and Nash simultaneously cleared their throats.

"What's going on here?" I demanded.

"Nothing," they replied.

"Jeb Halloran, who were you talking to just before one o'clock?"

"You know I don't wear a watch."

"But you wear a brain, don't you? Can't you remember who you saw at the Jamboree?"

"I saw lots of people, Whiskey. I sold sixty-three CDs! Tomorrow I hope to sell twice as many, if the weather doesn't get any worse. My Celtic Collection's a local hit."

"If you don't mind my asking, how do you advertise?" said Nash.

At which point, I once again pulled the blankets over my head. It must have been five minutes before they noticed. Then they moved their conversation outside. As he left the room, I sneaked a peek at Nash Grant's ass. Very nice. But to be fair, so was Jeb's.

It was Nash, though, who made me feel as if my IV drip contained an intoxicant.

"Grandma," indeed.

THIRTEEN

I MUST HAVE EATEN something for dinner, but hospital food is about as memorable as it is tasty. All I could recall was a delicious dream: Nash Grant, Jeb Halloran, and David Newquist were tag-teaming the dog-and-baby-sitting duties at Vestige. And this was the best part: their job descriptions included giving *me* Day Spa treatments. Nash was shampooing my hair, Jeb was massaging my back, and Dr. David was clipping my claws, I mean nails.

I could have spent the whole night, if not longer, inside that fantasy. Unfortunately, I was rudely awakened by a commotion in the hall outside my room. It took a moment—a very disappointing moment—to realize where I was, and that there were no attractive men attending me.

A nurse I hadn't yet met entered my room in that stealthy way night nurses do.

"What's up?" I asked, and she jumped in alarm.

"Sorry," I said. "Did you think I was dead?"

"I thought you were sleeping. I hoped you were sleeping." She sighed. "Everything takes longer when we have to talk to the patients."

She explained that an ice storm had started a few hours earlier, followed by scattered power outages. When the grid to Coastal Medical Center went down, they had switched to emergency generators.

"Since you're not on life support, it won't much affect you," said the nurse. "Except that your meals will be cold."

"Aren't they, anyway?"

"I'm going to remove your IV before we get busy. . . ."

"Do you have to? Whatever's in there is good stuff." I yawned, wishing to drift back to my Alternate Version of Vestige. Then it dawned on me that an ice storm spelled disaster for the Jamboree.

"Will the weather be better tomorrow?" I asked.

"It's already tomorrow," the nurse said, activating the glow-in-the-dark face of her watch for my benefit. It read 4:17.

"Uh-oh. Doesn't look good for the tourist trade."

"You can say that again. Most roads are closed. I won't be able to leave till they're plowed, or it thaws, whichever comes first. Why rush home, anyhow? We got no heat. At least here it's warm."

I nodded. Then Chester popped into my head. Chances are he was not only in trouble but also in the cold. And in the dark.

"I've got to get out of here!" I blurted.

The nurse, a large woman close to retirement age, laughed. "Honey, that's what they all say!"

"But I've really got to get out of here! I've got a lost kid to go find!"

"Yeah, the nurse from last shift said you mentioned that. We figured you were disoriented from the hypothermia. She marked it on your chart."

"I'm not confused," I said, sitting up. "I know exactly what's going on! Well, maybe not exactly, or I could tell Jenx where to find Chester. But I'm not confused! Where's the phone?"

"Phones aren't working," the nurse said flatly. "And you need to lie back down."

"I'll bet cell phones are working." I reached toward the bedside stand for mine.

"No cell phone use allowed," she barked. Dark though the room was, I thought I saw her scoop my cell phone into her pocket.

"You can't take that!" I said.

"Take what? You need to close your eyes and get some rest. Unless you want me to recommend a complete psychiatric workup."

I knew then that I'd seen the last of Nice Nurse. From now on she would manage me by coercion. I recognized the strategy; it was the only way I could handle Abra. So I shut my eyes, pulled the blankets over my face, and tried to recapture my three-man Day Spa.

Around seven AM, the night shift went off duty, even if they couldn't go off site. Or at least my night nurse took a break, because the next person attending me was a freckled young man whose nametag read C. RICHARDS, RN.

"I hear you got a little excited during the night," he said pleasantly.

"Not excited. Just concerned—for those without emergency generators."

I smiled. He smiled back. He was kind of cute for someone just out of nursing school. Actually, he looked just out of high school.

"I have a question," I said in my sweetest voice. "Is hospital staff allowed to confiscate the personal possessions of patients?"

C. Richards looked thoughtful, as if trying to recall that question from his New Employee Handbook.

"I don't think they can 'confiscate' things. But I know the hospital can hold on to personal possessions. For a while."

"See, we have an issue here . . ." I motioned for him to lean closer so that I could whisper my concerns. He did, and I conveyed my theory that the formerly nice night nurse had crossed a line by removing my cell phone against my will.

"Technically, I don't think she did anything wrong," C. Richards said, straightening. "But, if you really want your cell phone back, and you promise not to use it while you're here, I'll see what I can do."

"Cross my heart," I said, making the appropriate gesture over my left breast. His blue eyes followed my fingers. "I really need that phone back. . . ."

"Okay," he said, still staring at my chest. "Just let me finish rounds first."

"That's fine," I cooed.

Ten minutes later, C. Richards came through for me, confirming my faith in men, or at least in testosterone. Meekly, I thanked him and asked that he store the phone in my top drawer. As soon as he left, I removed it and checked the charge. How lucky that I'd carried it in a vest pocket that didn't get wet. Two bars left.

Now that it was daylight, I could see through my small window what the storm had wrought. The world outside appeared to be coated in glass. Earth and sky—both pearly white—were separated by no visible horizon. Neither humans nor machines moved. Everything seemed frozen solid.

I didn't have time for that. Fortunately, I knew one person with a vehicle that could probably get through anything. As part of both his veterinary practice and his animal rights activism, Dr. David Newquist owned and operated a 1989 Braun Type 3 ambulance. Dubbed the Animal Ambulance, it was painted white with horizontal yellow stripes that matched his gaudy parka. And it bore a variation on the same slogan he always wore:

ANIMALS ARE PEOPLE, TOO.
WE SAVE ANIMALS.

Confident that David also wanted to save Chester, I dialed his cell phone number. The first two calls wouldn't go through, but I connected on the third attempt.

"David," I whispered. "Get me out of here!"

"Who is this? And why are we whispering?"

As soon as I identified myself, David said, "How are you? I wanted to come see you last night, but I had two emergencies, and by the time I finished, visiting hours were over."

I doubted that most men would let a little thing like visiting hours stop them from seeing a woman they hoped to impress. I forgave him, though, and explained the reason for my call. David agreed that the Animal Ambulance could handle the ice storm. In fact, it was how he'd gotten to the vet clinic that morning. What he had doubts about was my readiness to leave the hospital.

"As a medical professional"—he made it sound like "*medicoh pwofeshunoh*"—"I have to advise you to put your own welfare first," David said.

"Yeah, yeah. I would have said the same thing if you'd shown me Gil's contract before you signed it," I retorted. "But you didn't, did you?"

"And you would have been right!" he reminded me.

"Okay, bad example. I need you to come get me, David. Together we are going to find Chester."

"Isn't that Jenx's job?"

"She needs help. Manpower shortage."

"There was an ice storm, Whiskey," David reminded me. "I'm sure Jenx would prefer that we stay off the road."

"What better time to go door-to-door looking for Chester!" I exclaimed.

"And where would we begin?"

"Do you care about Chester, or not?" I demanded.

"Of course, I do! I also care about you, and you're supposed to be in the hospital!"

"Not when I'm needed elsewhere. Let's start with what we learned yesterday," I said. "Did you find any sign of him after you and I split up?"

"As a matter of fact, I did. I interviewed people in the parking lot, asking if anyone had seen a kid who looked like Chester. Two people saw a boy who fit his description get into a white Jaguar. But they didn't see who he was with."

I supposed it was too much to hope they had written down the license number. It was. However, David said the witnesses recalled seeing an Iowa plate.

"Iowa?" I repeated. "Are you sure?"

"I'm sure that's what they told me," David said. "But am I sure they were right? How could I be?"

"Why would someone from Iowa snatch Chester?" I wondered aloud.

"Chester's the son of a celebrity," David reminded me. "Anyone from anywhere might want to collect ransom."

My heart thumped. Why hadn't I thought of that? Probably because I hadn't wanted to. But nobody had asked for ransom. At least nobody we knew about. I recalled my strange phone conversation with Cassina. Did she and Rupert know something we didn't?

Just then I became aware of C. Richards, RN, peering at me through the glass panel of my hospital room door. Quickly I concealed the cell phone under my blanket. When he continued to stare, I remembered what I knew about men: What works once works every time.

Very slowly with the index finger of my right hand, I traced a large X over my left breast.

C. Richards grinned and walked away.

FOURTEEN

RELUCTANTLY, DR. DAVID AGREED to come pick me up in the Animal Ambulance. He made me promise, though, that I would check myself out of Coastal Medical Center the legitimate way, rather than try to sneak out. That sounded a little too much like my mother talking. Of course, I wasn't going to sneak out. I'm a responsible adult: I run a business with employees and other kinds of headaches. Not to mention a 24/7 daycare center for kids and canines. What kind of person did Dr. David think I was?

As soon as we concluded our call, I located the clothes I'd arrived in, including my now dry socks and boots. Someone had had the sense to discard the expended flotation device I "borrowed" from the helicopter. Fortunately, my pocket-sized purse and its contents had survived the slide into Lake Michigan. I dressed quickly. Then, grabbing my cell phone, I peered out into the hall. I would have to make a break for it if I wanted to avoid arguing with overworked nurses or the random attending physician.

My destination was Admissions. At least, I assumed that's where I should go, although what I needed to do was the opposite of admitting myself. If the folks in that office could sign me in, they could probably sign me out. They'd just need a different form.

As soon as the hall was clear, I bolted for the stairway, yanked open the heavy metal door, and plowed straight into C. Richards, RN.

"Getting some exercise?" he asked. "Or looking for a better signal for your cell phone?"

"Shh." I stepped all the way into the stairwell, closing the door behind me. "Don't tell anybody, but I need to check out. Do you know where I go to do that?"

To my annoyance, the young nurse was staring at my left breast again, with such intensity this time that I wondered if I'd left it uncovered. So I checked. Everything was secure.

"Hey," I said. "Here's a tip: Try looking your patients in the eye for a change. It makes for a better bedside manner."

"I know all about bedside manner," he said huskily. "I even know where there's a maintenance closet with a cot."

"I'm going to report you!" I sputtered.

"Oh yeah? Do you know where to go to do that?"

Disgusted, I pushed past him and literally ran until the stairway ended. That was a mistake since it landed me in the sub-basement boiler room. But, after adjusting my course and going back up two flights, I eventually found Admissions. The clerks there weren't pleased with my assumption that they could automatically check me out. They made a few phone calls and insisted on my signing a little form called AMA—Against Medical Advice. The whole process was more time-consuming and aggravating than necessary, considering we all knew that I was going to get my way.

When I did, Dr. David was waiting for me out front. His Animal Ambulance had attracted considerable attention from off-duty hospital staff who couldn't get their own cars out of the glassy lot.

"I was offered almost two hundred dollars to take folks home," he said.

"You should consider running this as an emergency taxi service," I said, climbing aboard. "Pick up a little cash on the side."

"That's exactly what I'm doing. There are four people in the back. We're going to deliver them first, then look for Chester."

I stared at David, hoping for a sign that he was kidding. Then I realized the truth: He had no sense of humor with humans. Oh, he could giggle and laugh and roll on the floor with critters, but people turned him deadly serious.

"I'm donating the proceeds to Fleggers," he added.

Fleggers was shorthand for Four Legs Good, the name of the Ann Arbor-based Animal Rights group to which David devoted his spare time. Their slogan was, "We love people of all species." Their goal was equal rights for animals, whatever that meant. I found the notion too ridiculous to fit inside my head. Did "equal" rights mean equal to human, such as the power to, say, own one's home? Marry? Vote? Just what this country needed—dogs and cats voting in the next presidential election.

"We're giving four people a lift?" I asked.

David nodded. He consulted a scrap of notebook paper. "Two live in the neighborhood, one lives north of town, and the other lives east of Sugar Grove."

"East of Sugar Grove? That's almost an hour away in good weather," I moaned.

"Then we'd better roll," David said. He pronounced the last word like "woe." Which was precisely what I felt.

"By the way," he said. "Do you know you have blood on your jacket?"

In my haste to break out, I hadn't noticed. Now in the flat morning light, I stared at my chest and sleeves. Not just any blood, but Gil's blood—from my struggle to get out of the frigid water back onto the ice where our mayor had hemorrhaged. I whipped off the jacket and wrapped myself in a wool blanket I found on David's front seat. My teeth were chattering, and not from the cold.

In the hands of a skilled driver like David, the Animal Ambulance could overcome most road hazards. The vet was proud to have purchased it used, online, for a mere five thousand dollars. As a contribution to Fleggers, he had re-fitted the back to accommodate and secure both large animals and small.

On the down side, the ambulance had no radio or heat, and the passenger seat was built for rides lasting less than fifteen minutes. By the time we'd delivered three of the four passengers and were heading east toward Sugar Grove, I'd been bouncing in place for an hour and a half.

"Do you think we could take a break? Maybe get something to eat?" I asked David.

"Nothing's open today," he replied. "Maybe you shouldn't have checked yourself out before breakfast."

"Maybe you shouldn't have agreed to chauffeur four passengers," I groused.

Silently David raised his right hand from the wheel to display five fingers.

"What does that mean?" I asked.

"*Five* passengers."

We rode in silence the rest of the way to Sugar Grove, a former railroad town slightly larger than Magnet Springs. I respected David's driving, which was confident but not incautious. The roads were terrible, varying from a sheet of glass to a bed of broken glass. Now and then the Animal Ambulance fishtailed wildly. When it did, I gripped the door handle with both hands, closed my eyes, and hung on. David remained calm, his hold on the wheel relaxed.

Passing the Sugar Grove Inn stirred my memories. There I'd had many romantic brunches with my late husband Leo and one not-so-happy meal with the local judge. Six months after Leo died, jurist Wells Verbelow and I dated without making sparks. Now I was beginning to doubt whether David and I could, either. Or whether he'd even ask me out. Or whether I wanted him to, for that matter. The vet was competent, dedicated, and not bad-looking. But, God help me, he wasn't Nash Grant.

I jumped when someone thumped the partition behind me.

"Yo, dude!" said a muffled voice. "This is where I get out!"

We were on the other side of town now, on the edge of a woody glen. David eased the Animal Ambulance to a stop. The rear door opened and closed. Then our fourth passenger slid past my window. In civilian clothes, C. Richards, RN, looked like the teen-age boy he probably still was. He grinned lasciviously at me and ran his tongue over his upper lip. I glanced at David, who was adjusting something on the dashboard and hence missed the show.

C. Richards, or whoever he was, stepped deftly across the narrow ditch running parallel to the road. In seconds, he had vanished into the woods.

"Where to next?" David asked, looking up.

Before I could reply, my cell phone rang.

"How's your left breast?" panted You-Know-Who. "Are you keeping it warm for me?"

I clicked off. The damn kid had copied down my number when he retrieved my phone.

It rang again.

"Listen, you little pervert," I began.

"I've been called worse." Police Chief Jenkins was on the line.

"Sorry," I mumbled.

"I hear you busted out of Coastal Med. What's up with that?"

"Dr. David and I are going to help you look for Chester, now that we've finished our morning deliveries. Any suggestions where to start?"

"Where are you?" she asked.

I gave her our approximate location just east of Sugar Grove.

"That's great!" Jenx exclaimed. "You're near Bear Claw Casino Resort!"

"So? We don't have time for games of chance."

"That's what we're playing, Whiskey. I just got a call from Chester. On his cell phone. Somebody made him hang up before he could say much, but I recognized the noise in the background. It was the ding-ding-ding of a casino floor. Get over to Bear Claw now!"

Thanks to David's expert driving and keen sense of direction, we arrived at the Native American-run resort in less than twenty minutes. On the way, I tried to talk about my discovery of Gil's body, but David wasn't having any.

"Listen, Whiskey, I'm not glad the guy got whacked—if that's what happened—but I'm not sorry he's gone, either."

"You realize that your contract with Best West still stands," I said. "Gil's business continues to exist even if he doesn't."

David seemed shocked to hear that. Sometimes I wondered if he had any business sense.

"But Gil's name's on my lease! He signed it!"

"Yes, but he signed it as an agent of Best West Realty. Read the document, David."

Once again the vet settled into a funk. After a few minutes I said, "But the good thing for you is that Gil won't be around to threaten you anymore. Whoever takes over Best West has got to be more pleasant to deal with."

"More pleasant for you, too."

That revelation had already dawned on me.

"Who'll take over Best West?" David asked.

I didn't know. Unlike Leo, Gil was single and had no kin in the biz. He had a couple part-time agents, neither of whom seemed likely to want to run Best West.

When we pulled into the Bear Claw Casino Resort parking lot, David and I remarked on the number of vehicles. Apparently, ice storms don't discourage gamblers—not if the back-up generators keep running. David had a plan: He would drop me off at the front entrance and then check every row in the lot for a white Jaguar with Iowa plates.

"Or any white Jag at all," I suggested.

My job was to find out whether someone inside had seen Chester, which way he went, and who he was with. Since Chester's a kid that folks remember, I figured we just might get lucky. If Jenx was right in assuming the phone call had come from here.

FIFTEEN

THE BEAR CLAW CASINO Resort desk clerk hadn't seen Chester or any children that morning.

"Most parents don't pull their kids out of school for a day here," he remarked. "We're not Disney World."

When I pointed out that local schools were closed due to the ice storm, the desk clerk looked surprised. "There was an ice storm?"

I thought he was joking until I realized that the front desk afforded no outside view. Moreover, the bulk of the casino's business was day traffic, patrons who came to gamble for a few hours and didn't stay at the hotel. They used a different entrance. I headed that way.

From the smoky casino floor came a cacophony of artificial sounds. Not just the ding-ding-ding reported by Jenx, but also electronic chords and scales, and the occasional cascading clink of quarters when somebody's slot machine paid off. Bored cocktail waitresses roamed the room. They wore leather headbands with bedraggled feathers, beaded suede mini-dresses and four-inch heels. The costume suggested a nubile Native American princess, but every waitress I saw was Caucasian and had a name like Mindy or Megan.

I interviewed Mindy first as I ordered a tall Pepsi and some pretzels. She was a stocky dishwater blonde with sallow skin and watery eyes. When she complained about an allergy to cigarette smoke, I questioned her choice of employment.

"I got pregnant the first month of my junior year in high school," Mindy said. "So, after Christmas break, I didn't go back. Now I got three kids under five and two deadbeat dads. Why do I work here?" She scratched her nose. "Daycare's good, and they pay full benefits. Where else am I going to get a deal like that on the reservation?"

"You live on the reservation?"

"Sure. My kids are half Kickapoo."

Having children of her own, Mindy seemed likely to sympathize with Chester. Or so I guessed. But I guessed wrong.

"He's eight? What's a kid that age doing with his own cell phone?" she asked. "He sounds way spoiled."

"Well, his mother travels a lot on business, so she needs to keep in touch."

"The kid's mom is rich, right?"

"Right," I conceded. "But the point is that the kid is missing. Possibly kidnapped. And we think he might have been here this morning."

"The kid's mom lets him gamble? That's illegal, you know. We could get in trouble if he even touched a slot. I could maybe even lose my job."

I could maybe even be wasting my time, I concluded. After over-tipping Mindy, I took my Pepsi and pretzels and walked away.

Megan was the next waitress I cornered. A wee thing with slightly crossed almond-colored eyes, she was instantly concerned when I mentioned Chester.

"Well, kids aren't supposed to be on the floor," she began, "but there was one here this morning. Light blonde hair, big glasses. Looked about six years old."

"That's Chester! He looks six, but he's really eight."

"Preemie?" Megan asked.

"Pardon?"

"Was he born premature? I was, that's why I'm wondering. Growing up, I always looked a couple years younger than I was."

In fact, that was Chester's story. He was born backstage at one of his mother's first concerts. But I cut to the chase: "Tell me what you saw!"

Megan had met Chester about an hour earlier, when he came up behind her and yanked on her beaded suede mini-dress.

"Excuse me," he said. "That is not an authentic Native American tribal costume."

Megan smiled and explained that she was not an authentic Native American, so it didn't matter. Chester disagreed. He felt she was disrespecting Kickapoo tradition by wearing that outfit. Megan told him her bosses were Kickapoo, and they didn't care. Anyway, she was hired to sling drinks, not make a statement about Native American rights and traditions. At that point, Chester motioned for her to lean down so that he could whisper in her ear. She did, and he asked her to tell him whether she could see a tall woman with black and gray hair who looked like she was looking for someone.

"You have a better view than I do," he added. "I'm only three foot four, and I can't see over the slot machines."

Megan was moved by her own story. She told me, "I'm only five foot four, but I used my two-foot advantage to help him out. Sure enough, I spotted a woman who fit the description. She was heading straight toward us!"

That was when Chester whipped out his cell phone and made a call. But the tall woman grabbed the device from his hand. She told Megan, "Thanks for finding my grandson for me. I've been looking everywhere."

Chester glanced back at Megan as the woman pulled him away.

"He didn't say anything out loud," Megan said, "but he moved his mouth like he was trying to tell me something. I'll never forget it. His lips went like this." She demonstrated two silent syllables. For the first, she pulled her lips back; for the second, she halfway blew a kiss. She repeated the action several times as I stared.

"What does that mean?" I asked.

"I have no idea!" cried Megan. "I was hoping you'd know!"

"Like this?" I tried the mouth movement myself. Megan coached me until I got it right. But I had no clue what I was silently saying.

"Tell me about the woman," I said.

In the commotion, Megan didn't catch the details of her clothing. But one thing was certain: she was wearing a long fur coat. Megan also noticed that she was "kind of old, but not feeble."

"She reminded me of somebody who used to be like a dancer or something when she was young. She moved that way, know what I mean?"

I did. I pictured Mrs. Oscar Manfred Gribble the Third.

When I flipped open my cell phone to call Jenx, Megan stopped me. She said I'd have to make the call from the lobby. Casino rule.

"Of course, I would never have busted the little boy for it," she added.

I fished a ten-dollar bill out of my coat pocket and tossed it on her tray. Megan said, "For that kind of money, let me get you a real breakfast. Something better than Pepsi and pretzels."

She said she'd be right back. While I waited, I watched a couple octogenarian women with cigarettes dangling from their lips pump coin after coin into three slot machines at a time. Clearly, they were professionals.

Megan returned with a gooey bear claw pastry on a paper plate.

"It's our House breakfast," she said, her slightly crossed eyes sparkling. "Enjoy."

I took the pastry, which was large and extremely sticky, and crossed to the lobby.

Here's what I learned: Never try to use a cell phone while eating a bear claw. You'll get the sugary goop all over your phone. My fingers were too sticky even to speed-dial Jenx. I ended up washing my hands twice in the lavatory sink before I could make the call. I don't know what the pastry chef at the casino used to glaze those things, but it had the consistency of glue. On the plus side, it was delicious.

Not surprisingly, Jenx was in the field when I called. The dispatcher offered to patch me through. As I waited, David bounded into the Casino lobby, his green-blue eyes round with excitement.

"I found the Jag! I found the Jag!" he panted. He was waving a scrap of paper.

"Iowa plates?" I asked.

He nodded, breathless. "I also found a second white Jag! With Illinois plates."

By now I was familiar enough with David-ese to translate "iwwinoy pwates."

"I wrote that number down, too," he said. "Just in case."

When Jenx picked up, I gave the good vet the phone. Listening, I gathered that he had tried to get the hotel desk clerk to tell him whether either of those cars belonged to overnight guests, but the Bear Claw employee wouldn't say.

Jenx must have explained to David that he'd need police intervention for that kind of info.

"Then send somebody in a uniform right now!" David insisted and handed the phone back to me.

"It's sticky," he said, examining his fingers.

I asked Jenx whether she planned to dispatch Officers Swancott and Roscoe to the Casino.

"That's State Police jurisdiction," she replied. "I'll see if I can get the MSP out there. Brady and Roscoe are already on the case. They're following up on your suggestion of a door-to-door wardrobe search."

"They got a warrant to see people's fur coats?" I asked.

"Nope, it's voluntary," Jenx said. "So, technically, it doesn't have teeth. But when folks open their door and see Officer Roscoe, they tend to want to comply."

Understandable, given that Officer Roscoe was a German shepherd of impeccable breeding and imposing stature. Though highly trained in the field, the canine officer's greatest asset was his ability to stare people down.

"That's all well and good," I said. "But the fur coat you want is currently being worn by Mrs. Gribble the Third. A waitress described the woman who pulled Chester away, and it's got to be her!"

Both Jenx and Dr. David listened to my story. The vet wasn't interested in waiting for the MSP; he wanted to knock on every door in the hotel until he found Mrs. Gribble himself.

I asked Jenx to hold a moment while I reminded David that the woman in question was wearing a coat. Ergo, she was probably on her way out.

"Or on her way in!" David and Jenx blurted simultaneously.

"Was Chester wearing a coat?" said David.

I had forgotten to ask Megan. Jenx chided me for the oversight, and David demanded the name of the waitress so that he could go ask her himself. Before he walked away, I grabbed the now-sticky slip of paper from his hands.

"Can you run the plates David saw?" I asked Jenx.

She promised to try, so I read them to her. The one from Illinois was a vanity plate: IMGBLN.

"'I am gambling'?" I guessed aloud. "Nothing like advertising your vice."

"Maybe that's how they earned the Jag," Jenx said. "Speaking of vices, did you catch the big commotion this morning at Coastal Med?"

"What happened?"

"Some nurse got caught playing peeping Tom."

"Male nurse?"

"Yeah, but it gets better: the nurse wasn't really a nurse. Turns out he was using a fake ID."

"Don't tell me," I said as my stomach did a double back-flip. "C. Richards."

"So you heard about it," Jenx said.

"Not exactly. I let the guy stare at my breast. Then I gave him a ride home."

SIXTEEN

"TECHNICALLY, IT WAS DAVID who gave the guy a ride home. And not exactly home. More like to the edge of a woods," I told Jenx.

"A woods where?" she demanded.

"East of Sugar Grove. We had just let him out when you called about Chester being at Bear Claw."

"Could you give a description of the guy who's not C. Richards?" Jenx said.

"Yeah. But I've got to tell you, he looked a lot different out of uniform."

"How do you mean?"

"On the job, he looked young. Off the job, he looked too young. Like barely out of high school." I cringed.

"Stop by the station before you go home."

"Okay. But there's something else you should know: he has my cell phone number."

"How'd he get that?" Jenx asked.

"Long story. . . ."

"You're sure he's got it?"

"He called me!"

"What's his number?"

I hadn't thought to check until she asked. As I did, I realized David was right. Some parts of my phone were still sticky.

"The creep blocked his number when he dialed," I told Jenx.

"Smart perverts are predators," she said. "Dumb ones get caught and go to jail."

Jenx updated me on the state of the Jamboree: all activities postponed till tomorrow. Peg would be Acting Mayor until we knew more about Gil's fate.

We were concluding our call when David returned, munching a bear claw.

"Let me talk to Jenx," he said through a mouthful of pastry. As if he wasn't already hard enough to understand.

"You'll get my phone all sticky!" I protested.

"Your phone's already sticky."

When I handed it over, he told Jenx, "Chester wasn't wearing a coat. He had on a navy-blue turtleneck sweater and jeans."

I knew that turtleneck. I missed that turtleneck. Dammit, I missed Chester.

Returning my phone, David saw the tears in my eyes. I hate it when I get sentimental. I hate it even more when there are witnesses.

"We'll find him, Whiskey," David promised. "Jenx says the State Police will be here soon." He took another bite of his bear claw. "Delicious. Now I know where they got the name for this resort."

"From the pastry?"

"The pastry's a happy coincidence. According to legend, the Kickapoos and Shawnees used to be part of the same tribe. They split up after a fight over a bear paw."

"Did Megan the waitress tell you that?"

"I read it on the men's room wall."

Mentioning Megan reminded me of Chester's last known lip movements. I demonstrated them for David. His eyes bugged out.

"Abra!" he cried.

"What about her?"

"That's what you're lip-synching! That's what Chester was trying to say!" The good vet beamed. "Let's go to Vestige and pick her up. Abra will help us find him!"

I couldn't imagine Abra being helpful, period, and I said so.

"Are you forgetting? Abra has police training," David argued. "Jenx told me."

"Did Jenx tell you what her 'police training' consisted of? Abra demonstrated how to steal purses so that the cops could better understand the crime."

I didn't have the energy to add that in the process, Abra had stolen yet another purse, this one essential to a police investigation. In general, contemplating the topic of Abra made me very tired.

When we emerged from the dimly lit casino, I was startled by the brightness of the day. The sun smiled in a clear azure sky, making the layers of ice that coated everything sparkle like crystals on a chandelier. I reached for my sunglasses.

"Let's make sure those two Jags are still here," David said, squinting.

But they weren't. In the Animal Ambulance, we circled the vast parking lot twice without spotting either car. David became agitated.

"Did that woman drag Chester out in this weather without a coat?"

Although that question was rhetorical, I knew the next one would have my name on it.

"Whiskey, did Chester have a coat on when he left Vestige?"

"He had a coat on at my office, which was the last place I saw him. So far."

When David pressed me, I admitted that I hadn't checked Chester's closet at Vestige to see which clothes were gone and which remained.

"And you call yourself an amateur sleuth," he fumed.

"Actually, I call myself a real estate broker. I never intended a career in crime-solving. Or child care."

"I know what you mean," David conceded. "I never intended a career in messianic politics, but it called me."

"You're talking about . . . Fleggers?" I asked cautiously.

"I'm talking about the whole animal rights movement. I first got involved years ago. Before I even went to vet school."

"How? Why?"

David took his eyes off the road to study me. "You don't get it, do you, Whiskey?"

"No, I really don't. I mean, I like animals—in small doses and at an appropriate distance. But I don't think they should be competing for our jobs."

David burst into laughter. I'd never heard him guffaw before.

"Is that what you think I'm advocating?" he asked.

"Aren't you? What does 'equal rights for animals' mean?"

"Before you can understand what I advocate, you need to understand what I oppose. I'm against *speciesism*."

"What's that?"

"The practice of giving preference to a being simply because it's a member of our own species—in other words, the human race."

"But—"

"Let's start small, Whiskey. Let's start with cruelty to animals. It's ethically indefensible, do you agree? I mean, you wouldn't club a baby human to death, so why a baby seal?"

"Okay—"

"Okay! That's animal rights advocacy, in microcosm."

"But I thought—"

"Yes, there's more to it, but let's leave it there for today. Shall we?"

The good vet gave me his most winning smile, and so help me, I felt a small flutter. Was it possible that Dr. David was going to ask me out, after all? I waited. But he didn't speak again until we reached Vestige.

"I didn't know your late husband, but I assume he wanted the best for Abra, am I right?"

"Oh yes."

"Then I'm sure he wanted her to have the best training."

"Actually, Leo wanted to breed her—with an AKC stud in Chicago. But they didn't hit it off. She ran away and . . . well, you know the rest of the story."

David nodded solemnly. "My point, Whiskey, is that I'd like to make you a proposition."

"Yes?" The moment felt very sexual.

117

"I understand you have in your employment a woman named Deely Smarr."

In David-ese, her name came out "Deewee Smaw."

"Yes. Avery hired her for damage control—I mean, child care. She's the Coast Guard nanny. Why do you ask?"

"She's also an experienced dog trainer and animal rights advocate. Deely helped me found Fleggers."

"She did?" The conversation had shifted from titillating to icky.

"I would like you to authorize Deely Smarr to train Abra in rescue and retrieval," David said.

"Abra's got the retrieval part down already, provided you're talking about other people's purses."

"I'm talking about training her to find humans, dead or alive."

I gasped. "You think Chester's dead?"

"I think Chester's missing, and Gil's dead. Deely can do it, Whiskey. She can train Abra to find them both."

"But isn't that *speciesism*?" I ventured. "I mean, I wouldn't want the job, so why give it to a dog? Besides, Officer Roscoe's already trained. He's a paid professional."

We pulled into the driveway at Vestige just as Deely was coming around the side of the house with Abra and Prince Harry. Everyone was dressed for the weather. Identically. I couldn't imagine where Deely had found Mother and Son olive-green parkas that matched her own. Or was Deely wearing Avery's parka?

Neither Abra nor Prince Harry was on a leash, yet both walked companionably at Deely's heel.

"How did she do that?" I wondered aloud, more impressed by the behavior than the wardrobe. If it weren't for Deely's alleged involvement in Fleggers, I would have suspected either electroshock treatments or severe beatings.

"It's called The System," David said proudly.

"Is that anything like Dogs-Train-You-Dot-Com? Because Chester couldn't get that to work."

"The System is very advanced," said the vet, his voice husky with awe. "It's for difficult cases placed in the hands of skilled professionals. Like Deely Smarr."

"I didn't know they trained dogs in the Coast Guard," I remarked.

"She didn't learn The System in the Coast Guard," said David. "She learned it . . . underground."

"Underground?"

"Deely has been an animal rights activist since she was a kid. Her father was Arthur Smarr. He died for the cause."

"Her father died for animal rights?" We were both whispering now.

"He was trampled by a circus elephant at an Anti-Captivity Rally. It was tragic."

I couldn't help but flash on the *Mary Tyler Moore Show* episode in which Chuckles the Clown, dressed as a peanut, is crushed by an elephant. Like everyone in the WJM newsroom except goody-goody Mary, I was seized by inappropriate laughter. David glared at me.

"Deely was eight years old," he said.

The same age as Chester. That stopped my giggles.

"Arthur Smarr invented The System," David continued. "But Deely perfected it. Just look at her."

The reverential way he spoke caused me to look at David first. No question about it: the good vet was in love.

My cell phone rang.

"Do you know a waitress named Megan?" Jenx began.

"You mean the one at Bear Claw?" I asked.

"She told the MSP she remembered something else: the woman who grabbed Chester had a coat over her arm, a coat for a little boy."

"Chester wasn't under-dressed," I informed David, who was still mooning over Deely. I relayed Jenx's update, plus her repeated request that I get to the station ASAP to fill out a description of the guy who wasn't C. Richards, RN.

"What are you talking about?" said David, finally giving me his full attention.

"There's a pervert on the loose. He's supposed to be a nurse, but he's not."

My phone rang. Jenx again.

"How soon can you get Abra out to Pasco Point?"

"Why?"

"Brady and Roscoe's door-to-door wardrobe search is taking too long. They need backup."

"You're recruiting my dog?" As soon as I used the pronoun, I shuddered. I generally tried to deny ownership.

"And you," Jenx said. "We're deputizing you both. For that neighborhood, Abra should wear her rhinestone collar. Make sure you look good, too."

Pasco Point is the site of about a dozen multi-million-dollar lakefront estates. I could understand why going door-to-door was slow work: the homes were a quarter-mile apart, and most employed a battery of servants to process every request.

"But Abra's not trained for that kind of work," I protested. "She's more likely to steal something than find something!"

"Finding the fur coat is your job," Jenx said. "Use Abra to get in the door. She's a local celebrity, Whiskey. Face it, the bitch has class."

SEVENTEEN

WHEN I TOLD DAVID that Jenx was deputizing Abra and me for duty at Pasco Point, he said, "Abra has training. What about you?"

We were sitting in my driveway in the Animal Ambulance, a good vantage point from which to admire Deely and the dogs. The identically dressed trio pranced around the yard in a perfect circle.

"Watch this," David said. "Now they'll go in reverse."

Ever graceful, Abra made it look easy. Although Prince Harry stumbled, by God the pup tried to walk backwards. And when Deely gave him his treat, he did not pee on her feet.

"Wonderful trainer!" David sighed.

"But we hired her to be the twins' nanny," I reminded him, which made me wonder who was watching Leah and Leo.

"This is what Deely does on her break," David said. "Give her free rein to train Abra, and you'll be amazed."

"But can Abra make a good first impression?" I asked.

David said, "Can you?"

Though dubious about my qualifications, David agreed to deliver me, with Abra, to Pasco Point. I went inside to fetch the dog's rhinestone collar and a clean, blood-free jacket for myself. Upstairs in Abra's room—yes, she had her own room—I peered out the window. David and Deely were nose to nose in what looked like an intimate conversation. Were they about to kiss? Or just exchanging hot Flegger gossip? Maybe a whispered reference to *speciesism* was all it took to get them both excited.

Even from this angle, I was taken by how much Deely looked like Avery. If she ever lost the glasses and let her hair grow, She'd be a dead ringer.

———

"That one's your listing, isn't it?" Officer Brady Swancott asked, pointing toward the ivory castle that loomed before us. It would be our fourth stop, and we were tired already although the dogs remained enthusiastic. Why shouldn't they? So far, they were getting treats at every house. And the residents of Pasco Point didn't hand out dog biscuits. They wowed their canine guests with table scraps that included filet mignon.

"Yes, that's our listing," I said, afraid to look up for long from the slippery surface beneath my feet. We were making our way down icy Scarletta Road. Even the super-rich couldn't get the County to clear their street after a major winter storm.

Ahead loomed Iberville, a 10,000-square-foot French chateau with a panoramic view of Lake Michigan. It was one of the properties Odette and I had told Mrs. Gribble the Third about the day we signed her as a client.

"It's unoccupied, right?" Brady said

"Right. The owners moved to Miami right after Christmas."

"Has Abra been here?"

"Of course not. Why?"

"She acts like she knows the place."

I glanced up again. He was right. Brady had assigned Officer Roscoe to me and taken Abra's leash himself. Nice try at damage control. The blonde deputy dog was pulling hard as we approached the Iberville driveway.

"Let's humor her," said Brady. "See where she leads."

Three-quarters of the way up the long unplowed lane, I said, "Technically we're trespassing, you know."

"It's okay. You're with a cop. Heck, today you are a cop." Brady winked at me. He was young and sweet in a goofy, geeky way. Law enforcement was not Brady Swancott's destiny. In his mid-twenties, he already had a wife and a son, and was halfway through an online graduate degree in Art History. His career goal? Either art conservation or stay-at-home fatherhood.

Abra whimpered pathetically, straining toward the rear of the house.

Brady commanded her to halt, and to my amazement, she did. He crouched in the icy driveway and studied what I realized was a pair of faint tire tracks.

"Ice doesn't register good prints," he remarked. "But somebody was here, probably just a couple hours ago."

As Roscoe dutifully sniffed the ice, Abra whined again.

"What's wrong with her?" I said impatiently.

Brady replied, "She's trying to tell us."

He released her leash. Freed of constraints, Abra spun in place on the icy drive until her claws found friction. Then she loped away, her graceful blonde body disappearing around the corner of the mansion.

"There's a delivery entrance back there," I mused. "But there shouldn't have been any deliveries."

"Let's go see," said Brady. "I assume there's an electronic lockbox?"

"On the front door. The owners insisted that Mattimoe Realty oversee all showings. So far, only Odette has taken people through."

Abra's sudden shrill bark prickled the back of my neck. It wasn't her usual yip, but rather the higher-pitched yelp she saved for emergencies. Without waiting for Brady's command, Officer Roscoe woofed a reply and bounded after her.

"She found something," Brady said, breaking into a jog.

I managed to keep up with him, so we took in the scene simultaneously: The double-wide delivery door ajar. The two dogs planted in place, heads and tails erect, bodies electrified, as they peered inside.

Abra emitted a low moan.

"Good girl," Brady whispered. To me he said, "She knows better than to contaminate a crime scene."

More likely she didn't care for the smell. Or she was trying to impress Officer Roscoe.

I scanned the area. The tire tracks ended in front of the delivery door, where the earth looked churned and scarred.

Brady drew his sidearm.

"Somebody dragged something in." He motioned for me to wait with the dogs. "Is your cell phone working?" he asked.

I nodded.

"If I'm not back in five, call Jenx." Noiselessly he slipped inside.

Abra actually seemed to grasp the situation. At least she knew enough to take her cues from Roscoe. Silent and still as statues, the dogs stared after Brady. I did the same, keeping one eye on my watch. After four excruciating minutes, my stomach clenched. After four and a half minutes, my finger arched over Jenx's number.

Brady returned as stealthily as he had departed. His impassive cop face offered no clue to what he'd seen.

It can't be an emergency, I thought. *He's too calm.*

"It's Gil Gruen," Brady said without preamble. "He's inside."

"Gil's inside?" I echoed numbly. "Gil's dead."

"You need to see this." Holding my right elbow, Brady steered me toward Iberville's delivery door. "Come on."

Abra yipped excitedly. Though not directed at her, the words were a familiar command, one that she rarely chose to obey. But this occasion must have promised excitement because I'd gone green around the gills. Eagerly Abra trotted through the door ahead of us.

"No!" Brady bellowed. Roscoe leaped to his aid, taking the Afghan hound down. When she rolled onto her back, I recognized her come-hither look. She had interpreted the German shepherd's passionate action as foreplay. He restrained himself, however. The canine officer was a gentleman.

"I saw Gil's body already," I told Brady with a shudder. "I don't want to see it again."

"Trust me," he said. "This is . . . different."

Numbly, I let him lead me through the delivery door into what the owners of Iberville called their "service area." The partitioned extension of the kitchen-slash-pantry was an immaculate, bright-white room lined with benches, shelves, and a walk-in refrigerator. Brady pushed open the next door. We were in a hallway.

Since my only tour of Iberville had begun at the front door and proceeded in a clockwise circle through each of the three floors, I was already disoriented. At the next juncture, I paused. I may have even stumbled as the smell that Abra had no doubt discerned from outside finally penetrated my senses.

"Oh, god," I gasped. It was a sharp almost metallic stench, and it reminded me of the odor present in the ice shanty where I had found Gil's body.

"It's not what you think," Brady said. "Keep moving."

Shaking now, I half-closed my eyes and wished I could close my nose. The odor grew stronger when we entered the conservatory, a round room with a wall of leaded glass. No matter that the owners had removed their greenery; I was nearly gagged by the stink of organic decay.

"Open your eyes, Whiskey," said Brady. "It's all right."

Cautiously I did. Silhouetted against the window stood Gil Gruen in full Western regalia. His eyes and mouth were open, his hands raised.

I swooned. The questions formed just before my legs failed: How could Gil be here? And what *was* that god-awful smell?

EIGHTEEN

I HAD TO BE dreaming.

In my ear Brady whispered, "It's all right, Whiskey. There are three more Gil Gruens."

And someone was scrubbing my face.

When I tried to push the face-washer away, my hand made contact with a soft, furry muzzle. I didn't have to open my eyes to know whose. But I opened them anyway. Brady Swancott was holding my head in his lap as Abra tried to clean it.

"Three more Gils?" I asked.

"Yup. They're each a little bit different. One's in the main foyer, one's in the living room, and one's in the master suite."

"What are you talking about?" I said, struggling to sit up.

Brady nodded in the direction of the conservatory window-wall, where Officer Roscoe stood guard next to a life-size card-board cut-out of Gil Gruen.

"Recognize that?" Brady asked.

I did. It was Gil's habit to set up self-replicas next to the FOR SALE signs at his properties. Until, that is, the seller made him take them down, or local kids stole them. Gil called the cut-outs his "action figures." As far as I knew, he'd had them made in several poses. This one was a freeze-frame of Gil in mid-spiel: lips apart, arms outstretched, fingers splayed.

I sniffed the air. The putrid smell was fainter now, but not gone.

"What still stinks?"

"Are you sure you want to know?"

"Yes!"

"Well, along with each cut-out, there's a dead rat."

That got me to my feet. Fast.

"Where?" I demanded, scanning the room.

"The one that was in here is gone."

"Gone?" Temporary deputy though I was, I knew that nobody's supposed to remove anything from a crime scene until the initial investigation is complete.

"Uh . . . yeah. . . ." Brady cast a sidelong look at Abra.

"You mean . . . Abra took the rat? The dead rat?"

"She didn't exactly take it. She . . . ate it."

I stared at him. *And you let her lick my face?!*

I was already frantically wiping it with the sleeve of my parka. Make that both sleeves. I would never stop cleaning it. Lady Macbeth had nothing on me.

"She didn't eat the whole thing," Brady said in an apologetic tone. "Just the torso and the—"

"Are you trying to kill me?!"

"No! I'm trying to calm you down! Please calm down! Jenx is on her way over here. So is the MSP."

That stopped me. "Why call in the State Boys? This is just a trespassing, isn't it? Or maybe a simple B&E?"

When Brady didn't answer, I said, "Well, isn't it? What's going on, Swancott?"

"Remember the marks we saw in the ice outside? Where it looked like somebody had dragged something in?"

"Yeah?"

"Somebody did."

"You mean something besides the cut-outs and the rodents?"

Brady motioned for me to follow. I glanced back to see Abra happily tagging along.

"No!" I shouted. "No more dead rats for you!"

"I've secured the other rooms," Brady promised.

He led me through the first floor to the focal point of the house, the flared central staircase with its ornately carved walnut banister. A second cut-out of Gil helpfully pointed the way up the steps; a dead rat lay at his feet.

"Uh-oh, I forgot about that one," Brady said. He simultaneously whistled for Roscoe and body-blocked Abra as she lunged for her prey. The canine officer entered barking. I don't know what he told her, but Abra meekly trailed him back to the conservatory.

"You said there were three more Gils?" I asked Brady.

He nodded. "The one in the main foyer is holding a WEL-COME sign."

I knew that cut-out well since it was the one Gil displayed at Best West's Open Houses. Whoever did this was counting on visitors to enter through the front door.

Before we started up the staircase, I stole a peek at the dead rat Brady had shielded from Abra. Decomposing, it lay on its back, beady eyes still open, four feet in the air.

Brady followed my gaze. "They were all placed like that. Somebody was trying to make a point."

"What kind of point?" I asked, mystified. "What's this about?"

"Wait till you see what's upstairs. . . ."

As we ascended, I recalled that the master suite took up the entire second floor. The third floor—accessible by a different staircase and by an elevator—featured an eat-in kitchen-slash-family room for guests staying in the four additional bedrooms, each of which had its own private bath.

The master suite was to die for. Upon reaching the second floor, Brady and I paused, not to regain our breaths but rather to take in the scenic overlook. The wall ahead of us was mostly glass. Although we seemed to stand among the treetops, their seasonal leaflessness opened the view to a vast expanse of lake and shore.

The owners had left most furnishings in place so that the house could be shown in its nearly full glory. A California king-size canopy bed dominated the sleeping area. Arranged around it were matching nightstands and dressers, two sofas, two wing-back chairs, an entertainment center, and an antique writing desk. Chintz—never to my taste—was the fabric of choice in this room.

"Looks like they removed their best art," Brady quipped, nodding toward a couple of conspicuous bare spots on the inside walls.

As we walked on, I replayed sales points in my head: The master bath and dressing room comprised more than 400 square feet of luxury. Painted twilight blue, the dressing area featured wall-to-wall carpet, the same color as the ice now on the lake. The rest of the master bath was tiled: aquamarine alternating with midnight blue and gold. A twenty-foot-long alabaster counter with his-and-hers sinks matched the whirlpool bath, shower, commode, and bidet. Custom-made walnut cabinets and drawers under the counter provided ample storage in addition to the cedar closets and built-in cupboards covering two walls. The ornate plumbing fixtures were gold with a finish guaranteed never to corrode or stain. Ninety square feet of mirrors enhanced the drama and self-absorption one was sure to feel in this space. Or, as Brady put it, "If you live here, you better like the way you look naked."

"I thought you said the fourth cut-out of Gil was in here," I said, cautiously sniffing the air. "I see nothing and smell nothing."

Brady stepped toward the opaque privacy door that separated the whirlpool bath from the rest of the room.

"Are you ready?" he asked. Before I could reply, he pulled the door open, and the familiar stink wafted out.

I could not immediately grasp what I saw. The immense oval tub was crammed with slabs of ice, cut into odd shapes of varying thickness. Although the frozen chunks were melting, the tub still contained more ice than water. That wasn't all: wedged among the slabs was the fourth replica of Gil Gruen. This one was nearly submerged; pointy-toed cowboy boots poked up through the brine at a forty-five degree angle. The fourth dead rat was accounted for, too. Like the others, and like the submerged cut-out, it lay on its back. But this rat had been posed on the crown of a floating Stetson hat.

NINETEEN

"You're looking at the heavy part of the delivery—the ice," Brady said. "My guess is that somebody hauled it in using contractor-grade trash bags."

"Any sign of the bags?" I asked.

"Not yet, but I haven't searched the premises. The MSP will want to do that."

No sooner had he spoken than Abra and Roscoe set up such a ruckus that we knew we had visitors. Presumably official visitors.

Brady took one more look at the scene in the whirlpool bath.

"Do you think that's Gil's hat?" he asked.

"It could be one of them. Gil always wore black hats."

"Black hats are for bad guys, Whiskey."

"I've often thought so. Does that explain the dead rat?"

"What do you mean?" Brady said.

"I mean, was the person who pulled this stunt trying to say that Gil was a rat? Or that somebody else thought Gil was a rat—and that's why Gil's dead?"

Before Officer Swancott could reply, Jenx shouted from downstairs, "Anybody home? Brady, where the hell are you?"

"Up here!" he called, but she was already pounding up the steps in her steel-toed boots.

"Whiskey!" she panted when she saw me. "You and Abra need to get out of here before the State Boys come in. They don't look as kindly on temporary deputies as Brady and I do."

Too late. From downstairs we heard more frantic barking followed by the identifying cry of the Michigan State Police.

"I'll do the talking," said Jenx. She got no argument from me. When Trooper L. Hartmann found his way to the master bath, Jenx explained that I was the real-estate broker handling Iberville. She said I had noticed the open delivery door and asked for police assistance.

Trooper Hartmann nodded without interest. At least I couldn't discern any interest, possibly because he had not yet removed his sunglasses.

"What's with that crazy Afghan hound downstairs?" he demanded. "Why is she here?"

Jenx, Brady and I chewed over that one for a moment. Finally Brady said, "She's a civilian canine consultant."

"A what?" Trooper Hartmann removed his shades to squint at Brady.

"Do you remember the Warren Matheney case last fall?" Officer Swancott was talking fast. "The triple homicide that got Magnet Springs mentioned on every cable news network?"

Comprehension crossed the trooper's flat face. "Yeah, sure. You're saying she's the dog that helped solve that case?"

I wouldn't have gone so far as to say that she helped solve the case although Abra did contribute to it. She contributed complications.

"So what's her angle on this case?" Trooper Hartmann asked. I couldn't wait to hear Brady's response.

"She's ... uh ... she's a crime scene expert."

"*What*?" Jenx, Hartmann and I cried.

"Yeah," said Brady. "I thought she might help us out here."

"You mean she's like ... canine CSI?" said Hartmann. "How does she work?"

"Believe it or not," Brady began, "she works by ... tasting dead animals at the scene."

"That's disgusting!" Hartmann roared. "Not to mention, cops aren't supposed to consume evidence!"

"Yeah, well, that's the down side. On the plus side, she works cheap."

Brady quickly brought Hartmann up to speed on the evidence that Abra had not eaten.

The trooper studied the scene of each of Gil's cut-outs, lingering in the master bath.

He said, "They haven't recovered Gruen's body yet, right? Is there any way of knowing whether this is his hat?"

"We were discussing that before you arrived," I said, forgetting that I was supposed to keep mum.

"And what did you conclude?"

"That Gil only wore black hats," I said. "Black Stetsons."

"Well, this one is top of the line." Hartmann leaned low over the whirlpool ice bath. "My dad has owned a tack shop for thirty years. I help him out on weekends. This here's what Stetson calls their Black Beauty—a sleek genuine fur job with a suede finish. See the Spartan profile?"

Jenx, Brady, and I nodded even though we had no idea what he meant.

"The band is real sweet with that three-piece silver buckle," Hartmann continued. "And each piece of the buckle has a red stone. Do you remember seeing this hat on Gil Gruen?"

None of us could say for sure.

"What does a hat like that cost?" asked Jenx.

"That's a special order," the trooper said, straightening. "It runs around five hundred bucks."

Jenx whistled. "If that's not Gil's hat, then somebody spent a lot of money trying to convince us it was."

"If that is Gil's hat, how did somebody get it?" I wondered aloud. "And why did they bring it here?"

Everyone stared at me.

"A good question, considering you're the real-estate broker," Trooper Hartmann said. "Who else has access to this house?"

I explained that the owners had a cleaning service under contract to check the property once a month, but the first visit wasn't scheduled until the end of January.

"I'll need the name of that cleaning service," the trooper said.

"So will I," Jenx chimed in.

I promised to get it for them and added that Mattimoe Realty had placed an electronic lock box on the front door. The owners specified that either Odette Mutombo or I must be present whenever the house was shown.

Hartmann said, "So what you're telling me is that no other realtor can show this house?"

"Oh, another realtor can show it," I said, "but only if someone from my firm is present."

The trooper frowned. "The house has no security system. What's up with that?"

"The owners are technophobes. They had a couple bad experiences with their electronic alarm and ordered it removed. Pasco Point residents pay for an hourly Security Patrol, so the owners of Iberville rely on that."

The three officers shook their heads, presumably at the folly of trusting low-wage civilians to protect a castle. Hartmann said to Brady, "The back door wasn't forced. Did you find any sign of a break-in?"

"No," Brady replied. "If the house was locked, whoever entered used a key."

"*If* the house was locked," Jenx echoed.

Again everyone looked at me.

"When was the last time you showed it?" Hartmann asked.

"I'll check with Ms. Mutombo," I said.

It was a new listing. The only showing I knew of so far was the one that Odette had planned for the previous afternoon. She was scheduled to show Iberville to Mrs. Gribble the Third after our helicopter ride. When Odette visited me at the hospital last night, I'd forgotten to ask how it went. Or if it went.

Trooper Hartmann scratched his chin. "I was called to Bear Claw before I came here. Could this incident be connected to the missing kid?"

"I don't know how," said Jenx.

"Come on. In sleepy Magnet Springs the son of a celebrity disappears, and the mayor is murdered—and then this happens? All in the same week?"

Before she could comment, Jenx got a call from the dispatcher. An old tree in the center of town had suddenly split in two from ice overload and in the process pulled down a power line. One more complication from the storm.

"I gotta keep folks away from the hot line till the electric company shows up," Jenx told Hartmann. "Can you and Officer Swancott secure the house?"

"I'll handle it," said the trooper. "You take the dogs—and the realtor—and get out of here."

Jenx gave Officers Brady and Roscoe a lift back to their patrol car, which was parked at the entrance to Pasco Point. Then Abra, Jenx and I continued on to the police station so that I could write down what I knew about the fake C. Richards, RN.

On the ride back to town I used the last bar of my cell phone battery to reach Odette.

"Did you show Iberville yesterday?" I began.

"I would have told you about it last night," she said, "but you were more interested in other matters. Such as Nash Grant...."

"Last night I was in the hospital."

"From which I hear you've escaped. Did you run straight to Avery's ex?"

"He came to me. Listen, Odette, I've got one bar left on my phone, and I need to know—"

"I'll save you the bar. Mrs. Gribble did not love Iberville. She said it reminded her of Iowa."

"Iowa?" I repeated.

"My sentiments exactly. Isn't Iowa a land-locked state? It can't possibly have that kind of scenery!"

"I thought Mrs. Gribble was from Chicago," I said, picturing white Jaguars from two states that began with the letter I.

"Her husband is from Chicago. Mrs. Gribble grew up in Iowa and still owns a home there."

"If her Iowa home reminds her of Iberville, then it ain't no 'Little House on the Prairie,'" I muttered to myself.

"That was in Minnesota," Jenx contributed from the driver's seat.

"What?"

"Michael Landon's show. It was Walnut Grove, Minnesota—not Iowa."

I rolled my eyes, wishing that people would refrain from commenting on one-half of somebody else's overheard phone conversation.

Odette exclaimed, "No, not Walnut Grove—Cedar Rapids. I never heard of it."

Since leaving Zimbabwe, Odette and her husband had lived in London, Paris, Boston, and Magnet Springs. They were not inspired to learn more about the Midwest.

"Does Mrs. Gribble live in Chicago or not?" I asked.

"Oh, yes. She and her husband have a condo downtown."

"Is she a resident of Illinois or Iowa?"

"What's the difference?" sighed Odette. "As long as she buys a fabulously expensive home from us?"

Just then Abra poked her long nose over my shoulder and nuzzled my ear. Before I remembered the rat-eating incident, she burped loudly.

"Jeez!" cried Jenx. "What do you feed that dog?"

The police chief rolled down all four windows.

We drove in the freezing breeze to the site of the split tree that had pulled down the power line. Fortunately, the electric company crew arrived at the same time we did. Jenx decided we had sufficiently refreshed the air in the car, so she rolled up the windows and headed for the station.

I used my remaining road time and battery power to get Tina Breen on the line. My office manager isn't good at tasks that require sustained attention, but she does have an excellent memory for trivia. I needed the name of the cleaning service hired to maintain Iberville.

"Extreme Clean," she replied promptly. "Do you want their number?"

She provided it but couldn't come up with a contact person.

"Oh dear," she said. "I was afraid this would happen!"

"What?"

"The owners of Iberville were supposed to call me back with that information, but they never did. . . . And now they're on a cruise somewhere."

"No problem. Just call Extreme Clean yourself and ask who runs the show."

"Oh, please don't make me call them!"

"Tina, what's going on?"

"I'm sorry, Whiskey, but the last time I called that company, the person who answered got me very upset!"

"She was rude?"

"It was a he, not a she. And he wasn't rude, exactly. More like . . . lewd. Yes, that's the word. He was extremely lewd."

Whenever she grew upset, Tina's voice turned higher-pitched and more nasal than usual. By now it was making my teeth ache.

"Lewd? How?" This interested me on several levels.

"Oh, you know. He . . . *said* things. . . ."

"What kinds of things?"

"I can't repeat them! I'm a good woman with toddlers at home!"

"And how did you get those toddlers, Tina? You can say what he said."

"It was about what makes a woman . . . a woman. You know, her woman parts. . . ."

"Her *woman parts*?"

"Oh, Whiskey, don't make me say it!"

"Yeesh," I moaned. My battery quit the call before I could.

Naturally, Jenx had been listening to my half of the conversation.

"Tina Breen was talking about *woman parts*? I didn't think she knew the words."

"She may not," I said.

We had just pulled into the police chief's parking space at the station. I expected her to turn off the vehicle, but suddenly the engine roared. And then the siren wailed.

"What the hell—?" I said. The instant I looked at my driver, I knew. Her eyes were bugging out, and she had turned that alarming shade of puce that meant only one thing: Judy "Jenx" Jenkins was mad enough to mess up the local magnetic fields. The reason was apparent. Parked perpendicular to us was a nondescript late-model Chevrolet with U.S. Government plates and two men in dark suits. The Fibbies had arrived.

They stepped out of the car, tapping their watches. I checked mine; Jenx had set the numbers spinning.

"What do you boys want?" Jenx asked after turning off the engine and siren and joining them on the sidewalk.

The Feds proffered their IDs, and Jenx showed her own. The older agent said, "We're here about the kidnapping."

"So it's official now?" I said. "Chester couldn't have run away?"

The younger agent asked Jenx, "Who's she?"

"Meet Volunteer Deputy Whitney Houston."

"Technically, it's Whitney Houston Halloran Mattimoe," I said, extending my hand. "You can call me Whiskey."

The first agent ignored me. So did the second one.

"It's too cold to stand outside," Jenx said and went in. I followed her. Eventually the agents did, too. By then Jenx was rummaging through her desk, trying to find the form for me to fill out about the guy who wasn't C. Richards, RN.

"We got a call from Chester Casanova's legal guardian," the older agent announced.

"Chester *Casanova*?" I said, stunned to learn that he had a last name, let alone that one. His diva mother used a first name only, and as far as I knew, so did Chester.

"Cassina called you?" Jenx asked.

The younger agent checked a small notebook. "No. We got a call from a woman named Evelyn Huffenbach. The grandmother."

Jenx and I exchanged glances.

"Chester doesn't have a grandmother," I said. "He has a mother, but she has no living relatives. She was a foster kid who never got out of the system."

"And you're Whitney Houston," the older agent reminded me.

"Whitney—*Whiskey*—is taking care of Chester while Cassina does the world," Jenx explained.

"But she's not the legal guardian," said the younger agent. "That would be Evelyn Huffenbach."

"Who the heck is Evelyn Huffenbach?" I asked.

"That would be me."

We turned toward the foyer. There stood a tall auburn-haired woman, probably in her late fifties, wearing a fur coat and fur hat.

"Mayzelle is my only child," the woman said. "She started running away from home when she was six. On her twelfth birthday, she left for good. Ten years passed before we spoke again."

"*Mayzelle?*" asked Jenx.

"She changed her name to Cassina. When she gave birth to a son, I had to read about it in the *National Enquirer*." The woman dabbed at her eyes with an embroidered handkerchief. "For years she denied me access to the boy. Then, out of the blue, she asked if I'd be his legal guardian. That made me so happy."

"When was that?" the younger agent asked.

"Two days ago. I left Dubuque as soon as I could."

Wasn't Dubuque in Iowa?

Chester had disappeared two days ago. What did Cassina know that we didn't? What did the FBI know? What did Chester's legal guardian know?

"I think somebody kidnapped him," Evelyn continued.

"Somebody who looks like you," I observed. It wasn't just the fur ensemble that made me say that. Except for her hair color, Evelyn Huffenbach resembled one of my clients.

She nodded. "I believe the kidnapper may be my sister."

"Who's your sister?" the younger FBI agent asked.

I moved my lips in synch with Evelyn as she replied, "Mrs. Oscar Manfred Gribble the Third."

TWENTY

"WAIT A MINUTE," I said as if anyone wanted my input. "Cassina was a foster child. She had no family."

"She told that story just to hurt me," Evelyn Huffenbach replied, wiping her eyes again. "And to sell CDs. Cassina is her public persona—an ethereal creature who sings about love and clouds. She bears very little resemblance to my earthy daughter Mayzelle."

Except when drunk, I thought, recalling a nasty scene at my house last fall.

"I don't follow popular music," said the older FBI agent. "How famous is she?"

His partner replied, "She made the cover of *Rolling Stone*. And all her CDs have gone gold."

To Evelyn the older agent said, "What makes you think your sister kidnapped your grandson?"

"My daughter said Chester called her and told her he was with Beatrice."

"Who's Beatrice?" said the younger agent.

"Mrs. Gribble the Third," I supplied. "She also answers to Bibi."

The agents glared at me and then at Jenx.

One of them said, "Chief Jenkins, dismiss your volunteer deputy. Now."

"No way," said Jenx. "Whiskey's involved in this up to her hairline. Cassina left Chester in her care."

Evelyn Huffenbach snorted. "Clearly, Mayzelle hired the wrong person."

"She didn't hire me; I was drafted," I said. "Just ask Jenx. I'm not a child-care provider."

"I can vouch for that," Jenx said.

"If Chester's with Beatrice, he could be in real trouble," Evelyn insisted. "My sister is unstable."

"How so?" asked Jenx.

"She's capable of irrational, even violent, behavior. When she was thirteen, she killed the family cat."

"Why?"

"She didn't like the way he was looking at her. Romeo was a cross-eyed Siamese."

The phone on Jenx's desk jangled, and I jumped.

"Excuse me, boys," Jenx told the Fibbies. After a few mumbles, she held the receiver out to me. "It's the Coast Guard calling."

Deely Smarr was on the line. "We have a situation, ma'am. I recommend that you listen carefully and say nothing except yes or no. Got it?"

"Got it. I mean, yes," I replied.

"A certain individual recently hired by you wants to come in from the cold. If you know what I mean . . . ?"

"Yes. No." Did she mean Roy? Or Chester? I had business arrangements with them both. And by "come in from the cold" was she referring to the weather or a clandestine mission, à la John le Carré?

My eyes met the steely gaze of the older Fibbie. He was watching my every move.

Deely tried again. "I'm referring to a person from the past who recently appeared in the present. He's here now, and he needs sanctuary. Including a shower and a hot meal. Do I have your permission to assist him?"

Roy Vickers was at Vestige. My mind raced. If I let Deely help him, would I be aiding and abetting a felon? I feared that Roy had killed Gil, and I assumed that the ex-con knew something about what had happened to Chester. After all, Roy had delivered both of Chester's notes, plus Prince Harry.

"Uh—yes," I said. Then, for clarity and to prove I could talk military, I added, "Aye, aye."

"That's Navy jargon, ma'am, not Coast Guard," Deely said and hung up.

"Everything all right, *Deputy*?" asked the older Fibbie. "Or does the Coast Guard require your immediate assistance?"

"I thought you were a realtor," Evelyn Huffenbach said. "You work for the Coast Guard?"

"Only in the event of land-based emergencies," I said.

"Deputy Mattimoe, you're dismissed," Jenx said, "as soon as you fill out that report we discussed. . . ." She handed me an official form.

I frowned, my mind a complete blank.

"On C. Richards . . . ?" she prompted.

"Oh! Right!"

"C. Richards?" the younger agent piped up. "You mean, C. Richards, RN., a.k.a. Thomas McKondin, Service Technician at Extreme Clean?"

"The randy nurse is the perv at Extreme Clean?" I gasped. "He talked to Tina Breen about her woman parts!"

"'Woman parts'?" both Fibbies repeated.

"What's the FBI connection?" Jenx said.

The older agent shook his head. "You're not on a need-to-know basis."

Jenx planted her fists on her desk and leaned toward the Fibbies. "Boys, in this town I *am* the Need-to-Know."

Her face was darkening.

"You don't want to make her mad," I advised the agents. "She's got magnetic fields on her side."

The younger Fibbie looked at his partner. "Is everybody here nuts?"

"Just the local law enforcement," the other agent replied.

"That's not true," I said. "Magnet Springs has a long history of attracting eccentrics. It's part of our proud heritage."

Just then the front door opened and in bounded Abra, followed by Officers Roscoe and Swancott. As usual, Abra had something in her mouth.

"Check out Deputy Abra!" said Brady. He sounded proud, not horrified. Even so, I was afraid to look.

"Is that what I think it is?" Jenx said.

I squeezed my eyes shut.

"It's a purse," Brady confirmed.

"Of course it is," I groaned, visualizing yet another day in court with the incorrigible dog.

"Odette's purse," Brady added. "Her ID's inside."

My eyes opened. "It's her designer bag! The one she sacrificed to save the Gribble account!"

"Let's see," said Jenx, coming around her desk to examine Abra's find. To my astonishment, the dog sat down, opened her jaws, and deposited the purse in Jenx's latex-gloved hand.

"Deely's work with Abra is paying off," observed Brady.

Jenx said, "Whiskey, didn't this purse vanish at the same time Chester did?"

I nodded.

"Then maybe it can tell us something about where Chester went," said Jenx. "Officer Swancott, did you use gloves when you examined the bag?"

"I didn't touch it," he replied. "Abra opened it for me, and then closed it again. She let me see the ID inside, but nothing else. I think she was waiting for the right moment."

From deep inside the bag, Jenx withdrew a rainbow-colored poker chip.

"It's sticky," she declared.

"Bear claw," I said, recalling that Chester had mouthed the word "Abra" to Megan the waitress. "Proof that Chester was at the casino! Where did Abra find the purse?"

"At Pasco Point," Brady said. "Just as we were getting into the patrol car, something caught her eye, and she ran off. I thought she was gone again, but she came right back with the bag."

"There's something else in here," Jenx said, inverting the purse. A business card fluttered out. Jenx retrieved it and read aloud:

"Extreme Clean Indoor and Outdoor Services. Thomas McKondin, Jr., Service Technician."

"They have the Iberville account," I informed Jenx and Brady.

Jenx read the rest of the card: "'We'll clean up your mess. Even if you live like a pig.'"

"Or die like a rat," I said. Brady nodded gravely. Abra licked her chops.

As she did, the older FBI agent snapped on a latex glove and removed the business card from Jenx's fingers.

"Hey!" the chief bellowed.

"This may be needed as evidence in a Federal investigation," the Fibbie said.

"Why don't you tell us the real reason you're here," Jenx said, leaning back in her chair and propping her feet on her desk. "But first, what are your names again? I wasn't paying attention when you whipped out those fancy badges."

Turns out that the older agent was named Smith, and the younger one was Jones. Or was it the other way around? Once again, they flashed them really fast. But Jenx seemed satisfied.

"We're here about the missing boy," Smith said. "But we're also investigating complaints about identity theft, which may or may not involve Mr. McKondin."

"Identity theft? As in credit card scams?" asked Brady.

"Not necessarily," Jones said. "Identity theft—or impersonation fraud—occurs when one individual assumes another's identity in order to perform a criminal act. We have reason to believe that Thomas McKondin may be guilty of impersonation fraud."

"I can vouch for that," I said. "He pretended to be my nurse just to get a peek under my hospital gown."

The room was so quiet I might as well have farted. Then one of the dogs did fart, for which I was strangely grateful. Though unbearably stinky (surely thanks to Abra's fetid rat), it ended my Too-Much-Information moment. Jenx opened a window, and Brady herded both dogs outside. Poor Officer Roscoe. Condemned by the company he kept.

Agent Smith asked me, "What did you mean earlier, when you mentioned McKondin talking about 'woman parts'?"

I sighed and told him about my office manager's reluctance to call Extreme Clean because she had been sexually taunted during an earlier conversation.

Jones was taking notes. "We'll need to interview her," he said.

"Good luck," I offered. "Tina can't repeat those words."

"She can write them down," he said.

"I doubt it."

"What?" He looked up.

"I doubt she can write them, either. Tina has a mental block when it comes to certain vocabulary. She says it's because of Winston and Neville."

"Churchill and Chamberlain, the former prime ministers of England?"

"No, Winston and Neville Breen, her toddlers. Here's some advice: Don't point out that she must know the words because she gave birth. That'll only make her cry."

Smith and Jones exchanged glances. I knew they were silently agreeing that our whole town was nuts.

TWENTY-ONE

AFTER SMITH AND JONES took turns interviewing me about my embarrassing encounter with C. Richards, RN, who was probably Thomas McKondin, Jr., they quizzed me about Chester. Jenx cut short the interrogation, explaining that I had been hospitalized for hypothermia the day before and needed rest. The Fibbies weren't the least bit curious about that. They warned me not to leave town and sent me on my way. Me and Rat-Stink, the Afghan hound.

Driving back to Vestige, I fought off a wave of paranoia. If I had correctly interpreted Deely Smarr's phone call, Roy Vickers was waiting for me. Jenx had mentioned that the Michigan State Police wanted to question Roy, and now the FBI was in town. Any way you sliced it, I was probably harboring a suspected felon. Maybe a killer and/or kidnapper. Smith and Jones had asked me about the ex-con and his relationship to Chester. As far as I knew, they had no relationship, aside from Roy's role as a retriever of messages. Whenever I thought of my new handyman, I pictured his blood-soaked jacket and hoped to God he'd ditched it before showing up at my door.

The Coast Guard nanny greeted me and Abra as we entered the kitchen. Her first words were not quite the welcome I'd expected: "Did anyone follow you home?"

I said no but was forced to admit that I hadn't watched my rear-view mirror.

"Please don't tell me you took your usual route," Deely said.

"Okay, I won't tell you."

She groaned.

In my defense, I explained that my canine passenger was flatulent. And I wasn't feeling so great myself, having passed out twice within the past twenty-four hours.

"Your houseguest isn't in the best shape, either," Deely said. "I fed him, showed him the bathroom, and told him to lie down after his shower."

"What about his clothes?" I asked, dreading her answer.

"Taken care of, ma'am," she replied. "Damage control."

"But isn't that tampering with evidence?"

Deely frowned. "Roy arrived nearly naked. I found him some old clothes that must have belonged to your husband. They're too small, but they'll do until he can find something better."

"Nearly naked?" I was torn between shock and concern and prurient curiosity. Also, I wondered where Deely had found Leo's old clothes. I thought I had disposed of them all.

"Yes, ma'am. I treated Roy for exposure. I think he'll be fine once he gets some rest."

"But what happened to his clothes?" I asked, stuck on the image of a bare-assed buff Roy.

153

"Don't ask, don't tell. That's the first rule in these situations."

My expression prompted her to explain.

"If you don't know, you won't have to lie. Best not to know what Roy's been up to."

That reminded me of what Abra had been up to. As her unofficial trainer, Deely had a right to know. She handled the news with her usual calm.

"Eating a rotten rat won't make her sick, but it will make her unpopular. I recommend keeping her outdoors until the worst has passed."

I agreed and noticed that the nanny had, as promised, installed a doggie door connecting the kitchen to the new fenced-in exercise area.

"Great," I said, "except now the dogs can come and go as they please."

"That's the point: fewer interruptions for you. Plus, you can contain them where you want them." Deely inserted a wood panel in the opening. "This will keep them on whichever side of the door you like."

Exactly the way things had been before she installed the doggie door, back when I mostly kept them locked outside. This was progress? Deely removed the panel, and Prince Harry instantly appeared, shaking the snow off his paws and tail. The nanny beamed.

"He learns so fast! I only had to show him once."

Mother Abra trotted up to her son, sniffed his extremities, and contributed a very foul odor to my kitchen. Deely pushed her through the slot and slid the panel closed behind her. Prince Harry barked with delight at what must be a fun, new game.

"I'll get the air freshener," Deely said. We both knew we couldn't count on the pleasant scent of food cooking to cancel out Abra's stink. I never cook and rarely eat in. The same goes for Avery. My spacious kitchen, once the scene of Leo's gourmet concoctions, now functions mainly as eye candy.

"Did Leah and Leo's father come by to meet them last night?" I asked.

"Yes, ma'am, he was here," Deely said. "But I wouldn't recommend asking Avery about it. She's been locked in her room ever since."

"You don't happen to know where Dr. Grant is staying, do you?" I asked innocently.

"Yes, ma'am, I do. He's got a room at Red Hen's House. I think he plans to stay a while."

"Really?" I cleared my throat to erase my enthusiasm. "Uh, did either you or Avery notice . . . or care . . . that I failed to come home last night?"

"I noticed, ma'am. By the way, I think Jeb Halloran is cool."

"I wasn't with Jeb Halloran!" I said, wondering why I was blushing. And also why I felt I needed to clarify that for the nanny.

"Too bad. I've been a fan of his for a long time. He could have a brilliant career in Canine Music."

"What's that?"

"The wave of the future." Deely smiled in a way that was almost coy. "I talked to him about it at the Jamboree."

From the helicopter had I spotted Deely, not Avery, talking with Jeb?

The nanny continued, "I've noticed that both Abra and Prince Harry get sleepy whenever I play Jeb's Celtic tunes. So I'm integrating his music into The System. Remember how fast the dogs fell asleep when I crated them?"

I had wondered about that two nights ago.

"Jeb's version of *Danny Boy* is guaranteed to knock them out. David is testing it on some of his patients. If the results prove conclusive, and we think they will, we have a major find. Do you have any idea how many hyperactive dogs are out there with frustrated humans? Put Fleggers behind him, and your ex-husband's CD could go gold!"

"How nice," I said, doubting that there were enough extravagant *anti-speciesists* to make Jeb Halloran rich. Switching subjects, I asked, "You heard what happened to Gil Gruen, right? That's how you knew Roy was in trouble?"

"I heard the mayor disappeared, that's all. There's a rumor you saw his bloody body. Roy told me himself that he's in trouble. Like I said, I didn't ask what for."

So Jenx was keeping a lid on the murder until Gil's body was found. For now his fate was inconclusive—except to me, the only person who'd seen his corpse. Other than, of course, whoever had killed him.

When the phone rang, Deely answered it.

"Do you want to talk to Odette Mutombo?" she asked.

"Do I have a choice?"

"Now that their power's back on, Mother Tucker's is open," Odette began. "Since the Jamboree was cancelled for today, I thought you might be bored and looking for something to do. Or at least something to eat. Should I pick you up?"

"Where are you?" I asked, detecting a blur of cheery voices in the background.

"Mother Tucker's. I met a client for Happy Hour. And guess who's here?"

"Who?"

"I'll give you a clue," Odette crooned. "He's practically your stepson-in-law."

Images of the sexy professor from Florida danced before my eyes.

"He is not! He and Avery don't even like each other. Plus, he's fifteen years older than she is, which makes him three years older than me!"

"I'm relieved you know who I'm talking about," Odette said. "And you can still do basic math. Nash Grant is the client I met for drinks. If I do my job right and rent him a house, I'll keep him in town awhile. The rest is up to you."

TWENTY-TWO

THE PROSPECT OF SEEING Nash Grant again (and again) made me as giddy as a kid on Christmas morning. Never mind that sweet Chester was missing, smelly Abra wasn't, and a convicted felon had arrived at my house nearly naked.

By the time Odette rolled up in her Mercedes, I couldn't wait to start flirting. I had changed my clothes, brushed my hair, and applied a little perfume and make-up.

"Mascara!" Odette exclaimed. "Lipstick! You *are* in lust."

"It's still legal in forty-nine states."

"But coveting the father of your late husband's grandchildren? That must be taboo. Even if the guy's closer to your age, and you loathe your stepdaughter."

"They can barely stand each other," I insisted. "So no harm, no foul."

"There's another problem, Whiskey: The whole town wants you and Jeb to get back together."

When I laughed and she didn't, I stared at Odette. "You can't be serious."

"As the Apocalypse. You and Jeb have so much history."

"Which is why we're no longer in love. . . ."

Odette made that rude raspberry sound I've come to know and loathe. I changed the subject. "Did you hear from Jenx? She has good news and bad news for you."

"No. Tell me."

"The good news is Abra returned your designer bag. The one you sacrificed to land the Gribble account."

"That's not just a 'designer bag,' Whiskey. That's a Gucci."

"Whatever."

"What's the bad news?"

"You can't have it back."

"What?!"

"Not right away. Jenx had to impound it. As evidence."

Odette said, "It didn't have a finger in it, did it?"

She was referring to a disturbing incident that had occurred the previous fall. It had also involved Abra.

"No! Just a business card and a poker chip, I swear."

Despite still-icy road conditions and scattered power outages, Mother Tucker's was almost as busy as usual for a Friday night. We circled the parking lot looking for a space.

"Do you think he's still here?" I asked Odette.

"When I left to pick you up, Nash was settling in at the bar for a long night of sipping."

"He was getting drunk?"

Odette claimed a spot and turned off the ignition. "I said sipping, not tippling. Nash Grant doesn't strike me as a heavy drinker. More like a man who wants to meet people."

"He teaches in Florida," I said. "And he grew up in Mississippi. Why would he move to Michigan in midwinter? Don't tell me he's giving up his job just to be near the babies?"

"He's on sabbatical till August," Odette replied. "That's how long he plans to stay."

Inside Mother Tucker's a party atmosphere prevailed. The crowd, made up of equal parts tourists and locals, was rowdier than usual, all that pent-up Jamboree energy seeking immediate release. Proprietors Walter and Jonny St. Mary obliged by slashing drink prices in half. A banner announcing the discount festooned the foyer.

Odette and I made our way toward the bar, pausing every few feet to exchange greetings with tipsy friends and neighbors. Because my desire to find Nash Grant exceeded my interest in making small talk, my eyes swept the room like radar. I realized that I'd seen the professor from the back just once, when he walked out of my hospital room with Jeb the night before. I had been aiming low, and both their butts made favorable impressions. Now, if Nash were sitting at the bar, I'd have to recognize his upper half.

And I did. It was easy because his was parked next to a very familiar upper half: Jeb's. I surprised myself by feeling a completely illogical sting of jealousy. As if I were competing with Jeb for Nash's attention.

"Hey, guys," I said, inserting myself sideways between Nash's right shoulder and Jeb's left. I smiled at Nash.

To my annoyance, Jeb put his hand on my waist and turned me toward him.

"I hear you broke out of the hospital," he said. "Against medical advice."

"Was it on the news?" I asked.

"My cousin's neighbor works in admissions. Do you remember pissing off a thin blonde chick with freckles on her nose?"

"I remember *her* pissing *me* off."

"Then you probably won't care that you'll never get her real-estate business."

That made Nash laugh. I refocused my best smile on him.

"How's Magnet Springs treating the boy from Biloxi?" I asked.

"Just fine, thanks." Nash rose and offered me his bar stool. I glanced at Jeb, wishing he would give his seat to Nash. No such luck.

"I hear you met Leah and Leo last night," I told Nash.

He nodded enthusiastically. "I spent two hours with my kids, and it changed my life."

"Really?"

"I couldn't sleep a wink afterwards. 'Round about three in the morning, I figured out what I need to do."

"Which is—?"

"I can't believe Odette didn't tell you," Jeb interjected. "Nash is going to spend the rest of his sabbatical here. If somebody at Mattimoe Realty can find him a house to rent...."

I glanced at my ex-husband as he put his beer mug to his mouth, thereby covering the sly grin that we both knew was there.

To Nash, I said, "You're in good hands with Odette. She's the best agent I have."

"I'm sure she is," he agreed. "But I was hoping you might find time to lend me a little assistance."

My face flushed. Since I hadn't yet consumed a single drop of alcohol, I attributed the heat to pure lust. Before I could reply, Jeb took it upon himself to build Nash's case.

"After all, he's the daddy. And you're the grandma."

"Whiskey's too young to be anybody's grandma," Nash said gallantly. "But she'll always be important to the twins. I'll see to that." His copper-colored eyes sparkled seductively. "Leah and Leo give us something in common, don't they? Right from the get-go."

Good thing I was already sitting down.

"What do you drink, Whiskey?" Nash said, signaling the barkeep.

"This one's on me," said Jeb. He told the server, "A cool burn for the hot lady. Better make it a double, and put some ice in it."

"You like scotch?" Nash asked me.

"I used to," I said, glaring at Jeb—who winked. He paid for the drink, and then excused himself to join some friends at their table. Nash took his stool.

"What do you think of my plan to bond with my children?" he said.

"I think it sounds great, although I don't really know your plan."

I took a big gulp of my drink and felt the fire spread from my throat to my gut. Once again, thanks to Jeb Halloran, I was drinking scotch on an empty stomach. Where would it lead?

"I'm on sabbatical for six more months," Nash said. "Technically, I'm working on a book, but I can do that from anywhere."

"A book about what?"

"Advertising. 'Media Planning for the Sole Proprietor.' I reckon that sounds pretty dry."

"Oh, no," I said, unable to imagine how anything Nash Grant did could be boring.

"Advertising is sexy, Whiskey. Analyzing it isn't. True confession: I'd rather be creating ads than dissecting them, but that part of my life is behind me."

"You used to write ads?"

"Once upon a time, I was creative director for a big agency in L.A. But things change." He gazed into his beer mug for a long moment. "I went back to college, got my Ph.D. Now I'm an academic, and a pretty darned good one. The tenured life can be a good life."

I nodded, although I had no clue what the tenured life was like. My life involved running a business that required daily reinvention.

We talked about what Nash was looking for in terms of a place to live while in Magnet Springs. I was both touched and amused when he said he wanted the "whole white-picket-fence scene: big porch, fenced-in yard, lots of room to play."

I reminded him that his children were three months old. Nash sighed, finished his beer and ordered another one.

"Maybe I'm chasing some kind of fantasy here, but I'd like to prove that I'm going to be a good father. The best I can be, under the circumstances."

He looked at me so intensely that I automatically reached for and downed half my drink.

"I know you and Avery aren't close," he said.

"That's an understatement."

"But she does live under your roof. Listen, Whiskey, I hate to put you in an awkward position. . . . "

Just tell me the position you prefer.

I didn't say that out loud. At least I don't think I did. I kept staring into Nash Grant's eyes and squeezing a cocktail napkin in each hand.

He continued, "Avery is threatening to block my access to the twins. I may have to take her to court. Unless you can reason with her."

"Ha!" With that I swallowed the rest of my scotch. Nash offered me another, which I loudly declined.

"Avery reasons with no one, least of all me," I announced. "Why else would we need the Coast Guard?"

He frowned and offered to order me food. I gave him my blessing. I don't remember what he ordered, what we talked about, or what I ate. But I know I felt better after I'd eaten, even when the subject of Avery came up again.

"You may not like her, and she may not like you, but I think she respects you," Nash told me. "If only because she knows Leo loved and respected you. Avery adored her daddy."

The last sentence was true although I doubted that Avery would ever adopt any part of Leo's attitude. So far there wasn't a single sign of that happening despite my ongoing efforts to be nice—or at least helpful.

"I don't want to take the children away from her," Nash said. "As a matter of fact, I intend to be generous in terms of financial support. In return, however, I want what she doesn't seem willing to give me: access and time. They're my children, too, Whiskey."

I nodded. Suddenly his plight reminded me of my own. Although Chester wasn't my son, I felt responsible for him and ached to see him again. My keenly honed emotional-repression skills momentarily deserted me. Probably because Nash was so close, so handsome, so vulnerable, and he smelled so damn good. Without thinking, I placed my right hand on top of his left hand and squeezed. He placed his right hand on top of mine, and squeezed back. I added my left hand to the pile. By now our noses were inches apart. I felt his breath on my face.

"Well, well. If it isn't the Enemy, plotting their next move."

We literally jumped. Avery Mattimoe stood behind us in her olive-green parka. Her blotchy face was streaked with tears and snot.

"One man's not enough for you, Whiskey?" she demanded shrilly. "You need to sneak around town with your ex *and* my ex?"

TWENTY-THREE

NASH DROPPED MY HANDS as if they were scalding him.

"Avery, calm down," he said, rising to meet her.

"I'm not calming down until you get her out of here," my step-daughter said. She flicked her pink tongue in my direction, probably out of spite, although it could have been her tic.

"Man stealer! Child-care fake! Why don't you go make some babies of your own instead of borrowing other people's?" She was shrieking now. The once noisy bar had turned deadly quiet. Somebody touched my shoulder.

"Come on, Whiskey, let's go," Jeb whispered.

I ignored him. "I'm not borrowing your babies. I'm providing you and them with a good place to live, plus full-time care."

"We're in big trouble if you care for us the way you cared for Chester. By now the whole town knows he's missing, and Cassina fired your ass!"

"She couldn't fire me. I volunteered!"

"That's enough," Jeb said, louder than before. But I wasn't finished.

"Avery, the babies' father wants to do the right thing—by you and by them. Why don't you let him?"

"Why don't you listen to Boyfriend Number One and get the hell out of here!"

Jeb made sure I did. He grabbed my coat and my arm and steered me toward the exit. The bar crowd parted before us like the Red Sea.

"Why give her the satisfaction?" I fumed as he opened the door. The blast of air that greeted us was so frigid that it sucked the breath out of me. Jeb took advantage of my silence to speak his peace.

"The last thing you need right now is more trouble, especially with the people living in your house. Why can't you see that?"

"Deely likes me," I whined.

"Deely takes a check from you. But she takes orders from Avery and would probably follow her out the door. You may not like Avery, but you love her babies. And you need Deely to help you keep track of the dogs. Don't blow it, Whiskey."

He led me to his vehicle.

"You're still driving this?" I said, nodding at the rusted out Nissan Van Wagon, a relic of the late '80s. Even in the dim light of Mother Tucker's parking lot, I could see the wires holding the rear bumper in place.

"It gets me where I need to go, mostly."

The passenger door groaned when Jeb pried it open, and the interior light failed to come on. I didn't move.

He said, "Are you going to stand here till someone with a better car offers you a ride?"

I climbed in and promptly jumped out again. "There's something on the seat—and it's big!"

"Sorry." He reached past me to rearrange the interior. Hearing the squeaks, crunches and crashes, I wondered what the hell was in there. "Okay, try again."

Cautiously I entered and found the seat bare. With difficulty, he shoved my door shut. The car took a few tries to start, but eventually we were rolling.

"Where to next?" Jeb asked. "I'm guessing you're too wired to go home. How about a drink at my favorite dive?"

"Can I get something besides scotch?" I said acidly.

"As long as it comes in a can. The Blue Moon serves shots and beer. Cheap beer."

A whole lifetime in Magnet Springs, and I'd never set foot inside the Blue Moon, a ramshackle dive down by the docks. There wasn't even a sign outside, just a faded plywood crescent moon hanging crooked under a single floodlight. No parking lot, either. Patrons walked from their boats in summer, their ice shanties or snowmobiles in winter. We found a spot along the street. The place looked closed. I said so to Jeb, who laughed.

Closing my door, he said, "Just curious: Who's Evelyn Huffenbach, and what's she got on you?"

"She's got nothing on me!" I snapped. "Who said she did?"

"Everybody knows the Fibbies are in town. Rumor has it Cassina called in Grandma Evelyn from Iowa because you lost her little boy."

The grapevine in this town never failed to amaze me.

"I didn't lose Chester," I said through clenched teeth. "Even Evelyn didn't accuse me of that. At least not in those exact words."

"I hear she's his new legal guardian."

"Maybe. I didn't see the paperwork. Trouble is, Chester told me he didn't have a grandmother. Or any family at all. If Evelyn's story is true, then my client Mrs. Gribble the Third is Chester's great aunt. And possibly his kidnapper."

We had reached the Blue Moon's front door.

"Ready?" Jeb said with a mischievous grin. He swung it open to reveal a scene that wasn't nearly as dark or deserted as I had imagined. A pool table occupied the middle of the room, surrounded by card tables and chairs. The bar ran along the back. Vintage neon beer signs glowed on the walls, and every stool was taken.

"Where'd everybody come from?" I said.

"Most drove their snowmobiles. They're parked around the corner by the boatlift. What'll it be, Blatz or Schlitz?" Jeb asked.

"Is there a difference?"

"Oh yes."

"Then I'm in a Blatz mood tonight," I said. He fetched the brews while I located a couple of card-table chairs near the pool table. Everybody knew Jeb's name. I recognized almost no one.

"Who are these people?" I said when he returned with the frosty cans.

"Blue Moon regulars: farmers and factory workers from this side of Lanagan County."

"They know you because you're a regular, too?" I asked.

"They know me because they're fans of my music. Some of these good folks own all my CDs. They follow me from gig to gig."

I tried to imagine which of Jeb's several musical incarnations would have attracted this crowd. They didn't look like Celtic music types to me. More likely they'd found him during his Country or Rock-a-Billy days.

"Excuse me a minute," Jeb said.

I popped open my can and took a cautious swig. Blatz beer, all right. Nothing quite like it. That was one of the differences between Leo and Jeb: Leo liked the finer things—including imported beer, wine, and food; Jeb liked whatever he could get.

"I don't care what they say, Gil Gruen's dead."

The voice came from the pool table, where two middle-aged guys in snowmobile suits were chalking their cues.

"They ain't found a body," the second man said.

"That don't mean nothing. He's dead. And Roy Vickers killed him."

"I heard they had a showdown at the Town Hall."

"That's not why I think Roy did it," the first man said. "I saw Roy yesterday, and he wasn't right."

"How so?"

The first man dropped his voice so low that I had to lean hard toward the pool table to catch his answer. "When Big Jim arrested Roy for stabbing Leo Mattimoe, I was right there. I'd just come out of First Federal Bank next door. Roy looked the same yesterday as he did that morning."

The second man noticed me leaning and misunderstood.

"Did you want to join us in a game?" he asked.

"No thanks." I looked at the first man. "You knew Leo Mattimoe?"

"He was our real-estate agent when me and the wife bought our farm. Fourteen years ago now." The man squinted at me. "Say, aren't you Leo's widow? Never seen you in the Blue Moon before."

"That's because she needs me to show her all the best places," Jeb said. He shook hands with the men and introduced them as Bud and Chuck.

"Sure you don't want to play?" Bud, the first man, asked.

"Come on, Whiskey," Jeb said. "Let's see what you remember from our Glory Days on the road."

It had been that long since I'd shot pool. Jeb used to wind down after gigs by drinking a six-pack and shooting as many games. I played, too, mainly to keep the groupies at bay. Because I'd once been good, I figured I could still pick up a cue without embarrassing myself. Plus, I liked the prospect of learning more from Bud and Chuck about what Roy had been doing the day before.

Although, as rusty pool players go, I wasn't half-bad, Bud and Chuck were a couple of sharks. When Jeb and I got a chance to shoot, which wasn't often, setting up the right shots took all our concentration. By the time we finished, Chuck had run more consecutive racks of balls than I wanted to count, and Roy's name hadn't come up again.

I was reaching for my nearly empty third can of Blatz when Bud said, "Chief Jenkins says there's been no murder till we find a body, but I disagree. When I saw that blood on Roy, I knew somebody was dead."

"When did you see blood on Roy?" I asked, my heart thumping.

"Right around lunchtime yesterday. I don't wear a watch when I fish. I was in my shanty, in Fishburg, but nothing was biting, and hardly anybody was around. So I decided to stretch my legs and go check out the shanty to the north that went up the night before. I wondered who the hell would have set it there."

"Why?"

"Dumb location— on a shallow shelf with too much vegetation for a solid freeze. That's why Fishburg's where it is: the ice is more reliable."

"Roy was there?"

"I was eight, maybe ten, feet from the shanty when he came out, staggering like he was on a bender. I knew Roy back when he was a fall-down drunk. For a minute, I thought he'd been boozing again. His eyes had that crazy look. Then I saw the blood on his jacket."

"Did you talk to him?" I said.

"I asked if he was hurt. He said it was fish blood. I never saw that much blood on a fisherman. Roy shouted at me to get back. Said the ice was too thin. Sure enough, there were cracks, so I turned around and went back to my shanty. That was all we said to each other. But something wasn't right."

It must have been just minutes later when I encountered Roy on his way back to shore. I saw the same haunted expression that Bud had seen, but I went on. Why didn't I notice the cracks in the ice as I approached the shanty? Maybe it's true that we can't see what we're not looking for.

"Did you tell Jenx, I mean Chief Jenkins, about this?" I asked.

He nodded. "I missed the excitement when you and the shanty fell through. Had a walleye on my line. Later I heard you saw Gil's body go under the ice, so I called the chief and told her what I seen. She took my statement."

"Anything else strike you as strange?" I said.

Bud thought about it while he downed what was left of his Schlitz.

"Yesterday morning, real early, when I first saw the shanty, there was a guy out there, skating around it. He looked like a fairy."

"Gay, you mean? What made you think that?"

"He was wearing a full-length fur coat."

TWENTY-FOUR

WHY DID MR. OSCAR Manfred Gribble the Third circle the ice-fishing shanty on skates early yesterday morning?

What was Roy Vickers up to a few hours later when he staggered from the shanty covered with blood?

And where was Gil Gruen's body?

I pondered those questions as I replaced my pool cue in the rack. I didn't realize Jeb's cell phone had rung until he handed it to me.

"Deely Smarr for you," he said.

"We have a situation," she said.

"Didn't we already have one of those?" I groaned.

"Yes, ma'am, we did, and now we have another."

"Why are you whispering?" I said.

"Consider this a head's up: your stepdaughter returned here at twenty-one hundred hours and summoned a locksmith to change your locks. He's on his way now. I suggest you come home ASAP."

She pronounced the last word "ay-sap."

"You mean Avery's locking me out?" I said.

"Yes, ma'am, that's her plan. May I please speak to Jeb again?"

I passed the phone back to my ex-husband. He listened, murmured a couple responses and closed the call.

"Ready to roll?" he said before I could release the rage within me. "We want to stop the locksmith before he starts. Less of a scene that way."

Jeb waved good-bye to everyone at the Blue Moon.

"I'll be playing at the Jamboree tomorrow and taking your requests," he said.

And hawking CDs, I thought. Maybe he and Deely were already working out a plan to launch his new line of Canine Music.

"That bitch!" I said as soon as we stepped outside.

"Deely's just trying to be helpful," Jeb said.

"I mean Avery! Avery's the bitch! Where will this end?"

"At your front door if we're lucky. The locksmith she called is a fan of mine. I'm surprised I didn't see him at the Blue Moon tonight."

"It's my house!" I fumed. "Avery has no right to change the locks, whether the locksmith likes your music or not!"

"True. But what people should do and do do are two different things. I'm thinking of writing a song about that."

"Don't call it *Do Do*. If you substitute dogs for people and call the tune *Abra's Theme*, you might have a huge canine hit. Deely told me about the soporific power of your Celtic tunes."

"On dogs," he clarified. "People stay wide awake."

"Glad to hear it. Deely seems to think Fleggers could help you get rich."

"Nash thinks so, too."

"Nash?"

"He knows advertising. He has lots of ideas to promote my career. It's what we talk about, mostly. That and you."

"Me? Nash talks to you about me?"

Jeb didn't reply. He was straining to unjam the Van Wagon's passenger door.

"What does Nash want to know about me?" I insisted.

"He's just curious—about you and Avery and Leo and the twins. You're related now. Sort of."

"Do you think he's . . . attracted to me?" I asked, pretending the answer didn't matter.

"I think we'd better roll," Jeb said.

When we arrived at Vestige, we pulled in behind a van labeled Larry's Lock and Key Services.

"We're too late," I said.

"No we're not," Jeb countered. "He just got here. Let's go."

"Easy for you to say," I mumbled, trying vainly to open my door. That's when I realized that the Van Wagon's passenger door released only from the outside. I could have slid across the seat and over the gear shift lever to use Jeb's door, but I was annoyed enough to let him walk around and do the honors.

"You need a new car," I said as I stepped out.

"That's why I'm hustling CDs," he replied. "Let me do the talking here, Whiskey. Larry didn't like you in high school."

"I don't remember Larry in high school."

"Uh-huh," Jeb said.

When I met Larry the Locksmith, I instantly knew why I didn't remember him. Larry was one of those types who blend into the background: average face, average height, average weight (well, a little overweight by now) and absolutely zero personality. But who says you need showmanship to be a locksmith? Jeb supplied that element by making a dramatic entrance and immediately taking center stage. Fortunately for us, Larry hadn't changed the front door lock yet, so Jeb was able to fling it open. Both Avery and Larry were standing in the foyer. Avery, her eyes and nose still red from crying, was waiting, arms crossed, while Larry wrote up an estimate.

"Get out!" Avery shouted.

I assumed she meant me even though that was ridiculous since I owned the house. Jeb assumed she meant him.

"Easy, Avery," he said. "How's my man, Larry?"

The locksmith lighted up. "Good. Real good. How the heck are you, Jeb? Long time no see."

"I'm doing great. Hey, you need my latest CD. I've got a box out in the van. Let's go get you one."

"Not so fast!" Avery said. "We're doing business here."

Jeb said, "I don't think so. Larry doesn't violate the wishes of the homeowner."

Larry looked confused. "I thought Avery was the homeowner. She said she inherited this house from Leo Mattimoe."

"Well, she didn't," I said, unable to remain silent one moment longer. "Hi, Larry. How the heck are you?"

Larry stared.

"Leo left the house to my ex-wife," Jeb explained. "Come on, let's get you a CD!"

Jeb tossed an arm over Larry's shoulder, and the two men exited.

If ever Avery could have set fire to my hair just by breathing on it, that was the moment. She seethed.

"Get out of here," she repeated.

Deciding that silence was the safer, if not better, part of valor, I crossed the foyer toward the staircase. Time for bed.

"Not so fast, Whiskey!" Avery called after me. "We have issues to discuss."

Without turning around or even breaking my pace, I replied, "Not tonight we don't. Unless you want to turn in your key and move out before breakfast."

"I'm not going anywhere. Neither are my children. And their father isn't coming here to see them, even if their step-grandmother invites him in!"

That stopped me. I was on the third step already, so I seized the banister for support.

"Here's the bottom line, Avery," I said quietly. "Nash wants to help you and the twins, and believe it or not, so do I. You're the only person working against your children's and your own best interests. Get over it."

I slipped into bed thinking I had never been more eloquent. Leo would have been so proud. Roy, too, would have appreciated my oratory skills. Roy?

It hit me then that the ex-con was somewhere in my house, probably sleeping naked. What if Avery found out? Assuming she knew he was in trouble, she'd have him and me busted for sure. How much trouble was he in? I didn't think there was a warrant out (yet) for Roy's arrest. Maybe I couldn't be convicted of aiding and abetting a killer as long as I didn't know what he'd done. I winced. Except that I had told Jenx about seeing the blood on Roy. That didn't make me look innocent.

Someone knocked on my bedroom door. I tried to remember whether I had locked it and decided my best bet was to feign sleep.

Whoever was out there knocked again.

"Whiskey?"

I couldn't identify the voice.

"Who is it?" I whispered back.

The door opened. I pulled the covers up to my chin. Against the dim light from the hall was a hulking silhouette.

"It's me. Roy. Can I come in?"

TWENTY-FIVE

WHAT DO YOU SAY when a well-built septuagenarian ex-con who's under-dressed and on the lam knocks at your bedroom door?

I said, " Come in."

He did, silently closing the door behind him. I switched on my bedside light. Roy was wearing Leo's old bathrobe. The sleeves ended at Roy's elbows, the hem an inch above his knees.

"Where did Deely find that?" I asked.

Roy said, "Whiskey, we need to talk. I don't have much time."

I motioned for him to sit down in the Morris chair across from my bed. Although Deely had coached me to play don't-ask-don't-tell, I couldn't help myself.

"Where's Chester?"

"I don't know," Roy said. "I wish I did."

"But you retrieved two of his notes. Plus his puppy."

"I was on his trail for a while, but I lost him. That's why I need to get going again. I have a hunch where to look."

"Tell me!"

Roy shook his head. "You're better off not knowing. At least for now."

Exasperated, I punched my pillow. "Then what do you want from me?"

"Clothes, for one thing. I had to dump mine."

"Was that Gil's blood?" I said boldly.

"Don't ask."

"If you killed Gil—or were involved in Chester's disappearance—then I'm assisting a felon. That's obstruction of justice."

"I would never hurt Chester!" Roy exclaimed, his voice no longer a whisper. In fact, he'd spoken so loudly that we both held our breaths. Had anyone else heard?

There was a knock at my door. Roy's eyes were round with terror.

When I didn't answer, a familiar voice said, "Open up, Whiskey. I know where you sleep."

I signaled for Roy to go into the bathroom. Then I went to the door and peered out.

"Thanks for getting rid of Larry," I told Jeb. "You can go home now."

"No wham-bam, only thank-you, ma'am? I saved your locks."

"And I'm grateful, but not in the carnal sense. Please leave."

Jeb had braced himself against the door frame with one hand. Now he used the other hand to stroke my hair. I hated that . . . because I loved it.

"Please," I repeated, not moving.

"Please, what?"

I wished he wouldn't ask. Standing there in my PJs with Jeb's fingers in my hair, I was getting hot and bothered. Never mind how wrong it was. Never mind that I had a felon in my bathroom.

"We're not alone," I said, deciding that only honesty could save me.

He peered over my shoulder into the bedroom. "I don't see anyone."

"Come on out, Roy!" I hissed.

When he did, the men exchanged uneasy greetings.

Jeb said, "I may have underestimated you, Whiskey."

"It's not what you think."

"I'm thinking you're in way more trouble than I knew about."

"Speaking of trouble, how did you get back in the house? I was sure Avery would lock you out."

"She did. But Deely let me in."

Roy returned to the Morris chair, which left Jeb the choice of standing by the door or sitting on my bed. He chose my bed.

Roy said, "Now one more person knows I was here. That's not good for any of us."

Jeb the Unflappable told Roy not to worry. "Nobody takes a musician seriously," he said. "Besides, your secret's safe with me."

That brought us back to the question of the hour. What did Roy want?

"I need to borrow your car," he said. "And a little cash. Say, a hundred bucks."

"Whiskey," Jeb said. "Can we talk a minute? In the bathroom?"

I was sure he was going to tell me not to help Roy. Jeb locked the bathroom door and leaned against the sink. I sat on the closed toilet.

"Roy can borrow the Van Wagon," Jeb said.

"Are you serious?"

"Sure. It's not the least conspicuous car in the county, but anybody who sees it will think I'm at the wheel. That should help Roy."

"Why would you want to help Roy?" I asked.

"Because you do. I want what you want. More or less." Jeb winked.

"But then you won't have wheels," I pointed out.

"So you'll have to drive me. I can live with that."

When we gave Roy the news, Jeb added, "The Van Wagon's a little temperamental. There's a trick to getting her started sometimes. Kind of like Whiskey. . . ."

I cleared my throat. "Not to mention that you can't open the passenger door from the inside."

Roy wasn't fazed. "No problem. My job was maintaining the prison fleet."

"By the way," I said, "did you ever replace the antifreeze in my company truck?"

"Yes. And your car. Plus, I tuned up your company snowmobile."

I'd forgotten about the snowmobile, mainly because Leo used to take care of it. Since his death last spring, I'd ignored its presence in my garage at Vestige.

I was removing five twenties from my wallet when a third person pounded on my door.

"Do you have a man in there?" Avery demanded.

"A man?" I looked from Jeb to Roy. This could be fun. "You think there's a man in here?"

"Deely said she let Jeb back in. I don't want him sleeping in my father's bed!"

"Oh, there's no chance of that," I said. "And even less chance of you telling me what to do. Go to bed, Avery! We'll talk more tomorrow."

I heard her thumping back down the hall, swearing with every step.

"No chance?" Jeb asked wistfully.

I shook my head and handed Roy the cash.

"I'll pay you back with interest, Whiskey, from my first paycheck."

"Yeah, well don't be gone so long I forget you work for me. Jeb's going to need his Van Wagon soon."

"I'll bring it back by Monday, I promise."

My newly recharged cell phone buzzed. Who would be calling at 11:30 on a Friday night? Caller ID offered no information.

"Hello?"

"Nice *ménage à trois* you got going on up there. I didn't know the hottie realtor was into threesomes."

Thomas McKondin, a.k.a. C. Richards, RN, again.

My instinct was to close my phone. But I kew he must be right outside watching us. Jenx had said he was a voyeur, a peeping Tom named Tom.

I activated my speaker phone so that the men in my bedroom could hear his response. Then I stretched out on my bed, where I knew no one outside could see me.

"Feeling lonely tonight, Mr. Nurse Man?" I asked. Jeb and Roy's jaws dropped.

"Not lonely. Helpful. Nurse Richards is standing by to heal you, baby."

"Heal me how?" I said, signaling my companions to relax.

"We're talking sexual healing. Like the Marvin Gaye song."

Jeb and Roy's eyes were about to pop out of their heads.

"What can you do for me that these two hunks can't?" I opened a couple drawers in my nightstand looking for something to write on.

"You'll have to feel it to believe it," the fake nurse said.

On a tablet I scribbled:

This pervert is wanted by Jenx and the FBI. He's outside watching us now.

Roy and Jeb read the note, nodded to each other, and then started toward the door.

"Stop!" I said. The men froze. Thomas McKondin said, "What do you mean, stop? I haven't got you started yet."

I motioned for Jeb and Roy to sit down, but they wouldn't. Roy moved between my north- and west-facing windows. Jeb headed into the bathroom, presumably to check the view from there.

"Your boyfriends can't see me," the peeping Tom sing-songed, like one child taunting another. "But I can see them. No way they could satisfy you, baby! The one guy's too old, and the other guy's James Taylor. Uh-oh. You must have me on speaker phone. Mr. Taylor just gave me the finger."

Bent low in order to keep out of sight, Jeb reentered the bedroom and signaled me to mute the phone.

"The asshole's on the west side of the house, but he's probably moving around. You got lots of trees for him to hide behind. I'm going out there."

"I wish you wouldn't," I said.

"Roy, stay in the window and give him something to watch. Whiskey, keep our friend on the phone."

"Let Brady or Jenx handle this," I pleaded. "The guy's so bad the Fibbies want him. Call 9-1-1."

"I will. But first I want to know where he is." Doubled over, Jeb rushed to the bedroom door, opened it as narrowly as possible and slipped out. For a musician, he liked to get macho sometimes.

"What's going on up there, baby?" McKondin asked. "You're too quiet. I like to hear my girls talk."

TWENTY-SIX

THE NEXT SOUND THAT reached our ears was a canine chorus. I'm not talking about Jeb's Celtic music, either. This was the kind of racket that only Abra and son could make.

"Uh-oh," Roy said from his post at my bedroom window. "Looks like Jeb let the dogs out."

I had to see for myself. The back porch lamp made my yard into a circle of white light fading to gray and finally black. I peered out in time to see Abra and Prince Harry lope into the darkness.

"You trying to sic your dogs on me?" asked Thomas McKondin.

"No way," I said into the phone. "My stepdaughter let them out. She likes to exercise them before bedtime."

"Why doesn't she use that nice new exercise pen right next to your house?" he said. "You're lying to me, Whiskey Mattimoe. People who do that pay for it. Big time. I'll be back."

The phone clicked in my ear.

"Dammit," I said. I turned to Roy. "I've got to go round up those dogs. This is your best time to leave—before the police arrive. Jeb's keys are in the ignition. Did Deely find you clothes that fit?"

"They'll do until I can get something else. Whiskey—." Roy's earnest blue eyes searched my face. "I know it doesn't look like it, but I'm working on my redemption, just as I said I would. You'll understand when I come back. I swear you will."

I nodded, but my mind was racing in other directions. "Good luck, Roy. Be careful out there."

I slipped on my socks and hiking boots and took off down the hall at a run. When I turned the corner, I smacked right into Avery.

"Jeb said you're on the phone with some guy who talks dirty," she said. "What are you, a whore?"

"That would imply that I work for a living. Wish I could say the same about you."

I slipped past her, ran down the steps, and paused at the hall closet long enough to grab my coat, earmuffs, and gloves. Casting a nervous glance back up the stairway, I hoped that Roy's time in prison had taught him about stealth. Surely he wouldn't attempt to clear the upstairs until he knew Avery was elsewhere.

The temperature outside seemed to have dropped ten degrees since I came home, mainly because a breeze had picked up. Anyone who lives her whole life in the North Country can instantly estimate wind-chill factor. My exposed flesh registered minus ten degrees Fahrenheit. And I was wearing pajamas under my coat.

"Abra! Prince Harry!" I called, crunching through the snow as fast as my feet would allow. "Here, girl! Here, boy!"

I had entered the Dark Zone, that nocturnal void beyond the circle created by the porch lamp. My property gave way to a deep forest on the south, to Lake Michigan on the west, and to Cassina's Castle, set off across a broad field to the north. My home faced east, toward the road, but I was in the back yard, following the barks. They were coming from the woods. Although faint moonlight glinted off the Lake, the forest swallowed all illumination. I slowed, listening. The last thing I needed to do was trip and fall. Or get lost in the woods. I cursed myself for not bringing a flashlight.

The dogs barked again. I swore they sounded closer than the last time. But a heavy snow cover can intensify sound, and wind can blur its origin.

"Here, Abra, here Harry, here baby!" I shouted.

"Oh-baby-ohhhhhh." The male voice was so close to my ear that my blood froze. "You didn't have to chase me all the way into the woods. You must want it real bad."

Instinctively, I swung around and kicked with all my might, my right foot connecting with something solid. Through the sole of my boot the shape felt right; I had hit my target. The male yelp confirmed it.

"Damn you, bitch!"

The darkness was so complete that I could barely discern McKondin's face, but I knew the voice. I also recognized my window of opportunity: I should kick him again to disable him and then get the hell away. I did, landing my second boot swing squarely in his jaw. I felt a bone crack. He made a sound like someone choking on his own tongue. No mercy for aggressors. Skin clammy, mouth dry, I stumbled on through the blackness toward the sounds of Abra and Prince Harry.

Gradually, my eyes adjusted to the pitch dark well enough to avoid collisions with trees. Yet I failed to spot a downed sapling, shin-high and covered in snow. Over I went, skidding along the ground on my face. I lay very still for a minute, evaluating my condition. Everything seemed to be intact although my flannel pajama bottoms were now soaked with snow. I shuddered, chilled to the bone. If I couldn't get back home, I could die of exposure. Scrambling to my feet, I battled a surge of terror. Which way should I go? The dogs had stopped barking, and the dense wall of trees obliterated my sense of direction.

In times of crisis, I talk to myself. Some remote part of my brain takes over as Coach and issues elementary commands. Coach was speaking now, using my mouth, and I was following orders: "Breathe. Step. Step. Rub your legs. Breathe."

I proceeded like that, not thinking, not worrying, just doing what Coach said . . . until I collided with a man. It was me who screamed, not Coach. And it was Jeb Halloran who held me in his arms till I stopped shaking.

"Good god, Whiskey," he said after I told him about landing two kicks against Thomas McKondin. "What were you thinking, calling out for the dogs like that? You made yourself a target!"

"On the phone he said he'd be back, so I assumed he was leaving, heading for the road. It didn't make sense that he'd be in the woods."

"When you're dealing with a whacko, never assume," Jeb said, "and never expect logical behavior."

"I don't suppose you have a flashlight," I said, "or any idea how to get back to the house?"

"No. But I know where Deely Smarr is, and she has both."

Jeb put his finger to my lips so that I would listen. I did. For a long moment, I heard nothing. Gradually, though, I became aware of a shush-shush sound growing ever closer. When I turned my head toward the noise, I saw a swinging beam of light.

"Over here!" Jeb shouted. "Whiskey and I are over here!"

Then Abra barked, and so did Prince Harry. Deely jogged toward us, flanked by the dogs. They were all three wearing matching parkas.

"So the dogs didn't get out by accident?" I said.

"Not entirely," Deely replied. "I was about to take them for a run, but Jeb dashed out the door before I could leash them."

"Sorry about that," my ex-husband said.

"No problem. Did you call the police?"

"Jenx is on her way."

Crouching in the snow, Deely stroked Abra with one hand and Prince Harry with the other. The dogs' erect tails ticked back and forth like the needle on a metronome.

"It's a good thing Abra got out," Deely said. "She made sure we found something the police need to see."

"What?" I said. "It's not a dead body, is it?"

Deely turned her wide face up to mine. "How'd you know?"

TWENTY-SEVEN

"It's GIL GRUEN, isn't it?" I said, trying not to picture the mayor's bloated body or imagine how it had ended up in my back yard.

"No, ma'am," said Deely. "It's a woman."

"A woman?!" I needed a moment to fit that notion inside my head. "Was she . . . murdered?"

"I don't know, ma'am. She's wearing fur."

The hostility in Deely's voice was unmistakable. Of course Fleggers would be down on fur.

"Chinchilla, by chance?" I asked, thinking of Mrs. Oscar Manfred Gribble the Third and her similarly clad sister Evelyn Huffenbach. If the dead body belonged to the former, Odette and I had lost a commission; if it belonged to the latter, Chester had lost his grandma.

"I think so, ma'am," Deely said. "Have you ever seen a chinchilla? While it was alive, I mean?"

"Not that I know of."

"They're the most innocent creatures on earth. They look like a cross between a rabbit, a mouse, and a squirrel, but they're no bigger than a man's hand."

"You don't say. . . ."

"Did you know, ma'am, that 75,000 chinchillas are killed every year to make coats like the one that dead woman is wearing?"

"I did not know that," I said, taking a small step backward. This was the first time I'd seen the Coast Guard nanny go all *anti-speciesist.*

She continued, "Chinchillas are crammed into wire cages and forced to breed three times a year. Then, when their fur is ready, they're either electrocuted or their necks are crushed."

"Is that a fact. . . ." I tried to catch Jeb's eye, hoping he might break into a Celtic tune or find some other way to calm her.

"Listen!" he said. We all did. From far off, through the trees and across the snow, came the sound of a coughing engine. It sputtered, gasped, choked, and gasped again before settling into a broken-muffler roar and fading away.

"The Van Wagon," Jeb concluded. "Roy's on the road again."

"You lent him your car?" Deely asked. Her tone was reverential.

"What can I say? The man's on a quest. I admire that."

"Sure you do," I said. "And you're hoping he'll fix your car while he's got it."

Jeb said, "Judging from the sound, Vestige must be right over there." He pointed.

"The wind is deceptive, sir," Deely said. "Actually, Vestige is *there.*" She indicated the opposite direction.

"Are you sure?" I asked.

"Positive, ma'am. I have a compass. And, when I passed this way earlier, I left a trail of tangerine peels in the snow." She played her flashlight beam across Nature's glistening white carpet flecked with orange-colored scraps.

"Man, you're good," Jeb remarked.

"Thank you, sir. You're good at what you do, too."

I said, "Here's a suggestion: Now that we know where the house is, why don't we go there? Unless you'd rather stand here praising each other while my snow-soaked pajama bottoms freeze to my flesh. . . ."

"Let's go," they agreed.

Abra barked her approval. But Prince Harry wouldn't budge until he'd taken a long, satisfying leak.

We reached the house at the same time Jenx did. Gratefully I observed that she had refrained from using the siren. No small sacrifice since Jenx loved to use the siren. Her flasher was on, though, a red streak of light rhythmically slashing the front of my house. I expected Avery to notice the crimson pulse and burst out the front door in yet another temper tantrum.

"Yo, Whiskey!" Jenx called out as our motley crew approached. "Everybody all right?"

"Everybody except the dead woman!"

Jenx cupped a hand around her ear to show that she hadn't heard me.

"We're okay!" I said, deciding to save the shocker until we could see the whites of her eyes.

As if on cue, Avery flung open the front door and surveyed the scene.

"How the hell is a brand-new mother supposed to get any rest around here?"

"Sorry," Jenx said. "I got a call about a peeping Tom on the property."

"Is that what Whiskey calls her men now?" Avery asked, sneering in my direction. She slammed the front door and clicked the lock.

"You don't happen to have a spare key, do you?" I asked Deely.

Damage Controlman Smarr produced one.

"Jeb's right," I said. "You're good."

I took the key from her. By now I was so chilled that my teeth were chattering. I told Jenx, "Deely will fill you in while I put on pants."

The dogs were intently watching Jenx. Abra probably wondered where Officer Roscoe was. Prince Harry probably didn't have a thought in his head; he just liked to look at people.

"Should I crate the dogs?" I asked Deely.

She scooped up Abra's son and handed him to me. He yawned.

"Prince Harry won't need Jeb to sing him to sleep tonight," Deely said.

"What about Abra? Shouldn't I crate her, too?" I said.

"No. She needs more sight and chase training, which she's about to get. But you'd better bring me her leash, just in case."

Prince Harry was asleep before I slipped him in his crate. Avery had retired, hopefully until tomorrow. Although I was exhausted, my nerves tingled when I thought about the unnamed body on my property. This threatened to be a very long and distressing night.

On my unmade bed lay a cryptic anonymous note:

The First Sun of Solace is to do the right thing. That's where I begin. Thank you.

I tore Roy's note into a dozen pieces and flushed it down the toilet. Then I got dressed.

By the time I rejoined my group, two more officers had arrived *sans* siren—Swancott and Roscoe. Abra could barely contain her excitement. She taunted Roscoe with in-the-face views of her private attributes.

"I know you're concentrating on the rescue and retrieval part of her training," I told Deely, "but her libido needs a time-out."

Deely agreed. When she put her hand out to receive Abra's leash, I realized I'd forgotten to fetch it. I offered to run back inside.

"No. Let's try her without it," the nanny said.

"Okay, sure." I shrugged. "What's the worst that could happen?"

Abra assumed the male-aggressor role and began humping Officer Roscoe, who stared off into space.

"You did finally get around to having her spayed, right?" asked Officer Swancott.

"Right!" I said, my face reddening. "It'll just take me a second to grab that leash."

"Slow down, Whiskey." Jenx was trotting along behind me. "I want to tell you something."

In the shadows at the corner of the house we stopped.

"I passed Jeb's Van Wagon on my way over here." Her voice was expressionless.

I said nothing. I couldn't read her face in the dark.

"Never fails to amaze me how generous he is for a man with so little," Jenx added.

After a long silence, I felt compelled to say something. So I stammered, "Yeah, well. I guess that's true. . . ."

"His good-for-nothing cousins can always count on Jeb to help 'em out," Jenx said. I could hear rather than see her kicking at the snow. "Wonder who's the lucky bastard this time? Which one gets to borrow the Van Wagon tonight?"

"I couldn't say. . . ."

"Yeah, Jeb wasn't sure, either. But then he's got about thirty cousins. Must be hard to keep 'em straight." She coughed. "Hurry up and find that leash, Whiskey. Deely says we got a corpse to recover."

The Michigan State Police arrived while I was inside. Unlike our thoughtful local force, they didn't mute their sirens. Either Leah or Leo was starting to fuss as I dashed from the house. I was grateful to escape before Avery could rise and whine.

When I caught up with my group, Deely had already told the MSP what she knew. The officer clicked on his flashlight and said, "Lead the way."

He seemed skeptical as Deely fastened Abra's leash in place.

"That's not a scent hound," he pointed out.

"That's right," she said. "Neither was Lassie."

True. But then Lassie wasn't a blonde bimbo.

Deely's tangerine-peel trail made Abra's contributions almost irrelevant. Any of us on our own could have followed the Coast Guard nanny's well-marked route to the corpse. We just wouldn't have wanted to.

As we drew near, Abra set up a howl. If you've never heard an Afghan hound in extremis, count yourself blessed. The breed makes an unearthly sound that rolls up and down your spine, particularly in a winter woods at night when the bare trees are shuddering.

"Stop!" Deely shouted. Everyone did.

Four flashlight beams crisscrossed the scene. After a few beats, they converged on a single object about a dozen paces ahead.

I thought I'd be afraid to look, so my reaction surprised me: I couldn't stop staring. A well-dressed woman was seated on the ground, her back against the spotted trunk of an old sycamore tree. She wore, as Deely had said, a chinchilla coat. Unfastened, it had slid halfway off her shoulders. Beneath it a short, beige dress was visible. She had no hat or gloves. Her legs were splayed, and her feet, incongruously, were bare. I wondered if anyone else had fixated, as I did, on her bright red toenails. They matched her fingernails and shone like spots of new blood in the snow. But there was no blood.

I couldn't see the woman's face; it was obscured by the down-turned angle of her head. Her ash-blonde head.

TWENTY-EIGHT

When I crouched for a better angle, my throat tightened. I knew the hair, the face, the dress. Or should I say, the uniform.

The dead woman was Mindy, the cocktail waitress from Bear Claw Casino. Mother of three. Allergic to cigarette smoke.

That wouldn't matter anymore.

Personal reactions to death are hard to predict, except in the case of professionals. Jenx, Brady, and the MSP officer were trained to be stoic and respectful, which they were, and to do their jobs, which they did. Deely's response didn't surprise me, either. Without a word, she led Abra away. I listened to the Afghan hound's lament fade into the night.

But Jeb shocked me. He stalked off beyond the range of the arcing flashlights and retched.

I considered going after him, to lay a hand on his shoulder. Except that I didn't feel so steady myself. I dusted off a snow-covered rock and plopped down, lowering my head between my knees.

"Breathe," Jenx reminded me as she passed by.

She was studying the scene. I heard the MSP officer tell her and Brady to stop messing up the snow. Jenx reminded him curtly that this was her jurisdiction, too. "I'm a trained tracker. You think you can read a crime scene better than me?"

"No," he conceded. "But I got the State Crime Scene Unit coming in to do it for me."

That shut Jenx up until he pissed her off again, a minute later, when he ordered her back to the house to escort his CSU techies.

"Meet and greet your own people," she said, leaning against a tree. "I got work to do here." She wedged her flashlight under her chin as she scrawled in her notebook.

I hadn't noticed Brady and Roscoe leave. But from somewhere in the distance I heard Roscoe's "pay-attention-to-this" bark. Unlike Abra, he speaks only when spoken to, or when he has something useful to say. Wherever he was, he was insisting on something. I stood up and peered into the darkness toward his faraway *woofs*.

Jenx said, "Breakthrough for our side. Brady's on the case."

Then Jeb rejoined me. "Sorry about that," he whispered.

"Hey, I'm not doing so well myself," I said. "What's up with Roscoe?"

The German shepherd came crashing through the brush, still barking. Jenx and the MSP officer trained their flashlights on him.

"Roscoe found something," Brady panted, jogging behind his partner. "Another body!"

I passed out.

When I came to, I thought Roscoe was crushing me. He was just following Brady's orders to keep me warm so as to prevent shock. By pressing his considerable mass against my torso, the canine officer imparted quite a few BTUs.

Jeb was holding my hand and stroking my forehead. "You're all right," he said.

"Who else is dead?" I moaned. "If it's Thomas McKondin, I killed him in self-defense."

"The second body isn't dead," said Brady. "But it is McKondin. You're saying *you* messed him up like that?"

"I kicked him in the balls . . . and in the face."

"You *kicked* him?" Brady looked baffled. "Who stabbed him?"

"He was stabbed?" I tried to sit up, but Roscoe wouldn't let me.

"Oh, yeah. Not a pretty sight. The EMTs are with him now."

"Will he make it?"

"Too soon to tell. He's lost a lot of blood."

My eyelids fluttered. Jeb whispered, "Think happy thoughts, baby. You're going to be fine."

I don't know if I fainted again or just drifted off to sleep. I was spent.

The next time I opened my eyes, I was in my own bed with Jeb sitting next to me, the room dark.

"I was thinking of getting under the covers with you, but I didn't want to push my luck," Jeb said.

"Wise move. What time is it, anyway?"

"Almost three."

"I don't remember getting back here."

"That's because I'm such a smooth escort."

"No, really, how did I get here?"

"Brady and I put you on a stretcher and carried you. You're a lot heavier than you used to be."

"And you just blew your chance of ever getting in this bed. Good night, Jeb!"

I rolled away from him and pulled the quilt over my head.

"I was kidding!" he said.

"Go away."

"I like you better with a few extra pounds."

"Get out!"

I could feel him sitting there, waiting. He was waiting for me to fall back to sleep, and then he'd slide between the sheets.

"Now!" I roared.

Jeb said, "I can't leave, remember? I loaned my wheels to your friend in need."

"Then use the guest room across the hall. Good night!"

He sighed and left; I was instantly asleep. Even if I'd let him stay with me, I would have been too tired to enjoy his performance. After thirty-nine weeks and four days of celibacy, I could wait a little longer for the ride of my life. And I wanted that ride to be with Nash.

The knock on my bedroom door was too loud and too early. Winter sunlight shone through my windows, and my bedside clock said 8:12. But my internal clock screamed middle-of-the-night.

"Open up, Whiskey! It's me, Jenx."

"Open the door yourself. It's not locked," I groaned.

Our chief of police strode in, all business.

"Can I get a statement from you?" she said.

"About what?"

"About what happened between you and Thomas McKondin last night."

"I didn't stab him," I said.

"I didn't think you did. Even before he exonerated you. . . ."

"What?"

"The guy's half-dead from massive chest wounds, but he says you didn't do it," Jenx explained. "We haven't found the weapon, and McKondin can't tell us what it was. Says he didn't get a good look at his attacker. But he's very specific that it wasn't you."

Why, I wondered. I wished I felt something less like anxiety and more like relief. Sure, I was pleased not to be a suspect. But I had a dirty little secret. I knew that Roy Vickers had had both motive and opportunity to stab Thomas McKondin in the chest.

Roy served time for doing exactly that to Leo Mattimoe. Circumstantial evidence suggested that he might have fatally slashed Gil Gruen. Was Thomas McKondin Roy's third victim?

The ex-con could have followed me out of the house and into the woods. Did he believe that redemption for his attack on Leo required him to defend me against all aggressors? If so, Roy might have been misguided enough to see both Gil Gruen and Thomas McKondin as bad guys who had to be eliminated. The thought made me very nervous.

"We haven't found the weapon used in McKondin's attack. You'd better tell me everything you know," Jenx said, pencil ready, notebook open. "Start from the moment he rang your cell."

I did, omitting, of course, all references to Roy. I wasn't ready to implicate him again since that would mean implicating myself and Jeb for helping him flee.

In the midst of my story, I stopped. The last name McKondin had suddenly appeared as a folder tab in the deep dark recesses of my mental files.

"Remember a Donald McKondin who used to work for Gil Gruen?" I asked Jenx. "He was his bookkeeper. For years. Then Gil fired him, and the guy wrapped his car around a tree."

Jenx nodded. "I was the first officer on the scene. McKondin was dead when I got there. The inside of his car reeked of scotch."

After I finished my story, I waited while Jenx scribbled the rest of her notes. Then I said, "The dead woman is named Mindy, isn't she?"

"Mindy Mad Hawk. How'd you know?"

"She's one of the waitresses I met at Bear Claw Casino yesterday. How'd she die?"

"Preliminary reports suggest alcohol poisoning, possibly combined with hypothermia. The corpse reeks of booze. She had vomited on herself although someone tried to clean her up."

"She had no shoes," I recalled.

"No shoes, socks, gloves, scarf, or hat. It looked like she was trying to take her coat off when she died, but she was either too drunk or too sick to manage it."

"Why would she try to take her coat off?"

"Who knows? Intoxication, panic, hypothermia. . . . She might have felt overheated even as she was freezing to death. It happens. We're waiting for the coroner's report."

"She had three kids," I said.

Jenx nodded. "There's never just one victim."

"You think this was a crime, not an accident?"

"Too soon to say, but it sure looks funny. Especially with that coat. No way a cocktail waitress living on an Indian reservation could afford a fur like that."

"Does it have a label?" I asked.

"Huh?"

"Does the coat have a label? Some women put their names in their coats. There's probably a furrier's label, at any rate. Maybe you can trace it back to point of purchase."

"Worth a shot, I guess. I'll get Brady right on it."

"What was Mindy was doing on my property?" I wondered aloud. "And how did she get here?"

"Good questions," Jenx said. "The MSP will probably want to talk to you. The FBI, too. Have fun with all that."

"You don't like playing with the big boys, do you?" I observed.

"Who said they were big boys?"

Jenx reminded me that the Jamboree resumed today. In fact, this would be the last full day of events, culminating in a cross-county snowmobile race and a bonfire. Tomorrow's festivities consisted of the closing ceremony, plus clearance sales by all the vendors.

"Do you feel well enough to participate?" Jenx asked. "I could use a couple more deputies on site."

"I don't think I'm up to handling Abra today."

"You don't have to. I've deputized Deely, and she's good with your dog."

As if Abra's behavior depended on her handler.

"Deely's on duty here today," I said.

"Not anymore. Avery's so pissed off at you and Nash that she won't trust anyone but herself to watch the kids."

"Don't tell me she fired Deely?!"

"She laid her off. For the weekend."

"Avery just wants to sulk," I muttered.

"That's right," Jenx said. "I hear sparks are flying between you and the daddy. He's a hunk, all right. If you like men."

"I do."

"Of course, we're all hoping you'll get back with Jeb."

"That's not going to happen," I said.

"He's living here, isn't he? I just saw him in the kitchen making coffee."

"No! He couldn't go home last night. He doesn't have his Van Wagon, remember?"

"Yeah, right. He loaned it to some cousin. . . ." Jenx studied me. "Anything else going on around here you forgot to mention?"

"Nope. Not a thing."

Jenx seemed to be mulling something over.

"I take it Dr. David's out of the picture," she said.

"Out of what picture?"

"You were flirting with him for a while."

"*He* was flirting with *me*. But I think he's with Deely now. Or she wishes he was. There's nothing between David and me except a desire to do real estate, which we can't because of his contract with Best West."

"Does that still hold if Gil's dead?" Jenx asked.

"I think so, even if David doesn't. The man needs to learn to sign contracts *after* he reads them."

Jenx cleared her throat. "You know Dr. David better than I do. Here's a hard question: Do you think he would engage in illegal activities?"

"Such as what?"

"Radical activism on behalf of Fleggers."

"You mean, like Greenpeace?"

"Less dramatic. More personal. Still illegal."

"I think you'd better tell me what this is about."

TWENTY-NINE

"NEVER MIND ABOUT DR. David." Jenx checked her wristwatch, a man's Timex. "I don't have time to go into it. I'm due at the Jamboree at nine, and I want to take one more look at the crime scene before I head out."

I crossed my arms over my chest and glared at her.

"All right, I'll give you the poop scoop," she sighed, sitting on the arm of my Morris chair. "But this is strictly confidential. Got it? The only reason I'm telling you is because you're a realtor. Maybe you can give me some advice."

"You want to buy, sell, or rent real estate?" I asked.

"No. I want to talk about Dr. David and the trouble he may be in. It starts with Best West."

"If it's about that contract he signed—"

"It isn't. It's about some damage he did, or might have done."

"Damage?"

"Alleged damage. Gil never got around to filing charges. You knew he had trouble with vandals, right?"

"Right."

I thought about the stories I'd heard in recent months concerning suspicious thefts from properties Gil had listed. In the beginning, it looked like the work of kids. Gil Gruen life-size cut-outs kept disappearing, along with Best West FOR SALE signs. Gradually, the thefts grew more troublesome: house numbers, outdoor lights, mailboxes, shutters, and doorknobs. Even plantings vanished. In one case, a twenty-foot-long row of serviceberry shrubs were removed overnight.

"David Newquist wouldn't play pranks like those," I said. "For one thing, he's too busy. For another, he has no sense of humor."

"There were more serious incidents. Somebody punctured Gil's tires. Smashed his windshield. Set a fire under his car."

Stunned, I fell back against my stack of pillows. "David was mad about the bad contract Gil had him in. But he's not violent."

"Are you sure? This was about animal rights, Whiskey. Gil made a practice of poisoning stray animals."

"What?!"

"He believed that the over-population of cats and dogs lowered property values. So he fought back."

"That's illegal! Isn't it?"

"Yes. If we could have caught him in the act."

"But you know he did it! You must have evidence."

Jenx shook her head. "He bragged about it, and we found poisoned animals, but we couldn't link them to Gil."

"Where does David fit in?"

"David put humane traps all over town. That pissed Gil off big time. He called them eyesores. The traps were stolen, and the poisonings increased. David started following Gil, trying to catch him in the act. 'Stalking' him, Gil called it. Monday—five days ago—our mayor took out a restraining order against our new town vet."

I was speechless.

"There's something else," Jenx said, rubbing her eyes. I wondered if she'd been to bed at all last night. "We have witnesses who say David's been stealing dog and cat treats from local vendors."

"Stealing treats?" That sounded ridiculous . . . until I recalled what I'd seen from the helicopter: Dr. David stuffing something from the concessions stand into his voluminous parka pockets. "Why the hell would he do that?"

Jenx shrugged. "Maybe he's nuts."

I reflected on my conversation with David about *speciesism* while riding in the Animal Ambulance. It verged on craziness. But was it the real thing?

Jenx stood up and pulled a folder from her hip pocket. "Read this. It's the Flegger Manifesto."

I smoothed the glossy tri-fold brochure on my bed. The cover declared:

FOUR LEGS GOOD
Our premise is simple:
Do you own your child?
Cats and dogs are not your property, either.
Like children, they deserve protection
and the recognition of their rights.
We love people of all species.

"Oh boy," I sighed.

"It gets better. Read on."

I opened the folder to a litany of similar propositions, including an argument in favor of criminal behavior to defend animal rights. The assertion: Great leaders have always demonstrated that immoral laws must be broken. Consider the Founding Fathers, Mahatma Gandhi, and Che Guevara.

"Does *speciesism* measure up to taxation without representation?" I said. Then I thought about the Coast Guard nanny, whom I respected. "Deely's a Flegger, too. But she doesn't seem whacky."

"Maybe she knows better than to show her true colors around you," Jenx said. "After all, you employ her."

"Or maybe all Fleggers aren't nuts."

Jenx grunted to show she doubted it. I handed her back the brochure.

"What are you going to do about David?" I said.

"Keep an eye on him. I'm ordering you to do the same, Deputy Mattimoe. Right now, I need to call Brady."

Jenx unclipped her cell phone and headed out. I was too jazzed by our conversation to get more rest, no matter how deep my sleep deficit, so I opted for a long, hot shower. But I forgot to lock the bathroom door. Midway through my delicious ablutions, the shower door slid open and then closed.

Jeb Halloran had joined me. Naked.

"May I soap your back?" he asked.

"May I slit your throat? Get out of here!"

"Aw, come on, Whiskey. We used to be married, remember?"

"And then we got divorced. I remember that."

He grabbed me and kissed me hard, pressing his firm self against me. I was at a distinct disadvantage, having soap and water in my eyes. No way a girl can fight off a guy in that situation.

211

So we kept kissing until there was no more hot water.

"I need a bigger tank," I panted.

"Your tank is just right, like the rest of you."

I moved us both out of the shower and into big fuzzy towels. The drier I got, however, the harder I had to defend myself. On a non-slippery surface, Jeb was even more confident.

Finally, I ordered him to stop.

"FYI: You're forcing your attentions on a Lanagan County deputy. Please cease and desist at once."

"Or else?"

"Or else . . . I might have to make a citizen's arrest."

"And handcuff me to your bed, I hope?" Jeb winked.

With his hair wet and spiky, and his smooth skin rosy from the heat, my ex-husband looked almost irresistible. Fortunately, someone started pounding on my bedroom door.

"Yo, Whiskey, it's Jenx again. Can I come in?"

Before I could reply, Jeb said, "Sure. Join the party."

Jenx looked us both up and down, admiring our matching towels. Her grin implied that we were made for each other.

"Jeb needed a shower," I said.

"And two people can shower as cheaply as one," he chimed in.

Our police chief had an announcement to make. Her news changed everything.

"We found Cassina's American Express card, the one Chester had with him when he left."

"Where?" I said.

"Near Mindy's body. We think she dropped it."

"How—how is that possible?"

"Chester was at Bear Claw, remember? He and Mindy must have connected."

"But she said she didn't see him!" I insisted.

"Either she lied, or she saw him after you talked to her."

When Jenx answered her cell phone, I could tell she was as worked up about Chester and the dead waitress as I was. Jeb slipped into the bathroom, presumably to put on clothes. My over-sized towel wrapped around me, I sat on my bed and eavesdropped shamelessly. I didn't learn much from Jenx's cryptic murmurs.

"That was Brady," she told me. "You were right about the coat having a label."

"And? What does it say?"

"It's from a high-end Chicago furrier called Magdalena's."

"Can Brady call them and trace the sale?"

"He already did," Jenx said. "The coat was sold in December to a Mrs. Oscar Manfred Gribble the Third. She and her husband checked out of the Bear Claw Casino Resort last night."

"Did they have a kid with them?"

"Officially, no."

"Do you know where they are now?"

"No, but the State Police issued an All Points Bulletin for Mrs. Gribble and two white Jaguars."

THIRTY

CONSIDERING THAT THIS WAS late January in Michigan, Saturday morning earned a B+. After the paralyzing ice storm, it arrived like a gift, blessing us with vivid blue skies and temperatures in the twenties. For the snowball battle and the ice-sculpting competition, we wouldn't have wanted milder weather.

Reluctantly, I agreed to assume deputy duties at the Jamboree. I would rather have been helping with the hunt for Chester and/or Mrs. Gribble—and I suspected that locating one would mean locating both—but Jenx insisted that I was too close to the case. She did promise me regular updates, however. So I comforted myself with the knowledge that my Jamboree job would be a cakewalk without Abra. Deely was welcome to her.

I was similarly relieved to offload Jeb at the Jamboree, where he planned to make music and money. Fortunately, he had remembered to remove his sales stock of CDs from the Van Wagon before loaning the car to Roy Vickers.

My amateur police duties consisted of patrolling the festival on foot while wearing what looked like a joke badge. Made of the cheapest tin, it proclaimed me Temporary Volunteer Deputy. The mood of the Jamboree was so exuberant and my job so ridiculous that I was tempted to cross my eyes and fake a limp that shifted from leg to leg, just to make things interesting. but there might be someone in attendance who wouldn't appreciate my humor. Someone who'd consider it inappropriate for a person wearing a badge. Someone like federal agent Smith or Jones. If they were on the clock today, earning their good government benefits, they should be chasing after Chester instead of watching red-nosed people sip hot chocolate. Or so I thought. But I thought wrong. The Fibbies were doing exactly what I was doing, minus the cheesy badge. We spotted each other near the concessions stand where I'd seen Dr. David stuff his pockets two days earlier. Did they know what Jenx and I knew about the good vet? That his animal activism bordered on madness?

"*Deputy* Mattimoe," one Fed said by way of a curt greeting.

"*Agent* Smith," I replied and then wondered if I'd correctly matched the name. Both Fibbies wore dark glasses and black wool coats with their wingtip shoes. When he didn't contradict me, I decided I'd been right.

"Are you here on business or pleasure?" I asked cheerily.

Neither agent fielded that question. They must have thought that the answer was obvious, or that they had dressed to blend in with tourists.

I asked Smith, "Anyone ever tell you that you look like Tommy Lee Jones in *Men in Black*?"

"No," he said. "That never happens."

I was beginning to think that Agent Smith was a cynic. Then I had a revelation.

"Hey, *Men in Black* stars Will *Smith* and Tommy Lee *Jones*! Smith and Jones, get it?"

Once again, neither agent replied.

"May I help you?" The querulous question came from Magnet Springs' oldest living retailer, Martha Glenn. Well into her eighties and long past her mental prime, Martha had showed alarming signs of senility in recent months. And yet she continued to run Town 'n' Gown, her upscale clothing store. Most Main Street business operators, myself included, assumed that Martha's part-time help was really running the business, possibly into the ground. At the moment, she appeared to be minding the concessions stand.

"How are you, Martha?" I asked.

She was wearing a pair of post-surgical sunglasses, the ugly kind provided by eye doctors. In response to my question, Martha adjusted hers as if to see me better. Then she said, "I don't discuss my personal health with strangers."

"I'm not a stranger, Martha. You've known me all my life. Whiskey, remember?"

"Never touch the stuff," she said. Having dismissed me, she smiled sweetly at Smith and Jones. "Would either of you boys care to support our Chamber of Commerce with a purchase? We have all kinds of homemade goodies for sale, including my own famous dog and kitty treats."

She gestured toward an empty spot on the counter and froze.

"Oh, no, not again. Somebody keeps stealing my treats!"

They were quick about it, but not so fast that I missed the furtive exchange of looks between Smith and Jones. So that's why they were here: to follow up on Dr. David. What could that have to do with Chester's disappearance? No way the good vet would harm a child, even if Fleggers believed that pets were as important as people.

"Tell me about your treats, Martha," I said.

"You can't have any. They're for dogs and cats," she snapped.

"I have a dog. In fact, I have two dogs at my house. They love treats."

"Do you see any treats here?" She indicated the space between the homemade brownies and the homemade peanut brittle. "Maybe *you* need cataract surgery!"

When I glanced toward the Fibbies, they were gone. Vanished into the crowd.

More confused than ever, I continued my shoreline patrol. The ice-sculpting event was well under way, so I decided to watch for a while. It never failed to amaze me how chain saws, hairdryers, and steam irons could be used to turn a block of ice into art. I was engrossed in the proceedings when Brady Swancott sidled up to me.

"I had to write a paper on this for one of my grad school courses," he said. "'Ice Sculpting: Is It a Culinary or a Visual Art?'"

"Art is art," I said.

"Not when you're in grad school," Brady sighed.

"Hey, where's Officer Roscoe?"

"He got stuck doing Public Relations: signing 'paw-tographs' over by the Main Street Merchants' Face-Painting Booth. That's a bust, by the way. Very few colors look good on a cold red face."

"What's the latest with Mrs. Gribble and the APB?" I said.

"No news yet. But Thomas McKondin has stabilized," Brady said. "We're hoping he'll tell us what happened after he gets some rest."

"You think his stabbing is connected to Mindy's death? And Chester's disappearance?"

"Who knows. For some reason, McKondin doesn't want your name involved. But he hasn't mentioned anyone else's."

"Where are Deely and Abra?" I asked. "I've been here a couple hours already, and I haven't seen them."

"That's weird," Brady replied. "I haven't seen them, either, and Jenx assigned them to cover the Snowball Battle." He checked his watch. "Uh-oh. That starts in five minutes. We'd better get over there."

I couldn't imagine what Jenx had been thinking. Putting Abra on duty at a snowball fight was like trusting a cat to oversee a bowl of goldfish. The Afghan hound was sure to chase the flying orbs and no doubt knock down a few kids. So I assumed it was for the best that Deely and Abra failed to show up at Vanderzee Park, the harborside playground where a few dozen children were gleefully making stacks of snowballs in preparation for a rule-bound battle. Brady read the rules aloud, but nobody listened.

As he was reading, I scanned the crowd. There was a good influx of tourists, promising money to be made for local merchants. Despite the disappointments caused by yesterday's weather, today's participants were in a buoyant mood, which could lead to extravagant spending. In the distance I heard Jeb Halloran singing the last bars of his Rockabilly standard, "I'll Park My Gun at Your Door and Lay My Heart at Your Feet." His audience cheered. Jeb knew how to read a room, or, in this case, a Jamboree. I hoped they would buy every CD he'd brought to sell.

Brady had barely finished covering the contest rules when the first snowballs flew. Nobody waited for the starting whistle, just as nobody intended to play by the rules. This was a snowball fight, not a chess game. Who were we kidding? To avoid getting smacked in the face, I stepped back from the action.

I did get smacked—not by a snowball, but by the shock of what I spotted across the ice.

Zigzagging between the shanties in Fishburg was a snowmobile driven by a woman in an olive-green coat. Her identically dressed passenger had long blonde hair and a Sarah Jessica Parker profile. And a tail.

THIRTY-ONE

"BRADY, LOOK!" I CRIED, pointing toward Fishburg. Before he could do that, I was knocked sideways by a thwack to the head. A snowball—more likely an illegal iceball—fired at close range sent me sprawling. By the time Brady had helped me to my feet, a bump the size of a tulip bulb was blooming above my right ear. I fingered it gingerly. The snowmobile was nowhere to be seen.

"This is a free-for-all," Brady said, ducking just in time to avoid two snowballs colliding in midair. "Nobody's listening to us, anyhow, and if anybody gets hurt, the parents will take over. Let's go check out Fishburg!"

As was the case two days earlier, Jamboree festivities had drawn most Fishburg regulars closer to shore. We found a half-dozen diehards hunched over fishing holes inside their shanties. One was Jeb's fan and Leo's former client Bud from the Blue Moon bar. All the fishermen had heard Deely's snowmobile, but only Bud had received a visitor.

"She was here and gone again," Bud said. "Just wanted to ask a question: Did I see anybody who didn't belong here? I said no. So she left."

Bud sounded like every ice fisherman I'd ever known. They all subscribed to a live-and-let-live philosophy. If you don't ask what the hell they're doing in their makeshift village way out on the ice, they won't ask what you're up to, either.

All six fishermen said that Deely's snowmobile had sounded like it was heading up the coast.

"That don't mean much, though," an old-timer said as he checked the bait on his line. "Them machines can turn on a dime. It could be a couple miles inland by now."

Brady and I stood on the north edge of Fishburg scanning the landscape.

"What should we do next?" I said. "It's not like Deely to disobey a direct order. Why did she skip the snowball battle? And where did she get the snowmobile?"

"The last question might be easy enough to answer," Brady said. He pointed to a RENT-A-SNOWMOBILE sign near one of the docks. "Let's go see if that's what she did."

It wasn't exactly what she'd done. The skinny teenage boy running the rental stand said that Deputy Deely had showed him her badge and declared a police emergency. She told him she needed to borrow one of his machines to pursue a fleeing felon.

I tapped my own tin shield.

"She showed you this cheesy badge and you gave her a snowmobile?"

The kid looked confused and frightened. "You're saying I shouldn't have done that? You're saying I should have told the deputy no?"

"No, we're not saying that," Brady told him. "You did the right thing."

"That dog she had with her—" the teenager stammered. "Something wasn't right."

"How do you mean?" asked Brady.

"It didn't look like a police dog."

"It isn't," I assured him.

"It didn't even look . . . like a dog. When it turned its head a certain way, it looked kind of like . . . a person."

I nodded sympathetically.

The kid added, "In that coat, with that blonde hair and everything—it creeped me out."

"She creeps *me* out," I confessed. "And I live with her."

"What if the deputy doesn't bring the snowmobile back in time for the cross-country race?" the kid whined. "My uncle will kill me! This is his business. He expects me to rent out every single machine. And the race starts in forty-five minutes."

"I'm pretty sure she'll bring it back," Brady said. "Aren't you, Whiskey?"

I was too distracted to answer. A vaguely familiar guy in his twenties was striding toward me, and he looked pissed.

"Hey!" He was still at least ten yards away. The aggressiveness of his tone made me want to turn and run. But I didn't.

"You owe me a flotation device!" he said. I recognized the What-Would-Jesus-Do newbie helicopter pilot, minus his affable demeanor.

"Yes I do," I admitted. "Would you take a check instead?"

"I'll take cash," he said. "My boss doesn't believe in anything else."

"Not even in Jesus Christ, our Lord and Savior?" I smiled hopefully.

"Faith will save your soul, but it won't inflate upon impact. You need cash for something like that."

"How much cash?"

"Two hundred dollars," the pilot said. "That's wholesale, by the way. No markup. I'm cutting you a break."

"Thanks. Could we—uh—do a little business?"

"What do you have in mind?"

I motioned for him to walk with me. I didn't want Brady or the snowmobile kid to hear my offer.

"You need something from me, and I need something from you," I began.

"All I know is I've got to replace that flotation device before my boss notices it's missing. Or else he'll fire me, and I just started this job!"

"Right," I said. "Here's my offer: I don't have it on me, but if you give me an hour, I can get you four hundred dollars."

"I need *two* hundred dollars—not four hundred!" the pilot said. He was talking to me as if I were senile Martha Glenn.

"That's where the what-you-can-do-for-me part comes in: I need you to fly me somewhere."

"You mean, like a charter?"

"Like a micro-charter. We won't be in the air long, probably twenty minutes or less. I'll give you the money up front—for the flotation device and the flight. If, when we're done, you decide that

I underpaid, I'll give you the balance due. If I overpaid, you keep the change. Or donate it to your church."

The pilot grinned. "See you back here at 2:15."

"Everything all right?" Brady said. He was standing so close behind me that I wondered how much he had overheard.

"I owe him for the flotation device I . . . uh . . . borrowed. If you can get along without me for awhile, I'm going to get some cash from my office."

"No problem," Brady said, studying my face. "You sure everything's all right?"

"Except that Deely and Abra are AWOL on a stolen snowmobile, everything's fine."

I didn't believe that for a minute, which is why I wanted the helicopter ride. I needed a fresh perspective on my hometown—a panoramic view of the crime scene, if you will. My brief time in the sky with Odette two days earlier had taught me something: What's familiar is still full of mystery. Big deal that I'd lived here all my life. I didn't know every corner or every soul in Magnet Springs. In fact, I had a long list of questions and just the vaguest hope that a second aerial view might help me answer them.

It would take thirty minutes, tops, to get the money from my office and return to the Jamboree. But there was something I needed to do first. And I didn't relish doing it. Avery had been more frazzled than usual when I left that morning. No one at our house, including the twins, had slept well, which meant that Leah and Leo were both cranky, and Avery's nerves were frayed. Although laying off the nanny had been Avery's own foolish choice, I couldn't help worrying that she was in over her head. On her best day, she probably wasn't up to the task of managing two infants without backup or a break. In her current state of high anxiety over Nash's intentions, she might be dangerously distracted. I flipped open my cell phone. Even though I knew she'd find a way to blame me for her misery, I felt obliged to check on her.

Before I could punch in the first digit, I got a call—from my own home number. Avery was on the line, and she was hysterical.

"They're gone! They're gone!" she wailed.

"Who's gone? Calm down, Avery. Take a breath."

"Damn him! I should have known Nash would do something like this!"

"What are you talking about?" But even as I asked, I had a sick feeling that I could guess the answer.

"He stole my babies! My babies are gone!"

"What do you mean, Leah and Leo are gone?" I asked.

"Missing! Stolen! Kidnapped! Arrrgghh...."

Avery was sobbing and sniffling so hard that her words faded into a choke. At least the phone spared me the aggravation of seeing her blotchy, snot-streaked face.

"Listen to me," I said as if talking her in from a ledge. "Avery, I want you to sit down and take some slow, deep breaths."

"I don't give a damn what you want. Nash stole my babies! You helped him do it, didn't you? I should have known you were capable of this kind of shit! Bring back my babies right now!"

"I don't have your babies, you stupid, lazy fool!"

I'd been mentally calling her that for so long that it finally slipped out. Nothing like a crisis to release the repressed goodies. I tried to redeem myself.

"Avery, I'm doing my best to help you keep your family together. And I think Nash is, too. He wouldn't have taken the kids without asking you. Now sit down and get a grip. Please. Then we'll call 9-1-1." My phone beeped, indicating another call on the line. "Hold on. Somebody's trying to reach me. Breathe!"

It was the Coast Guard nanny, a.k.a. Deputy Deely.

"Ma'am, we have a situation."

"I know!" I said. "When did Avery call you?"

"Avery hasn't called me, ma'am. This is about Chester."

I felt a second wave of the same emotion that was rocking my stepdaughter. Since I worked hard not to let most feelings in, I wasn't sure how to label the rare ones that grabbed me.

"What about Chester? Do you know where he is?"

"No, ma'am. But I think Abra's onto something. When we were at the Jamboree, she started barking and jumping, trying to pull me toward Fishburg. Then I saw what she saw: somebody in a chinchilla coat, like the one on the dead waitress. But this person was wearing a matching hat. So I borrowed a snowmobile and took off."

"Did you find her?"

"Not yet, ma'am. But I did find Chester's coat."

"Chester's coat?" I couldn't understand what she was telling me. "But he's wearing his coat. Isn't he?"

"Not anymore, ma'am. Abra saw it spread out on a rock by the shore. She barked until I saw it, too."

"How can you be sure it's Chester's?"

"It has his name in it, ma'am. I think he left it to dry in the sun."

"Why would Chester's coat need to dry?" No sooner had I asked the question than I answered it. From my own recent experience. "Unless he fell through the ice."

Deely must have heard the rising tension in my voice.

"Yes, ma'am, I thought of that, too. Before you panic, consider that he must have got out again and made it to shore. There's one set of tracks leading inland, and they look about Chester's size."

"Then where is he?"

"That's why I'm calling, ma'am. Abra and I abandoned the snowmobile and followed the tracks till they ended. They led us to the Broken Arrow Motel. That's where we are now."

"The Broken Arrow? Isn't that where Dr. David lives?"

She didn't answer right away. When call waiting clicked again, I knew Avery had had enough of being on hold. I asked Deely to wait while I switched lines.

"Sorry, Avery," I began, "but I've got *two* emergencies."

"Whiskey, this is Jenx. I hate to be the one to tell you, but now you've got three."

THIRTY-TWO

"SOME NUT JOB TOOK Leah and Leo," Jenx said.

"I know," I sighed. "That's Emergency Number One. You're counting it twice."

"No, there's *another* emergency, related to Number One. That adds up to three—if you have a Number Two."

"I do." I switched my cell phone to the ear that didn't have a throbbing bruise by it. "Just tell me how Three is different from One!"

"After Avery called you, the whacko who took the babies called her," Jenx said. "Why'd you put her on hold, anyhow?"

"Because of Emergency Number Two! Go on."

"You put Avery on hold, she hangs up, and right away the phone rings. A muffled voice says Avery can trade Abra and Prince Harry for Leah and Leo. But there's a catch."

"There usually is," I sighed.

"Avery has to bring the dogs herself."

"Where?"

"The caller says that info will come later and adds, 'You'd better be brave, or your babies are dead.'"

"Oh god," I groaned. "No way Avery's brave!"

Jenx said, "Emergencies One *and* Three."

I told Jenx that Deely borrowed a snowmobile to go after someone in Fishburg and then found Chester's wet coat on a rock.

"Deely and Abra followed Chester's tracks from the shore to the Broken Arrow Motel," I said. "That's where they are now, where David Newquist lives. *That's* Emergency Number Two!"

"I'm already on Broken Arrow Highway," Jenx said. "I can be at the motel in three minutes. Where are you?"

"Still at the Jamboree. I was planning to do some aerial reconnaissance—"

"You're going up in that helicopter again?"

"I owe the pilot a flotation device, so I thought I'd buy another ride while I'm at it. Do you want us to circle the Broken Arrow Motel?"

"Good idea, Deputy," Jenx said. "Tell your pilot to keep in touch by radio."

She told me the police frequency. I removed my mittens, found a pen in my pocket, and scrawled the digits on the back of my hand. Then I made Jenx promise to phone me if she found Chester.

Assuming that Deely was telling the truth—that she had followed Chester's trail to the Broken Arrow Motel—what would she do next? What was Deely's relationship with David? Although the veterinarian was living at the Broken Arrow, he might not be there right now. He worked Sundays, as needed, at his clinic downtown. Once again I wrestled with the notion that David could or would hurt anyone. It didn't compute, even if Gil Gruen had felt compelled to get a restraining order against him.

Most likely the Broken Arrow Motel was simply the first place Chester found in his search for help. Or maybe he knew where he was going, and he counted on his friend David to be there. In any event, we were closer than ever to finding Chester.

According to my watch, I had thirty-eight minutes until takeoff. Enough time to fetch my fare from the safe in my office and check around on the ground for suspicious characters. I hadn't counted on running into Tina Breen and Noonan Starr in the lobby of Mattimoe Realty. By their startled expressions, I knew they weren't pleased to see me, either.

"What brings you two to the office on a Sunday?" I asked. "Shouldn't you be down at the Jamboree?"

"Uh, no—thank you, anyway," Tina said nervously. But then Tina was usually nervous. Her job as my office manager didn't strike me as particularly stressful, given the haphazard way she approached her tasks. But her husband's recent layoff, plus the demands of her two toddlers, seemed to be pushing Tina toward the edge. I recalled her reaction to the foul-mouthed man at Extreme Clean and thought I knew how to make her feel better.

"Good news, Tina. That pervert at Extreme Clean will never bother you again!"

Tina's eyes filled with terror, and she covered her mouth with both hands. Choking back either a sob or vomit, she raced down the hall to the bathroom.

"I was trying to make her feel better," I told Noonan.

The New Age massage therapist nodded. "Tina is learning to confront her terrors, which is where all healing begins."

Taking a step toward me, she whispered, "That's why we're here, Whiskey. Tina's checking her work schedule so that she can set up a series of counseling sessions. We're going to start with her fear of foul words."

I had my own fears to deal with.

"Roy Vickers is on the lam," I confided. "He's trying to find Chester, but I think Chester's about to be found. Jenx is on the case, and so is Deely Smarr. If Gil is dead, Roy may be implicated in his murder. And in a second attack, too. I don't know what to do!"

Noonan couldn't have looked less perturbed.

"Roy Vickers knows the Seven Suns of Solace," she said. "He'll be fine."

"But the police don't, and I'm afraid they're going to arrest him. In fact, I'm afraid they're going to arrest me for helping him escape!"

Noonan took my hand in both her strong ones. "You need to work on trust issues."

"Okay, but first I'd like to make sure I don't get busted."

I saw a rare flicker of impatience in Noonan's pale eyes. "Follow the logic, Whiskey: If Roy is innocent, you have nothing to fear."

"Yeah, but from here, that's a really big 'if.' Roy doesn't look innocent. He looks like an ex-con who's headed back to the slammer."

Noonan closed her eyes. I figured she was doing some kind of meditation. Either that or I had made her so mad that she was counting to ten. Silently I counted along. On nine, she opened her eyes and smiled.

"Godspeed, Whiskey." Noonan released my hands and stepped back. Then, with a dramatic flourish, she extended her arms as if they were wings. "Fly where you will with faith in your heart!"

Was that some kind of metaphysical metaphor—flying equals personal freedom, for instance—or did Noonan know I was about to board a helicopter? And if she knew, how did she know? I demanded an explanation.

Noonan smiled like an amused mother. "Oh, Whiskey. You continue to underestimate the strength of your personal vibrations. The Seven Suns of Solace would enlighten you about your own power."

"That's a fact," another voice affirmed.

I peered past Noonan to see where the familiar tones were coming from. The visitor had entered Mattimoe Realty so stealthily that I hadn't heard her. Like me, Noonan knew who it was. Without turning, she said, "Cassina, welcome home."

I almost sank to my knees before the diva—not because I was a fan, but because I had failed as a child-care provider. As *her* child's care-provider.

"Cassina, I am so sorry about Chester—"

"Forget it, Whiskey. I forgive you," the superstar said, tossing about a mile of flame-red hair over one shoulder. "I'm a terrible mother, so you're allowed to make a mistake."

"You're not a terrible mother," I began. Except that she was, and the whole town knew it.

"Noonan," Cassina said, "I need a Personal Power Coach session. I'm way overdue for a vibration infusion."

"Personal Power Coach?" As usual, I was a few beats behind. I knew that Noonan had dozens of counseling clients for the Seven Suns of Solace, but I'd never heard anyone call her "Coach."

"Personal Power transcends the Seven Suns of Solace, Whiskey," Noonan explained. "It encompasses ongoing, larger life issues, for those of us working on a higher spiritual plane."

Or a superstar budget, I thought. Cassina probably kept Noonan on retainer.

"Did the FBI call you home?" I asked the singer. "Or did you just get bad vibes?"

"I wanted to do the right thing," Cassina said. "For a change."

"Cassina has postponed the rest of her tour," Noonan explained. "Until Chester can join her."

How utterly un-Cassina. I had long suspected that she loved to spend days in her recording studio and months on the road precisely to avoid motherhood. Even when she had Chester in tow, Cassina tended to misplace him. She had left him behind in hotel lobbies too many times to count. And her tendency to lock him out of his own home was legendary. Cassina always insisted it was an oversight, but I figured it was more like a Freudian slip. When he couldn't get in the door at his house, Chester found his way into mine, often through the window over my kitchen sink. He was resilient and resourceful, which gave me hope for him now. But, until I knew he was safe and whole, even his mother's forgiveness wouldn't ease my guilt. No matter who was involved in his disappearance, I knew that this time I had lost Chester.

"Did Rupert come back with you?" I asked.

"He's in the limo," Cassina said. "He thinks Magnet Springs looks like the set of a made-for-TV movie. Starring Angela Lansbury."

"Will we get to meet Rupert?"

"Probably not. He's a snob."

"Were you looking for Noonan or for me?" I asked.

"Neither," replied Cassina. "I told the driver to cruise the Jamboree, but it's so blue-collar. Not my fan base. We were heading back to the Castle when I saw you duck into your office. I thought I'd let you know I'm not planning to sue you."

She looked at her Personal Power Coach for approval and got it.

"Excellent soul expansion!" Noonan applauded softly.

"I don't want to build any false hope," I told Cassina, "but Jenx may be close to finding Chester."

"Where?" Cassina's Kabuki-white face brightened. "Has someone seen him?"

I shouldn't have started this, I thought. What if I'm wrong? What if the tracks Deely followed weren't Chester's, after all? What if we never find him?

"I—uh—don't think there's been a sighting, but there may be some tracks. All I know for sure is that everybody's looking."

Cassina sighed, and Noonan put her arm around her best client's waist. As Cassina fussed with the collar of her coat, I realized that it was made from some exotic fur I didn't recognize. Cassina's entire wardrobe was white, and the coat was no exception.

"What kind of fur is that?" I asked.

"Ermine," Cassina said. "This was made for Marlene Dietrich. I bought it at an auction in Paris."

"A word to the wise," I said. "Women who wear fur coats in this town have been getting into trouble. You might want to warn your mother—even though she looks good in chinchilla."

"My mother? What the hell are you talking about?"

"Evelyn Huffenbach? She showed up yesterday to talk to the FBI. As Chester's legal guardian."

"She was only supposed to take over in an emergency," Cassina raged, "in case I couldn't make it back to the States!"

The singer started for the door, shoved it open and then paused. Turning back toward Noonan, she said, "Call me later. I'm going to need some kick-ass coaching tonight!"

THIRTY-THREE

CASSINA AND HER ERMINE coat had barely left the building when Noonan declared, "She has made amazing progress."

"Her music may be soothing," I said, "but up close and personal, Cassina's as serene as an abscessed tooth."

"Would it surprise you to learn that people feel the same about you?"

"They think my music's soothing?"

Noonan gave me her tolerant-but-tired look. "People think you lack serenity, Whiskey. People who know and care about you."

"I'm as serene as the next guy!"

A mistake—since "the next guy" turned out to be Tina Breen, who emerged from the bathroom bawling.

I slipped into my office and locked the door behind me. Twenty-seven minutes before my scheduled voyage into the wild blue yonder. Still plenty of time, but I needed to get focused. It had been a while since I'd raided my own office safe. The combination was one that Leo had invented: a mix of his birthday, 7-30 (yes,

Leo was a Leo), and mine, 3-28 (I can't help it that I'm an Aries). Carefully, I typed the numbers on the electronic keypad, followed by "enter." When the door clicked open, I was relieved to find my modest stash of cash. I counted out four one-hundred dollar bills, re-secured the safe, and exited my office.

No sign of Tina or her new therapist. I hoped the Seven Suns of Solace would do more for my office manager than it had for my next-door neighbor. Or my stepdaughter.

My stepdaughter! Striding down Main Street toward the water-front, I speed-dialed Avery on my cell phone. Five times I called, and five times she failed to answer. When I reached the entrance to the Jamboree, I was bathed in the cold sweat of anxiety. My phone rang. Caller ID said Jenx. Her voice was so low I could barely hear her.

"He's not here," she said.

"Who's not where?"

"There's no sign of Chester at the Broken Arrow Motel."

My heart deflated like a cheap balloon. "You lost him?"

"Whiskey, he was already lost. Looks like he went from unit to unit, knocking on doors until somebody opened one. His tracks stop outside Room 19."

I caught my breath. "Is that . . . David's room?"

"No. The room is rented to Evelyn Huffenbach."

"Chester's grandmother! I should warn you, Jenx, something's not right about her."

Hastily, I filled the police chief in on my brief encounter with Cassina. Jenx asked if Chester's father was here, too.

"Yes, but don't expect to meet him. He's a snob. What about Huffenbach?"

"She's not in her room—or not answering the door. And the desk clerk's none too helpful," Jenx said. "We'll need a warrant to force our way in."

"I'm worried about Avery," I said. "She doesn't answer the phone."

"She's okay, just mad as hell at you for putting her on hold. She's checking Caller ID."

I groaned. "What are you doing about the babies?"

"I'm heading over to Vestige now to interview Avery. I'll have to let the Fibbies in. The State Police, too." Jenx was talking through clenched teeth. "Then the assholes will make us wait while they muck things up."

"Who says?" Threading my way through the Jamboree crowd toward the helicopter, I had an idea. Not so much a new idea as a revised version of an earlier one. "I'll be your eye in the sky! But maybe now I don't circle the Broken Arrow Motel. Maybe now I look for clues somewhere else?"

"Where?" Jenx asked eagerly.

"You're law enforcement!" I said. "You're supposed to tell me!"

I heard Jenx's police radio crackling in the background. "Got to go," she said. "I think you should still circle the Broken Arrow and then move out from there. Good luck!" *Click.*

As I hurried toward the helicopter, the pilot was pitching his services to a couple who looked around twenty years old. The male prospect reached into his pocket and withdrew his wallet.

"Not so fast!" I shouted, breaking into a trot. "The next ride is mine! I've got the money!" I waved my four one-hundred-dollar bills like a flag.

All three stared as if I was fanning my underwear at them. The pilot said something to the couple, probably something unflattering about me. They backed up a little.

Sliding to a halt, I said, "Sorry to cut in. Police business."

I pointed to my badge, which had slipped sideways. If it had worked for Deely and the dog, it should work for me and my money. "We're in pursuit of a potential felon! Maybe more than one!"

"What are you talking about?" the pilot said. "You owe me for the flotation device."

"Right. And there you have it." I handed him two bills and then extended two more. "Now you owe me a micro-charter."

"I owe you nothing. These folks were here first, so they're going up first. Hold your fare till we get back."

"You don't understand," I said, "there's been a kidnapping! Well, *two* kidnappings because they're twins. Actually, *three* kidnappings, counting Chester. Plus two murders and one attempted murder."

"What kind of town is this?" the young woman gasped.

"This week? A very dangerous one."

The guy returned his wallet to his pocket. "Maybe some other time," he mumbled, and they moved off.

"Thanks," the pilot said acidly. "Your micro-charter just got more expensive."

"Fine. Here's my deposit. We'll put the rest on my credit card. On all my credit cards, if necessary. Let's go!"

The pilot insisted on taking not only my cash but also my Visa. As a down payment. I was all right with that, provided we got off the ground right away. Of course he made me wear a flotation device.

"I guess you know how that works by now," he said into his headset; I was wearing one of those, too. Even though he didn't seem to like me, he let me ride in the seat next to his, which promised a truly panoramic, puke-inducing view.

The takeoff was so smooth that the copter seemed to levitate. My stomach lurched as the earth dropped rapidly away, so I closed my eyes and concentrated on breathing. By the time I was ready to see the world again, we were straight up in the sky, high above the Jamboree. Below us, the cross-country snowmobile race had begun. Dozens of machines were zooming out of town on a disused service road. The Chamber of Commerce had laid out a thirty-mile course made up of old roads and railroad beds, farmers' fields and woodland trails.

"Where to, Deputy?" the pilot asked.

It took me a moment to get my bearings. Flying from downtown Magnet Springs to the Broken Arrow Motel was a whole different matter than driving there. Simpler, yes, but completely disorienting.

"Can we fly at a lower altitude?" I said. "From up here the people look like dots."

"No problem," the pilot said and promptly dropped us about five hundred feet.

I must have shrieked into my mouthpiece because he told me never to do that again. I promised not to scream if he promised not to make me feel like I was falling from the sky.

"This craft is very responsive," he explained. "Whatever you want it to do, I can probably make it do. In a heartbeat."

I directed the pilot to fly north along the coast until I spotted a large, flat rock on which a child's parka was spread. From the air, it looked sickeningly like a murder victim's chalk outline. Nearby was Deely's abandoned snowmobile, meaning the teenage kid who'd lent it to her was in trouble with his uncle, for sure.

"Turn right!" I said. As the pilot tipped us too sharply, I revised my command. "Easy, please! Try heading toward two o'clock."

"Now you've got it!" He grinned at me, and I decided he was cute when he wasn't being a dickhead.

"Do you have a name?" I asked.

"Todd."

I told him my moniker. "Where're you from, Todd?"

"I grew up in Kissimmee, Florida," he replied, "but when I was in the Army, I was stationed at Fort Grayling, and I liked having four seasons for the first time in my life. So after I got out, I stayed. Now Michigan feels like home."

I thought about Nash Grant, lately of Florida, too. He was willing to call Magnet Springs home for the short term in order to have access to his kids. I didn't believe Nash had had anything to do with Leah and Leo's abduction. Whoever took the twins wanted to exchange them for Abra and Prince Harry, but only if Avery made the switch. Nash wouldn't toy with his own children or torment their already agitated mother. Who on earth would? And why?

Spotting the Broken Arrow Motel from the air proved easy enough. Not only did the sprawling scarlet one-story building have a large sign in front—featuring a broken arrow—but it was located right on the highway less than a mile from the Lake. How Chester had found it from the shore was the mystery. He would have had to trudge mostly uphill through pine woods and scrub. I could hardly imagine my diva dog enduring that hardship, except in pursuit of the boy she loved. Was it coincidental that Chester had come ashore so near the Broken Arrow after falling through the ice? Or had he known where he was?

Probably because I'd seen too many cop shows on TV, I anticipated arriving in the middle of the action. Sure, I knew that Jenx was no longer at the scene, but I expected some police authority to be there, guns drawn, lights flashing. At the very least, I thought I'd see Deputies Deely and Abra.

Nobody. Nothing. Not even Dr. David's Animal Ambulance. Just a few tourists' cars were left in the parking lot. Most of the Broken Arrow's guests had gone to town for the Jamboree.

I checked the back of my hand for Jenx's police-radio frequency and then asked Todd to tune it in. We were circling the motel when my headphone crackled.

Todd said, "Your chief's on the line. I'm patching her through."

"Jenx!" I shouted. "We're above the Broken Arrow. Where is everyone?"

"Brady's on his way. The State Boys are slow, as usual—"

"Hold on!" I said, leaning as far to the right as my seatbelt would allow. The door to one motel unit had opened, and a woman had emerged. Shielding her eyes with her hand, she peered up at us. The sun glinted off her bright auburn hair.

"Evelyn Huffenbach is down there!" I cried. "She's waving at us!"

THIRTY-FOUR

OVER THE RADIO, JENX asked, "When you say Evelyn Huffenbach's 'waving' at you, do you mean as in 'Hello there!'—or as in '*Help me!*'?"

I considered the question. "I'd say Mrs. Huffenbach's inviting us down, wouldn't you, Todd?"

My pilot agreed and tipped the helicopter to return Evelyn's wave.

Assuming that Jenx was about to tell us to get down there, I scanned the parking lot for a good place to land. Suddenly Todd shouted, "Over there! Look!"

He pointed toward a break in the pine woods bordering the motel. A small boy with a pale blue blanket over his shoulders appeared to be running for his life.

"That's Chester!" I shrieked. "Jenx! I see Chester!"

"Forget about Evelyn!" Jenx said unnecessarily. "Go pick up the kid!"

I looked at Todd, who was already pulling away from the motel.

"We need to get him out on the road," the pilot said. "I'm going down to treetop level. Whiskey, you're going to tell Chester what to do."

The copter dipped as promised, and my body lifted ever so slightly from my seat. We were skimming the pines now, accelerating toward Chester. Todd flipped a couple switches on his radio console and pointed at me. "You're on loudspeaker! Go!"

I peered at the blanket-cloaked form below. His white-blonde head down, Chester pressed onward. He must have thought the "bad guys" were above as well as behind him.

"Hello, Chester! It's me, Whiskey! It's okay! You're okay! We're going to take you home!"

When he looked up, my heart soared. We were low enough to see the sparkle of his glasses and the smile creasing his round face. When he waved, he dropped his cape and stumbled. The poor kid lay buck naked in the snow.

"Chester, this is Todd, your pilot, speaking. We'll have you warm and dry in no time, buddy! Just do what we tell you. Okay?"

Still grinning, Chester gave the thumbs-up sign.

"Brush yourself off, bundle up, and go to your left—out to the road!" Todd boomed. "That's it. To your left, Chester! We'll pick you up there in a minute! Follow me!"

I'm sure Chester was still smiling, but I could no longer see his face for my tears. I, the gal who never cries, was letting the dam break apart. Without comment, Todd handed me a box of tissues. He wasn't a jerk, after all. And he was a damn fine pilot. He nodded the copter at Chester, then slowly pivoted toward the road.

Aircraft and boy proceeded apace, with Todd broadcasting steady encouragement.

When we touched down, Chester was running toward us, his small body carnation-pink from cold. Todd handed me two wool blankets. I whipped off my headset and stepped out onto the road, ready to envelop Chester as he launched himself into my arms.

———

"We're six minutes by air from CMC," Todd said, referring to Coastal Medical Center, the nearest hospital. I'd checked myself out of there the previous morning . . . after meeting C. Richards, RN, now a Coastal Med patient himself under his real name, Thomas McKondin.

En route, we swathed Chester in additional blankets and cranked up the cockpit heat. I held him on my lap, my arms around him, my cheeks damp with tears. As soon as his teeth stopped chattering, Chester started the story of his remarkable seventy-two-hour adventure. The details would have to wait until after he was treated. But I heard enough during the six minutes we were in transit to know what I needed to do next.

"I only went with Bibi because she said she had dog problems. Like you do, Whiskey," Chester began. "Bibi read about me in the Chicago papers, so she knew I could handle Abra. She said her Saluki had behavior issues. She wanted to hire me as a canine consultant."

"You're good at that," I assured him.

"Bibi took me to her car, to meet her Saluki. But there was no Saluki. She pushed me and Abra and Prince Harry into the car and locked the doors."

Repelled though I was by that image, I had to admire Mrs. Gribble's dog-handling *chutzpah*. At home I could hardly push Abra through the doggie door.

"Abra didn't like Bibi," Chester said. "When we got to the casino, Abra bit her. That's how she got away!"

"Is that why you mouthed the word 'Abra' to the cocktail waitress when Bibi yanked you off the casino floor?"

"I didn't do that. I was trying to yell 'Help me!' But Bibi had my scarf so tight around my neck it was like a noose. I couldn't get the words out."

"I'm still confused," I said. "If you were kidnapped, why did you send a note saying you were 'on a mission'?"

"Bibi made me write that." Behind his thick lenses, Chester's eyes were shadowed. "She's not a nice lady . . . even though she kept telling me she was."

"She held you prisoner!" I exclaimed. "How could she call that being 'nice'?"

"Because she let Prince Harry go when I asked her to. And she left messages for Roy Vickers at your office to tell him where he could find my notes and also Prince Harry."

"Mrs. Gribble kidnapped you," I insisted. "That's a federal crime."

Chester shrugged. "She said it was Cassina's fault for keeping us apart my whole life. Bibi's my grandmother."

"No, Evelyn Huffenbach is your grandmother," I said.

Chester screwed up his face. "Who's Evelyn Huffenbach?"

"The red-haired lady at the motel? You were in her room."

"Ohhhhhh." Chester pondered the new information. "Well, that would explain the pictures."

"What pictures?"

"Her motel room is full of pictures—of *me*: baby pictures, school pictures, pictures backstage with Cassina. I thought she was a stalker. That's why I went out the window, and why I was only wearing a blanket."

"I was wondering about that—"

"I fell through the ice. So I took off my coat to dry."

"What about the rest of your clothes?"

"It's a long story, Whiskey," Chester sighed. "Let me tell it my way, okay?"

"Okay."

"I was planning to come back for my coat, but first I needed help. I started walking toward the highway. There wasn't a trail, so I followed car sounds when I could hear them. Finally, I saw the motel! I knocked on doors, one after another. Nobody answered till I came to the red-haired lady. When she saw me, she went wild—laughing and crying. She wouldn't stop hugging me. She called me God's gift. The answer to her prayers. Then she pulled off my wet clothes and wrapped me in a blanket from her bed. She started running my bathwater.

"'Uh-oh,' I thought. 'I've got to get out of here.' So I told her I had to pee. I locked myself in the bathroom and climbed out the window. I was almost too cold to keep going. But no way was I staying with a crazy lady!"

Todd had radioed ahead to CMC, and while Chester was talking, he set us down on the helipad. Two men with a gurney dashed out to meet us.

Over the helicopter's roar, one shouted, "Is this Cassina's kid?"

Jenx must have given someone a heads up.

"Yes!" I yelled back. "His name is Chester!"

"Relax, Chester," the orderly said. "You're fine, and your mom is on her way!"

I squeezed my favorite neighbor's hand. "See you in a little while, Big Guy!"

He waved as they rolled him away. I wished I could stay with him, but I had to go find Leo's grand-babies. Hastily I used my mittens to wipe my cheeks and nose so that nobody would know I'd been crying.

"Call coming through for you," Todd announced in my headset.

"Hello?"

"You've been crying," Jenx declared. "I'm at Vestige, with Avery. The State Police are here, and our favorite Fibbies are on their way. So's an ambulance."

"An ambulance?" My heart wobbled. "What happened?"

"Just what you expected: Avery lost it. She's hysterical—can't talk, can't think, can't breathe. No way she can exchange the dogs for the babies." Jenx exhaled heavily. "No way we can meet the kidnappers' demands."

I had an idea.

"Can we find Deely?" I said. "I looked for her around the motel but didn't see her."

"That's because I brought her and Abra back here with me," Jenx said.

"Avery will calm down if she knows that Deely will stand in for her."

"Say what?"

"Jenx, haven't you noticed? Deely looks like Avery! Take off the glasses and put her in a parka like Avery's, with the hood up. I swear to God, you can't tell them apart."

"Yeah?" Jenx sounded doubtful.

"Yeah! And Deely can do *anything*. Except wear fur. Can you talk to her?"

I heard a phone ringing in the background—my phone at Vestige.

"Hang on," Jenx said. "This could be another call from the kidnapper. Let me get back to you."

"Where to next, boss?" Todd asked.

"Don't you have to return this thing?" I said, indicating the helicopter. We were sitting on the helipad, blades churning.

"Sure, but what's the rush? I've got your credit card. . . ." He grinned lazily.

Jenx's voice came through again. "Okay, Whiskey, she's up for it. Deely Smarr is reporting for duty!"

"Was that a call from the kidnapper?" I said.

"Yup. Deely wrote down the instructions. And here's where you come in—"

Jenx talked fast. I listened. When she had finished, I checked my watch and turned to Todd.

"Let's go get us a pair of skybox seats for the cross-country snowmobile race!"

THIRTY-FIVE

As the roof dropped away from us, I pointed out a vast expanse of snow to our west: the Shirtz Brothers' farm. A thousand acres devoted to corn and soybeans in season, it was the last family dynasty in Lanagan County.

"If the race is on schedule, the lead snowmobiles should be crossing those fields any minute," I told Todd.

We tied with the fastest contenders, flying in from the east just as three motorized winter chariots darted out of the woods to the south. Their brightly dressed drivers bounced across the undulating white landscape below us.

"Take her down a bit!" I said. My pilot obliged as four more snowmobiles exited the woods. Now that their route had widened, the vehicles tried to pass each other.

"What are we looking for?" Todd said. "If you don't mind my asking."

"I'll know it when I see it. I just hope I see it."

A few minutes later, we both saw it: another snowmobile running parallel to the racers along a low ridge about a half mile to the west. The outsider vehicle appeared to have more than one occupant.

"Hey, they're cheating," Todd said. "Looks like they're taking a shortcut!"

"No, they're running a different race."

More contenders rocketed across the Shirtz Brothers' fields, but they didn't interest me. We hovered, focused on the lone snowmobile; it followed the ridge to the end and then dropped out of sight on the far side.

"What now?" Todd said.

"Find the missing chariot."

We whirred across the fields and over the ridge. Between the high ground and Lake Michigan lay a swath of naked deciduous forest. I recognized it as part of a state preserve. A wide trail intended as a firewall had been carved through its center, parallel to the shore. I squinted and leaned forward in my seat, straining to decipher a detail farther north along the trail. Without speaking, Todd passed me a pair of binoculars. Once I had adjusted the focus, I identified Deely and the dogs. Abra appeared to sit upright like a human passenger while Deely carried Prince Harry in a mesh backpack. I recognized the snowmobile, too, by its bright blue MR inscription. Deely had managed to start up the Mattimoe Realty snowmobile that my late, great Leo kept in our garage. When Jenx had told me that the strange voice on the phone ordered Avery to use a snowmobile, I knew I owed Roy Vickers a debt of gratitude for servicing it.

The Coast Guard nanny veered off onto a service road that led away from the preserve. We kept her in sight while climbing higher and hanging farther back. I was sure Deely could hear us; yet we kept enough distance between us to avoid attracting the kind of attention that might broadcast her approach.

"Mind if I ask what this is about?" Todd said.

I took a deep breath and told him what I was sure of: that the woman below was on her way to exchange two dogs for two missing babies.

"You mean, they were kidnapped?" he asked.

"Yes."

Todd said, "Are the dogs valuable, like ransom?"

"Not really. The puppy's cute enough, but the older dog's a pain in the ass."

Suddenly it hit me that we were about to give away Chester's pup. And we'd only just rescued Chester. The poor kid had been traumatized enough already. How long till he insisted on seeing Prince Harry? How could I justify sacrificing his dog?

I assumed Jenx had a plan in place for rescuing the dogs after we rescued the babies. But what if she didn't? Or what if her canine recovery plan failed? Would Chester forgive us? Would Prince Harry? I knew Abra wouldn't. If anything went wrong, the Afghan hound would haunt me the rest of my days.

I didn't recognize the land we were flying over now. It continued to be mostly tree-covered and rolling. Deely stayed on the winding service road; there was no other traffic.

"Nobody lives around here," Todd commented.

I was about to agree when I spotted a small, peak-roofed structure tucked in among the trees ahead of Deely. "Except over there," I said, pointing.

"That's just a hunting cabin," Todd said. "A retreat off the grid. Deserted this time of year."

Except it wasn't. A thread of smoke curled from the chimney. And that wasn't the only sign of habitation. Near the cabin stood a circle of pines. Through the dark green boughs, I detected something bright white. Something the size and shape of a car. A white Jaguar? I had barely processed the thought when Deely turned off the service road and began zigzagging between trees on a diagonal route toward the cabin.

Todd announced, "I'm patching your police chief through."

"How's Avery?" I asked Jenx.

"A little better. She's been sedated. Peg Goh is staying with her till you get back."

"Thanks."

"Don't thank me. Peg's the saint. Can you see Deely?"

I told Jenx what the Coast Guard nanny was doing down below.

"She must have found the landmark," Jenx replied. "Her instructions were to turn left off the service road when she came to a broken tree. Can you see where she's headed?"

I filled Jenx in on the cabin and the possible white Jag, which were still ahead of Deely.

"As this unfolds, I'm going to need you to have a panoramic view," Jenx said. On cue, Todd pulled us up and back, distancing us from whatever was about to occur.

"Wait," I said. "I see something else!"

I immediately regretted that announcement, for the "something else" I'd noticed was Roy Vickers. Technically, what I'd seen was Jeb's Van Wagon parked just off the service road to our north. Although I was in the sky, and the car was in the trees, I was sure that no other vehicle still running in Lanagan County was quite that shade of rust.

"What do you see?" Jenx demanded.

"Uh—nothing. Sorry. My mistake."

"I left Vestige when Deely did," Jenx said. "The State boys are right behind me. We're in cars, though, not snowmobiles, so we're still at least eight minutes away. The Fibbies'll probably show up, too."

"Smith and Jones?"

"Yup. They can't stand to be all dressed up with nowhere to go."

On the ground, Deely Smarr was slowing. She must have sighted the cabin.

"So there's nobody else around?" Jenx asked.

"No sign of anybody," I lied.

Jenx reminded Todd to keep the radio clear for her calls. Then she turned on her siren and signed off the air.

Roy Vickers was approaching the cabin on foot, still too far off through the trees for Deely—or whoever was inside—to see him. But those of us in the sky had a clear view.

"Hey! There's a guy down there! We need to tell Jenx." My pilot reached for the radio switch. I clamped my hand over his.

"Todd, this is complicated."

During the long moment while he stared into my eyes, I expected Mr. WWJD to flick my hand aside. He was reading my expression—or what lay behind it. I couldn't tell what he found there, but finally Todd withdrew his hand from the radio.

"Okay," he said. "You're the boss."

"And you've still got my credit card. . . ."

Deely had stopped the snowmobile and was proceeding on foot with Prince Harry in the doggie backpack and Abra on a leash.

"She's waving to whoever's inside," Todd observed.

Both Deely's hands were raised in salute, probably to show she was unarmed.

"Can we get a better angle on this?" I asked.

"Not if Jenx wants us to hang back," my pilot replied. After a beat he added, "Are we still doing what Jenx wants?"

Good question, I thought, watching Deely and the dogs vanish into the cabin.

What happened next gave us our answer. Spry septuagenarian Roy Vickers emerged from his woodsy cover at a run. He was closing in on the cabin from the northeast, the side opposite Deely's entrance, when his body spasmed in mid-air: We saw his arms flex sideways, his head tilt back toward the sky. Roy seemed to dangle, electrified, before folding onto the snow, where a red pool encircled him.

THIRTY-SIX

"Take me down! *Now!*" I screamed at Todd.

"Where?" he asked, sounding plain stupid.

"Just *down!*" I roared. Focusing on Roy's crumpled form, I couldn't comprehend much else. Such as the fact that a copter may be convenient, but it still needs a clear and level spot to land.

"Okay, but we're calling Jenx," Todd said calmly. As he lowered the craft toward the service road, a wall of trees replaced our view of the drama.

Jenx's voice was in my ears. "Whiskey, what the hell's going on?"

"Roy Vickers just got shot!" I blurted. "He was running toward the cabin, and somebody inside must have shot him!"

The full horror of the situation seized me. "Oh my god, Jenx, the babies are in there! So's Deely. And the dogs!"

"I'm four minutes away, tops, with backup right behind me," Jenx said. "Do not panic. And do not do anything stupid, which is more likely in your case."

"It looks like Roy's hurt bad," I said. "He's losing a lot of blood. I know first aid, Jenx. I've got to help him."

"So you can get shot, too? What did I just say about not doing anything stupid?"

"Maybe I could help—by creating a distraction." That was Todd talking. "While Whiskey approaches Roy, I can buzz the cabin. Most folks stop what they're doing when a helicopter's overhead. It makes 'em nervous."

"Nervous enough to shoot more people," Jenx snapped.

I said, "If you're four minutes away, you'll be here by the time I reach Roy. So I'll be covered, no matter what."

"Since when do you know first aid?" Jenx said.

"Since . . . high school."

"Yeah? When was your latest certification?"

"Come on, Jenx," I groaned. "I remember stuff!"

"I'm certified in first aid, CPR, and AED," Todd interjected. "I'll coach her. I won't let her do damage—not even to herself."

Jenx didn't give us her blessing, but she didn't outright order me to stay inside the helicopter, either. As soon as she clicked off, I asked Todd what AED stood for.

"Automated external defibrillation. You *are* out of date." He went on, talking fast, "If Roy has a chest wound, there's not much you can do—except apply pressure and try to keep him talking if he's still alert. The bullet might have gone right through him. If it did, he has entrance and exit wounds. The bottom line is watch him closely. Be sure nothing you do makes it harder for him to breathe. If he has a sucking chest wound—"

"Oh god, what's that?"

"Never mind," Todd said. "Just don't do anything stupid. And keep your head down."

Todd and I synchronized watches. This time I remembered to remove the flotation device before I left the helicopter. Todd gave me the thumbs-up sign and then pointed me in the direction I needed to go. Good thing he did. I was completely turned around.

The cabin was too far away to see clearly through the trees, but now that I knew where to look, I could just discern it. My plan, if you could call it that, was to follow the service road until I reached the far side of the house. Then I'd cut in toward Roy. If I was lucky, there would be enough tree cover to disguise me until I got close. Fortunately, I was wearing my khaki jacket and not my crimson parka. My Higher Fashion Power had helped me today.

I checked my watch. In less than two minutes, Todd would be heading back up to make his contribution. If we timed this right, the roar from the helicopter should claim the complete attention of whoever was inside the cabin while I helped Roy.

Now that I was off the road, picking my way through the snow-covered woods, I felt a pinch of panic. This was slower going than I had anticipated, not only because the terrain was uneven and slippery, but also because I was headed straight into the slanting late-afternoon light. The low-angled glare sliced through the latticework of bare limbs and ricocheted off the snow, blinding me at intervals. I still couldn't see Roy.

Then I spotted his blood: a large scarlet blot on the snow, maybe ten yards ahead of me. But no Roy. When I squinted, I made out red droplets trailing into the woods—a darker, more alarming version of the tangerine peels Deely had left in the snow at Vestige. So Roy could walk. And we would have cover.

I heard the helicopter's approaching whine.

"Roy!" I shouted. "Roy Vickers! It's Whiskey Mattimoe! I know you're hurt. Let me help you!"

There was a crash nearby, the sound of imploding snow, ice, and broken branches. I jumped. Roy loomed before me, the yellow-white sun a halo around his head and shoulders. He appeared to be wearing part of a tree. I needed a moment to process the scene: a snow-laden branch hung around Roy's neck like a yoke.

"Whiskey," he moaned and collapsed near my feet.

I dropped to my knees next to him. A jagged, three-foot-long piece of a tree had snagged him. With both hands, I carefully removed it. Roy moaned. His right cheek was in the snow; the only eye I could see was closed tight.

"How bad are you hurt?" I said.

A new stream of red was seeping into the white stuff by my knees. I shuddered. Roy lifted his head enough to speak.

"Upper chest, near the shoulder. She got me." I assumed he didn't mean the tree.

By now the helicopter's engine was deafening. Despite the trees and the glare, I could see the craft, hovering above the cabin. Todd would know by now that Roy had moved, but I didn't know if he could see us.

Jenx and backup should be less than a minute away. I hadn't done a thing to staunch Roy's bleeding and didn't know whether I could. Or should.

With a leonine roar—the sound of a wild animal psyching for battle—Roy pushed himself into sitting position. His bloodshot blue eyes met mine.

"I'm okay," he panted. "I can do this."

Do what? The blood on Roy's jacket—on what had once, ironically, been Leo Mattimoe's jacket—suggested he was in no shape to do anything.

"I'm going in there," Roy grunted, gathering his energies to stand.

"No, you're not—" I began, as another voice cut through the stutter of the helicopter.

A woman was shouting. Roy and I turned simultaneously in the direction of the cabin. At first, I couldn't make out her words. Then I realized that she was repeating a sing-song refrain, a childish taunt:

"Roy-Boy, oh Roy-Boy! Come out, come out, wherever you are! Try to save Leo Mattimoe's family like you never saved your own!"

THIRTY-SEVEN

CROUCHED ON THE SNOW-COVERED ground next to Roy, I peered through the brush toward the origin of the voice. But I couldn't see the cabin for the trees.

"Who's that?" I asked Roy, over the mechanical chop-chop of Todd's helicopter.

The wounded ex-con was still sitting in the snow. Whatever reserves of strength he had drawn were spent. Closing his eyes, he said, "That . . . is my past talking."

"Your ex-wife is in that cabin?" I asked, stunned.

"No. I lost my wife because I got involved with that woman."

Roy leaned forward, supporting himself with his good arm.

"How are you feeling?" I said anxiously.

"A little dizzy."

Roy ran his tongue over his chapped lips, and I remembered what I'd learned in that long-ago first-aid class: Blood loss makes you thirsty. How much blood had Roy lost? How long till Jenx and the paramedics found us?

"Who's the woman?" I said, desperate to keep Roy alert.

"I'm tired," he moaned. His eyelids fluttered, and he slumped forward as if in prayer.

"Who's the woman, Roy?" I insisted.

"Baby" was his reply. Or what I thought I heard. I repeated it back to him as a question.

Weakly he shook his head. "Bibi."

"Bibi?" The white Jag. "You mean Mrs. Gribble the Third?"

Roy whispered, "She was Bibi Bosworth then. We were both married to other people . . . when she had my baby."

"You and Mrs. Gribble—I mean Bibi—had a kid together?" Suddenly I recalled how Roy had turned pale upon seeing my prospective client in the lobby at Mattimoe Realty.

Roy nodded ever so slightly, his head still down.

"I didn't know . . . till almost twenty years later. She sent a copy of a birth certificate—'Mother: Bibi Bosworth; Father: Unknown'—and pictures of a girl from childhood through her teen years. The numbers were right, and the kid looked a little like me."

"What did Bibi want?" I asked. "Back child-support?"

"Emotional blackmail. She said she didn't need money, just satisfaction. If I didn't tell my wife I had a grown daughter, Bibi would tell her for me."

"What was the point?" I asked. "After all those years?"

Roy hesitated. "I think she was striking out at me from a place of pain. Her own life had become so miserable, she wanted to hurt anyone who had ever done her harm."

"Did you tell your wife you were a father?"

"No. I was drunk all the time in those days and couldn't figure out where to begin. So Bibi told her. And my wife left me. A few days later, I stabbed Leo Mattimoe."

I pressed my palms to my ears, mostly to shut out the din of the helicopter but also to block the pain in Roy's words. His lips moved again, but I couldn't decipher what he was saying. Then our soundscape changed. Todd's helicopter suddenly withdrew, pulling its thunder with it. A gun fired, terrifyingly close by. A woman shrieked, and I jerked Roy flat to the ground with me. Someone was crashing through the brush.

"Magnet Springs Police!" Jenx yelled.

I sat up. Roy didn't. He moaned, but I couldn't rouse him.

"Whiskey Mattimoe!" I shouted. "Over here!"

Jenx was threading her way through the woods toward me, moving as fast as she could with a rifle in one hand, a walkie-talkie in the other.

"Roy took a bullet in the upper chest," I called out.

"EMTs are on the way," Jenx replied. "Are you okay?"

"Yes—except for a runaway heart rate! Who just got shot?"

"Nobody, thanks to my excellent marksmanship."

Jogging up to me, Jenx said, "I saved Mrs. Gribble's life. She was about to turn her gun on herself, but I shot it out of her hands."

"Where are Leah and Leo?"

"The crew from the first ambulance is examining them. Cover your ears!"

The police chief checked overhead, then raised and fired her rifle into the air.

"That's so the second EMT crew can find us," she explained. "They had to leave the ambulance on the service road and proceed on foot."

Jenx knelt by the wounded ex-con. Feeling for his pulse, she said, "Roy Vickers, can you hear me?"

He stirred faintly.

"You're doing good, Roy. Hang in there."

"Are Leah and Leo all right?" I asked.

"They're fine," Jenx confirmed. "So are Deely and the dogs. While Mrs. Gribble was calling for Roy, Deely got everybody out the other side of the house."

"Talk about damage control. . . ." I sighed.

"No way you're paying that woman enough."

When the paramedics came into view, I knew my work here was done. I squeezed Roy's hand, and he squeezed back although he didn't open his eyes.

"You helped save Leo's family," I whispered. "We'll talk about your family later."

Stiff from the cold and anxious to see Leah and Leo, I worked my way back out to the service road. Deserted when Todd and I had landed, the scene was now Command Central. No wonder the helicopter had sounded so loud: there were two of them.

Todd was helping Deely board his. She had Leah and Leo in her arms and Prince Harry in her backpack. Near the second copter—a bright white machine emblazoned with the letters FBI—stood identically dressed agents Smith and Jones. They watched as a Michigan State Police officer led my client toward them in handcuffs. An unleashed Abra lunged menacingly at Mrs. Gribble the

Third until Officers Swancott and Roscoe succeeded in luring her away. Mrs. Gribble wasn't wearing her chinchilla coat.

From the first helicopter Todd and Deely were waving at me. I hurried over.

"I'm taking your nanny and your family home!" Todd said over the din of two helicopter engines.

"Let me see those babies," I said, stepping aboard. Deely handed me Leo and then Leah. Both looked as flawless as they had before their misadventure.

I thanked Deely for her service and looked around for Abra.

"Where did my dog go?" I asked. *Damn.* I used the possessive pronoun again.

"Deputy Abra's assisting Officer Roscoe, ma'am. Over there." Deely pointed. Roscoe and his human counterpart Brady appeared to be checking out the perimeter of the cabin. Abra appeared to be checking out Roscoe's private parts.

"You call that 'assisting'?" I asked.

Deely shrugged. "It keeps him moving."

As I watched in disgust, Abra broke into her by-now familiar "sighting" pattern. It vaguely reminded me of a cat about to stalk a bird: her stately head erect, her glossy body tensed, Abra focused on something in the distance. Then she bounded after it in full running glory.

Roscoe barked, probably the equivalent of "Hey, get back here and keep doing that thing you were doing that felt so good."

But she was gone.

"Don't worry, ma'am," Deely said. "Trust The System. My daddy knew what he was doing."

I understood the reference. She meant her animal trainer guru father, Arthur Smarr, whom Dr. David had told me about. But the inventor of The System never met Abra the Afghan hound. She had already vanished into the woods.

"You go ahead," I told Deely. "I'll find another way home—after I find Abra."

To Todd I shouted, "Thanks for everything. Leave what's left of my credit card with Deely. I expect it'll melt before you're done with it."

He grinned.

I cleared the craft and waved as it rose into the fading sky. On the ground, the engine of the FBI helicopter still thrummed. I could barely hear the ambulance siren when it started up.

Jenx stood next to me, finishing some notes in her pad. "The EMTs think Roy will make it. And Chester's fine, by the way. Cassina's taking him home to the Castle as soon as he's released."

"I don't understand why Mrs. Gribble was holed up here, of all places," I said, indicating the shambling structure in front of us. Now that the excitement had ebbed, I could see how basic the building was—a small, serviceable hunting cabin with a vented woodburner for heat and little more. Not the likely hangout of a woman who owned Jaguars, furs, and multiple lovely homes—and who claimed to be in the market for yet another piece of real estate worth seven figures.

"Uh-oh," Jenx said. I looked where she was looking. Her blonde head held high, Abra trotted toward us, followed by Brady and Roscoe. Ordinarily, that might have been a good thing. Except she had something grotesque in her mouth. Nothing as mundane as a handbag this time.

"You take it," I told Jenx. "I'm not touching whatever that is." I couldn't even look.

The police chief whipped a couple latex gloves out of her hip pocket and slipped them on while Abra sat patiently, tail thumping the ground.

I closed my eyes. Jenx exclaimed, "Well now, this is interesting."

"'Interesting' as in . . . a decomposing dead rat?" I asked.

"It's not a rat," Brady confirmed. "But it is related to what we found at Iberville."

"Another black Stetson?" I said, afraid to peek.

"Do you want to play Twenty Questions or try acting like a grown-up deputy?" Jenx said.

I opened one eye. Then I opened the other. Jenx was holding Gil Gruen's head. The head from one of his life-size cut-outs, that is. Definitely the worse for wear, it looked like it had been roughly torn off and cast into the snow and mud of a hard Michigan winter. In fact, it had been trod upon. A muddy boot print was planted squarely across Gil's grinning face.

"Good work, Deputy!" Jenx said. She wasn't talking to me.

THIRTY-EIGHT

ABRA'S DISCOVERY OF THE head from Gil Gruen's life-size cut-out probably meant that the cabin was one of Gil's listings. To find out, I called Tina Breen, my office manager. Unfortunately, her cell phone was answered by a toddler, presumably Winston or Neville, neither of whom proved helpful. So I phoned Odette. She knew every rumor about Lanagan County real estate, if not the actual facts.

"You're talking about the cabin on the land north of the state preserve?" she asked.

"Yes," I said. "I don't know the name of the service road."

"Gil owned that cabin," Odette said. It sounded like she was chewing. "He used to boast about his deer-hunting weekends there. Have you forgotten?"

"I hope so." I had strived for years to forget things Gil Gruen said. "What are you eating?"

"Roast buffalo. It's delish."

Something else I'd forgotten: the Jamboree tradition of holding a buffalo roast before the bonfire.

"Save me some sinew," I said. "Back to Gil . . . did he rent out that cabin?"

"I don't know." Odette gagged noisily. "Sorry. Bit of gristle. Hold on—I recall Walter St. Mary saying that Gil bragged about it to Mr. Gribble just before they had their big blowup in the bar at Mother Tucker's. Gil told him it was secluded. A good place for a tryst. When Mr. Gribble said he wanted to rent it, Gil laughed in his face and said, 'Too late again, pal. Somebody beat you to it.'"

"I think I know who," I said. I hated to tell my best agent that Mrs. Gribble the Third had done business with our competitor and was no longer in a position to buy. But the sooner Odette knew, the sooner she could apply her considerable sales talents elsewhere.

"A difficult woman to work with," Odette said after I'd told her. I could envision the indignant toss of her ebony head. "Impossible to please. And she didn't return phone calls."

"She was probably too busy playing kidnapper." I filled Odette in on what little I knew about Mrs. Gribble luring Chester away and then stealing Leah and Leo.

"Why on earth would she do that?" Odette said. "She didn't need ransom money. No woman in her right mind takes other people's babies!"

I suspected that Mrs. Gribble's motivation was tied to her own illegitimate child, though I couldn't see how. As much as I wanted to be the bearer of juicy gossip, I kept to myself what Roy had said about Bibi having his baby. That story was so good I wanted to share it in person rather than by phone. Plus I needed a few more facts.

I surmised that one or both of the Gribbles had brought Chester to Gil's cabin after leaving Bear Claw. But I didn't understand the casino connection, or how Mindy the cocktail waitress had ended up dead in my yard wearing Mrs. Gribble's fur coat. Who stabbed Thomas McKondin, the nurse-impersonator and pervert? And where on earth was Mr. Gribble?

Odette asked if I planned to attend the annual bonfire, which would start in four hours. I hadn't missed one yet, and I wasn't about to break with tradition tonight. Besides, my favorite tourist Nash Grant might be there. And what was more romantic than a bonfire?

I was ending my call to Odette when Agent Smith entered my field of vision.

"Deputy Mattimoe," he said, inclining his head in what was surely a mock bow. "Good work rescuing Chester Casanova."

Considering I'd only just learned that Chester had a last name, hearing it paired with his first name jarred me.

"Thanks," I said. "I'm relieved he's all right. Any luck locating Mr. Gribble the Third?"

"There's an APB out for him. And we have his wife in custody. She'll probably tell us his whereabouts, eventually."

I glanced toward the FBI helicopter; Agent Jones was assisting a handcuffed Mrs. Gribble aboard.

"Could I talk to her? For just a minute? After all, she stole my step-grandchildren."

I clapped a hand over my mouth. Had I, at age thirty-three, actually used the G-word?

"Why not?" Agent Smith said cheerfully. "If she's willing to talk to you. But make it snappy. We're taking her to Lansing."

Agent Jones had already fitted Mrs. Gribble with a headset. He lent me his so that we could communicate over the helicopter's racket.

"Remember me?" I said, sitting across from my client and giving her my most leveling glare.

"Of course. You're a very lucky woman," Mrs. Gribble replied.

That startled me. "What do you mean, lucky?"

"People like to be on your side. Good people. How do you manage that, Mrs. Mattimoe?"

"I guess I pick the right friends and sometimes the right husband—. Wait a minute," I said, stopping myself. "I'm asking the questions here."

"Very well." Mrs. Gribble the Third made herself as comfortable as possible on the helicopter's bench.

"Why did you kidnap Chester?" I demanded.

"I didn't. You can't steal what's rightfully yours. Chester is mine, yet he has been withheld from me his whole life. As was his mother before him."

"His mother? You're saying you have a 'right' to both Chester and Cassina?"

"Of course," Mrs. Gribble said evenly. "Cassina is my daughter. Chester is my grandson."

"But your sister, Evelyn Huffenbach, is Cassina's mother."

"Only in the eyes of the law."

"You mean . . . you and Roy Vickers are . . . *Cassina's* birth parents?"

"Ah. He told you we made a baby." Mrs. Gribble's dark eyes narrowed. "I only knew Roy for one night. I was working in Vegas, at the club my husband managed—not Mr. Gribble, my first husband. The one who died and left me rich. It was a miserable marriage."

"Why was Roy Vickers in Vegas?" I asked.

"Believe it or not, Roy was on vacation with his wife. They'd had a fight—over his drinking, as usual, and the way he handled money. Roy came into the Emerald Dream, where I danced. Okay, where I stripped. My husband was out with his girlfriend *du jour*. Roy kept buying me drinks. Finally it got late, so we got a room. Cassina was born nine months later."

"Did your husband think she was his?"

"When I started showing, I tried to tell him she was. He knew she couldn't be. We hadn't been together in a while. He didn't divorce me, but he made me give her up. My sister and her husband agreed to adopt her. Evelyn couldn't have children."

"You named your daughter Mayzelle," I observed.

"I certainly didn't! I named her Cassina—a nod to her Vegas casino heritage. Evelyn changed it."

"Were you close to Cassina while she was growing up?"

"Evelyn controlled everything. I was allowed to be Cassina's long-distance 'aunt.' Nothing more." An eerie gleam shone in Mrs. Gribble's eyes. "My daughter knew she didn't belong with Evelyn. When she was little, she started running away. By age thirteen Cassina was a ward of the court, placed in foster care. When she turned eighteen, I found her and told her who she really was."

"Did she believe you?" I said.

"What do you think?" Mrs. Gribble asked nastily. "She reclaimed her birth name and reinvented herself as a singer."

"So," I mused, "Cassina knows that you and Roy Vickers are her parents."

"I didn't tell her Roy's name," Mrs. Gribble said quickly. "And I've never told Roy that the famous Cassina is his daughter. Why should I? He took no responsibility for giving her life."

"He took responsibility for helping us find her son," I said. "Why did you take Chester?"

"Isn't it obvious? To see what it would be like to have a grandson. That's why I took your grandchildren. I never got to hold Chester when he was a baby, but now at least I know what it would have been like. As I said, you're very lucky, Mrs. Mattimoe."

Agent Jones stepped up then to reclaim his headset. "We've got to go!" he shouted.

"Just one more question!" I turned to Mrs. Gribble. "Why the dogs? Why did you insist that Avery bring Abra and Prince Harry?"

Mrs. Gribble's expression was indignant. "Your damn dog could identify me. I followed Abra's story in the Chicago papers, remember? I know she's a crime-solving canine."

I surrendered my headset to Agent Jones and allowed Agent Smith to escort me from the helicopter. It was almost dark out, and I needed a ride home. Fortunately, Brady and Roscoe were still at the scene with Abra, so we all climbed into the patrol car together. I stared at the Afghan hound sitting demurely next to me on the back seat. Was it possible that she actually was a *good* deputy? I removed my battered tin badge and pinned it to her rhinestone collar. Abra flashed me a self-satisfied grin.

THIRTY-NINE

ON THE DRIVE BACK to Vestige in his patrol car, Brady relayed the good news: Chester had given the Michigan State Police sufficient information about Mr. Gribble that they were now hot on his trail to the next Native American-run casino up the coast.

Oscar Manfred Gribble the Third apparently had a serious gambling problem, although, according to Chester, he called it his "pricey hobby." Mr. Gribble enjoyed his vice, as long as his much older and wealthier wife could afford it. Hence the vanity plate, IMGBLN.

Chester learned a great deal about the Gribbles during his enforced time with Bibi. As she had told me herself, she inherited a tidy sum from her first husband, a Las Vegas club owner who liked the ladies. He died of a gunshot wound inflicted by a jealous boyfriend, leaving Bibi more money than she'd dreamed of. She sold the club and started investing. Some years later, she met a charming gambler who'd squandered his family fortune. She fell for him and became Mrs. Oscar Manfred Gribble the Third.

Manny, as she called her husband, had the name and social connections she longed for, provided she could supply the cash. Unfortunately, Manny set to work demolishing her savings just as he had his own.

According to Chester's report, the two did nothing but fight when they were together, which wasn't often because Manny was more interested in gambling and otherwise spending money than he was in keeping company with his wife. We already knew that he had planned to invest some of the marital assets in real estate of his own choosing. But Bibi short-circuited that plan by personally tipping off Gil Gruen that her husband had no money of his own. Ever the jerk, Gil took pleasure in publicly humiliating Manny.

Chester told police that Bibi confiscated his cell phone. His first opportunity to escape occurred Friday morning when he distracted Bibi, fished his phone out of her purse, and ran through the casino looking for help. But she intercepted him before he got very far and hauled him off to Gil's cabin.

"I'm calling Chester right now," I informed Brady. "I've got to hear the rest of this firsthand."

Fortunately, Chester answered the phone, so I didn't need Cassina's—or Rupert's—permission to speak to him. He sounded like his usual buoyant self. "I'm getting ready to go to the bonfire!" he informed me.

"I'll see you there. But I want to ask you a couple questions about what happened. Can we talk?"

"Sure. I'm not traumatized or anything. I've already been interviewed by the FBI!"

I said, "The police think Mindy the waitress had your mother's credit card. Do you know how she got it?"

"When we were at the casino, Manny took it away from me and gave it to her." Chester's tone turned somber. "I heard a policeman say Mindy's dead."

"I'm afraid so. Do you know what happened to her?"

"No. Manny told me that they had a fight. He called her a real bad name. He was mad because he gave her a thirty-thousand-dollar coat, and she treated him like . . . another bad word."

I was sure the coat he'd given her was Bibi's.

"He said he gave her a designer purse, too," Chester said, "but she lost that when he took her to see a house that Bibi might buy."

I flashed on the Gucci bag that Odette had temporarily sacrificed to win the Gribble account. The one that Abra had later recovered at Pasco Point . . . with a Bear Claw Casino poker chip inside. Abra had the purse when Bibi forced Chester and the dogs into her car. Manny must have seized it later as a present for his girlfriend. But there had been something else in that handbag. Something besides Odette's ID that either Manny or Mindy had added later.

"So Bibi took you from the casino to the cabin," I said. "What happened next?"

"Manny broke in while we were still asleep this morning," Chester said. "He shouted and waved a gun around just to scare us. Even though Bibi knew there was a rifle in a case by the wood-burner, she couldn't get to it till after Manny dragged me out the door. Then she shot at his tires, but she missed."

"Where was Manny taking you?"

"He said we were going north, casino by casino, till somebody came through with enough money to send me home," Chester said. "I think he meant ransom. From Cassina or Bibi. Or both."

I took a deep breath. "So how did you end up falling through the ice a mile from the Broken Arrow Motel?"

"We didn't drive far before Manny said he needed a little nap. I think he'd been drinking."

I didn't ask how the eight-year-old would know. I didn't have to since I'd witnessed his own mother over-indulge in front of him.

"Manny pulled off on a dirt road by the Lake," Chester continued, "and told me he was turning on the child-proof locks. I'm way smarter than that! I waited for him to fall asleep and then, when he was snoring, I let myself out."

"Good for you!"

"I went down to the Lake because I knew I could walk along the edge and end up in Magnet Springs. Except we were farther up the coast than I thought. I went north when I should have gone south. Then I fell through the ice. The water wasn't deep, but I got soaked. And I was real cold. So I went inland looking for help. You know the rest of the story."

"Thank goodness you came to the Broken Arrow Motel!"

"Thank goodness I got away from the crazy lady," Chester said, "and you were there in the helicopter to save me!"

Chester and I made a date to meet at the bonfire. He promised to introduce me to Rupert, if Rupert felt like talking to locals.

Brady had been on his patrol car radio while I was talking. When I finished my call, he said, "The State Police want to question Mr. Gribble about Mindy's death. Gil's, too—if they find the body. First they have to find Mr. Gribble."

I thought about the third item found in Odette's Gucci bag and knew I had to see someone at Coastal Medical Center right away.

FORTY

Back at Vestige, there was no point trying to have even a quick conversation with Avery, who had secluded herself in her room with the babies. Deely informed me that Nash was on his way over, but she doubted Avery would let him in. Though tempted to linger for another look at the handsome professor, I didn't care to get caught up in their domestic drama. Plus, I had pressing business of my own. So I entrusted the dogs to the nanny and drove to CMC.

My first stop was the information desk, where I learned that no one named Roy Vickers had been admitted. Assuming that meant he was still in the Emergency Room, I headed there. Sure enough, a team of physicians was working to stabilize him. All anyone would reveal about Roy's condition was that he was conscious. I said a quick prayer and moved on to the Intensive Care Unit, which was more chaotic than the ER. I overheard two nurses griping about how woefully short-handed they were that shift, which might have explained why it took almost five minutes for me to locate the unit clerk. Then I told a small lie: in order to see Thomas McKondin, I pretended to be his sister.

My ruse amused the patient.

"I'm not into incest," he wheezed.

"That's all right," I said pleasantly, "because I'm not into you."

McKondin looked terrible. I had braced myself for a disturbing sight, but he was worse off than I had imagined. Multiple tubes, wires and monitors, all of them pumping or beeping or flashing, were attached to him. His chest was heavily bandaged, and so was most of his face. No doubt the latter damage was due to my handi-work—or footwork. I figured I wasn't to blame, though, for the fact that he needed oxygen.

"If you don't like me, why'd you come?" he asked.

"I want to know what your business card was doing in a dead girl's purse." I recounted Abra's retrieval of the Gucci bag at Pasco Point. McKondin claimed he had no clue.

"Okay," I said patiently. "Here's a question you can answer: Why are you making sure I don't get blamed for your injuries?"

"You didn't stab me, did you?"

"No. But I did hurt you—in self-defense. Why not let me take the fall?"

McKondin motioned for me to draw closer. Given his history, I declined.

"You're a sexy lady," he said. "Sexy but scary. That's one mean-ass kick you got. I don't want to mess with you again, unless we're in it for fun."

"That will never happen," I promised. "But there's more going on here, McKondin. Who's to blame?"

Before he could reply, a male nurse appeared brandishing a hypodermic needle.

"I'm sorry, but you'll have to go," he said in a jarringly high-pitched voice. "It's time for me to draw blood from Mr. McKondin, and then he'll need some rest."

"Of course," I said, getting to my feet. When I turned to say good-bye, McKondin's bloodshot eyes were darting back and forth between the nurse and me.

"Wait," he croaked.

"Now, Mr. McKondin," the nurse said soothingly, "you know I have to do this."

"I'll come back tomorrow," I told the patient. "Think about what I said."

McKondin made some kind of reply, but the nurse's jovial comment drowned it out: "Oh, yes, I know you hate needles, Mr. McKondin. Everybody does! But this is all part of what we do to make sure you get better."

I had almost reached the door beneath the ICU's exit sign when I froze. Something about the scene I'd just witnessed didn't compute. Granted, I knew less than the next guy about medical procedures. But a nurse about to draw blood wouldn't arrive with a syringe full of clear liquid, would he? If it weren't for the fact that Lanagan County's death rate had recently spiked, I might have ignored my paranoid instincts. With no plan whatsoever, I headed back to McKondin's room, where I slammed into the male nurse hurriedly making his departure.

When I tried to step around him, he said, "You can't go back in there! This is a critical care unit, and Mr. McKondin's asleep."

For the first time I looked closely at the nurse. He was around forty years old, a bald, stout man with piggish eyes and a small nose. A glaze of perspiration shimmered on his pink face. My eyes shot directly to his hands. No syringe.

"Where's the blood sample, Mr. . . ." I glanced at his nametag to finish my question. "C. Richards, RN?"

The absurdity of the moment struck me before he did. But I had no time to brace myself. It was a supreme sucker punch, and it snapped my head around. I reeled backwards into the glass partition outside McKondin's room, then slid to the floor. Blood gushed from my nose. I let loose a strangled cry.

By the time I could focus my eyes again, two bona fide nurses were bending over me. Mr. Oscar Manfred Gribble the Third was gone.

Thomas McKondin was gone, too. Permanently. The *faux* nurse had jammed a syringe full of adrenaline into his carotid artery, or so one of the real nurses surmised. Breathing through my mouth, I did my best to report what had happened. A nurse immediately notified hospital security and local law enforcement.

Mr. Gribble was grabbed before he could flee the building. I explained to police that I had seen the man only once before, at a distance, on Opening Day of the Jamboree when Odette pointed him out. He had avoided us, skating away before we could approach. If only I had recognized him today in time to save Thomas McKondin's life.

Like Roy Vickers, I ended up in the Emergency Room, where a pleasant female physician assured me that my nose was not broken and would heal looking exactly the same as it had before. That would have been comforting news had I actually liked my original nose. At least I wouldn't have to get used to a different one. For now, though, it was swollen, stuffed with cotton, and reddish purple. Not the look I'd planned to wear at tonight's bonfire. Maybe if I stayed far enough back from the flames, no one would notice.

That was not to be—even though I added a floppy-brimmed hat as a last-minute accessory when I changed out of my blood-splattered clothes at home. Without fail, every single acquaintance I saw at the bonfire asked what had happened to my face. A few couldn't resist warning me that I'd probably have lingering sinus problems as a result. God love the doomsayers—because I don't.

Still, I had a pleasant evening. Jeb entertained the crowd with more Rockabilly hits, including my personal favorite, "I Had All the Angles and She Had All the Curves." Eventually, he brought me a beer and his Blue Moon pool-playing fan, Bud.

"Hey, Whiskey. Bud just told me something you've got to hear."

I took a sip of my beer, blandly expecting either a fishing story or a pool-shooting story.

"Remember how I told you a lady came to my shanty today? Asking if I'd seen anybody?" Bud said.

I nodded.

"Well, I remembered something else."

"What?"

"Two things. I didn't look at her for more than a second, but she was wearing a fur coat and hat—kind of silver-gray, like. Not what you'd wear to the Jamboree, more like what you'd wear to the opera. Not that I've been to the opera."

My heartbeat quickened. That was proof Deely had seen what she said she saw when she commandeered the snowmobile. But what did it mean? Bibi's chinchilla coat was on the dead waitress. So Bud and Deely must have seen Evelyn Huffenbach. Except that Mrs. Huffenbach had been at the Broken Arrow Motel.

"What's the other thing, Bud?" I said.

He slid his eyes toward Jeb, who nodded encouragingly. "Well, it dawned on me later that the lady didn't exactly seem . . . like a lady."

"What do you mean?"

Bud cleared his throat. "Well, I glanced at her just long enough to see she was ugly. And now, well—now I think she might have been . . . a guy. You know, a guy with a kind of high voice dressed like a girl." He appeared sickened. I figured it wasn't his slowness in putting the pieces together that bothered him, but rather the fact that he'd been that close to a possible transvestite.

I comforted Bud by assuring him that the man wasn't a female impersonator, just a nurse impersonator and a killer.

Jeb bought me a few more beers, which was nice of him considering I kept scanning the crowd for Nash Grant. Jeb was celebrating the return of his Van Wagon—in improved condition. Roy the handyman-mechanic had repaired the passenger-side door and replaced the overhead light bulb.

Dr. David and Deely joined us after a while. Grinning happily, they appeared to be out on their first official "date."

Deely explained that Avery had excused her from duty when Nash arrived at Vestige. My heart sank because that meant I probably wouldn't see the professor tonight. Still, I hoped their meeting had turned into a conversation and not a confrontation. The twins' recent kidnapping just might help both parents realize what was important.

The abduction served to remind me that I should use the expensive alarm system Leo had installed. I seemed to have a mental block against activating it, probably because it reminded me of my late wise husband—and all the reasons I needed to be nice to Avery. Leo had always looked out for his family. How could I turn my back on his only daughter and her children, no matter how much I disliked her and lusted after her ex-boyfriend?

Maybe it was the beer talking, but I had a question for Dr. David. I asked him point-blank if he'd been harassing Gil Gruen.

"Harassing? No. I used an approach Fleggers call Conscience-Calling." David made it sound like conscience *cawing*. "We alarm someone in small ways as a means of reminding him that he's doing something wrong."

Or *wong*, as David pronounced it.

"Okay," I said, "but how does Conscience-Calling excuse your theft of Martha Glenn's homemade dog and cat treats?"

"That's what we call a Community Intervention," David said. "We tried talking to Mrs. Glenn, but she doesn't get it. She insists on putting chocolate in her pet treats. Chocolate is toxic to cats and dogs."

I lingered by the bonfire until the last flames faded to embers. Jeb lingered with me, neither of us talking. I think he knew I was disappointed that Nash Grant never showed up. With some effort, I managed to interpret the professor's absence as a good sign. A sign that he and Avery were working things out.

My night was hardly a bust, however. Besides my informative conversations with Bud and Dr. David, I enjoyed a brief chat with Chester.

"Rupert likes dogs!" he announced. "He might convince Cassina to let me bring Prince Harry home."

"I hope so," I said sincerely. "One dog for the long term is definitely my limit."

We chatted about dogs and how to train them, a subject I clearly knew nothing about. Chester was losing interest in Dogs-Train-You-Dot-Com now that Deely had started teaching him The System.

Changing the topic, I asked Chester how he felt about Bibi going to jail.

He shrugged. "She'll get what she deserves, I guess. But I'll still have a grandmother."

"You mean, Rupert's mom?" I knew nothing about Chester's paternal lineage.

"Her, too, but she's in London. I mean Mrs. Huffenbach. She's not crazy, after all, just lonely." Chester pointed toward a long-haired man wrapped in a cape standing next to a red-haired woman in a chinchilla coat. "Rupert likes talking with Evelyn because she's an Anglophile. That means she loves everything about England—even the pub food."

"Maybe Rupert will change Cassina's mind about Evelyn," I suggested.

"Maybe," Chester agreed. "It would be nice to have a whole family."

FORTY-ONE

Two weeks passed before the Gruen-Gribble-McKondin-Mindy-the-waitress connection became clear. News about that arrived the same day I hosted my first solo dinner party.

There was no Leo Mattimoe to plan the menu or do the cooking for me. And bear in mind that I had never cooked. As I fretted over the menu, my poor mother received more phone calls from me than she had in her whole life. She said she appreciated hearing my voice. But I could tell by about the fortieth call that she was getting annoyed by my questions. Finally, she recommended the Cooking Channel and wished me luck.

I decided to make something simple, yet satisfying. Then I asked Odette what that would be.

"Simple for you, or simple for a normal cook?" Odette said.

When she found out I meant me, she suggested spaghetti.

"You can boil water, can't you?"

I honestly wasn't sure. But the more I thought and read about spaghetti, the more confident I became.

Brainstorm: If I could manage to cook the pasta, the only other things I'd need were sauce, garlic bread, tossed salad, and dessert—all of which could be purchased pre-made by somebody else! For that matter, I could have bought the whole meal from Mother Tucker's, but that seemed dishonest.

"Baby steps," Leo used to say when teaching me something new.

I planned my dinner party for the night before Magnet Springs' annual Groundhog Day Dance Extravaganza. Our town's traditional celebration offered a chance to be either sexy or silly, depending on your talents. It began in the 1950s as a flimsy excuse to attract moneyed tourists who wanted to dress up and dance. At the Town Hall there was still a formal dance, complete with live big-band music. But now there were as many as twenty casual to downright crazy dance parties at locations all over the area. Peg Goh hosted one of the most popular: a Specialty Costume Dance that required participants to come as rodents. You wouldn't believe how many people enjoyed dancing the night away dressed like chipmunks and squirrels.

My pre-Groundhog Day dinner guest list included Roy Vickers, Jeb Halloran, Deely Smarr, David Newquist, Nash Grant, and—of course—Avery Mattimoe. I felt awkward inviting Jeb when I wanted to flirt with Nash. But since I would have to deal with Avery, I counted on my easy-going ex to be the social lubricant.

Roy, convalescing in his new apartment downtown, referred to my venture as a Redemption Dinner. The phrase set my teeth on edge. I was experiencing waves of guilt because I knew something about Roy that only one other person on earth knew: that he was Cassina's father and Chester's grandfather. When Bibi Gribble was hauled off to prison, I became the sole possessor of her earth-shaking secret. What I had at first regarded as potentially hot gossip quickly morphed into an ethical burden. I wasn't sure what I should or would do with the information. So, in typical fashion, I tried not to think about it.

Odette helped Nash Grant obtain a short-term lease on a small house in Magnet Springs. I thought he was being silly to insist on so many family-friendly amenities when his children were just a few months old. Peg explained it like this: "Nash wants to show his true colors, his commitment to doing the right thing."

Avery was as chilly as ever. Since her crisis with Bibi and the twins, however, she seemed less inclined toward temper tantrums and crying jags. I could only hope that the change was permanent.

On the day before Groundhog Day I left work early. In fact, I took the afternoon off. I needed lots of time to prepare my spaghetti.

By six o'clock, I had lined up all my ingredients and equipment on the kitchen counter. Boiling water for the spaghetti was beginning to loom as a fearsome task. So I was distracting myself by setting the dining room table when Jenx arrived. Slack-jawed, she first surveyed my kitchen and then froze in the archway to my dining room.

"I heard about your Redemption Dinner, but I had to see the evidence for myself."

"It's not about redemption—" I began.

"Oscar Manfred Gribble the Third could use some of that," Jenx said. Without waiting for an invitation, she pulled out two chairs, one to sit on, the other to prop her booted feet on. "This morning the Grand Jury indicted his sorry ass: one count murder, one count kidnapping."

"Do we know why he did what he did?" I asked.

"Blame it on a triangle of warped personalities," Jenx said.

That sounded like a great excuse to postpone my culinary destiny. I pulled out a chair and sat down to listen.

If Noonan had been telling the story, she would have said that Manny Gribble, Thomas McKondin, and Mindy Mad Hawk were three lost souls doomed to collide and implode. Jenx called them "three complete losers looking for revenge."

"Manny Gribble resented his wife because she made him beg for money," Jenx began. "Thomas McKondin blamed Gil Gruen for wrecking his life because Gil fired his dad. And Mindy Mad Hawk had a grudge against anybody whose life wasn't as screwed up as hers. These three charmers found each other at Bear Claw Casino."

According to Jenx, McKondin was a little older than he looked —twenty-one, to be exact. Before Manny Gribble came to town, McKondin liked to hang around the casino and brag to Mindy about his criminal exploits. Another waitress overheard him. She told police that his boasts ranged from stealing Gil Gruen's life-size cut-outs and his best Stetson to embarrassing women with lewd talk and impersonating a nurse at area hospitals.

"The waitress—I think her name is Megan—reported that McKondin showed Mindy and Manny his fake-nurse nametag," Jenx said. "Manny offered him twenty bucks for it—and McKondin sold it."

"Worst deal he ever made," I remarked.

"After Gil Gruen publicly humiliated Manny Gribble at Mother Tucker's, Gribble and McKondin found common ground hating Gil," Jenx said. "They sat around the casino buying drinks from and for Mindy, hardly aware that Megan was listening. The boys hatched a payback scheme that went like this: The night before the Jamboree, McKondin would set up an ice shanty north of Fishburg. He knew the ice was dangerously thin there due to too-shallow water and thick vegetation. On Opening Day, he would lure Gil to the shanty on the promise of meeting a wealthy prospective client. There McKondin and Gribble, wearing flotation devices and ice skates, would scare the crap out of Gruen by *almost* letting him fall through the ice."

"What went wrong?" I said.

"Everything. McKondin lost his temper and stabbed Gil with a fish-cleaning knife before Gribble even met them at the shanty."

I recalled my Jamboree memory of Oscar Manfred Gribble the Third on skates. He was probably still waiting for McKondin's signal. By then he must have surmised that something had gone awry.

Jenx went on: "McKondin was so shocked by his own actions that he left Gil's body in the shanty and got the hell out of there. Roy Vickers saw the kid skating madly away and entered to investigate. He tried to revive Gil. In the process, he got blood all over himself. Roy admitted he was having a 'post-Leo Mattimoe flashback' when you saw him making his way to shore."

"Why didn't McKondin just leave town?"

"You're forgetting: he was a loser," Jenx said. "McKondin decided to blackmail Gribble, threatening to tell the police that Manny had hired him to kill Gil for revenge. Gribble told the cops that much himself. He said McKondin demanded fifty thousand dollars to keep his mouth shut."

"Money that Gribble preferred to spend on his gambling habit, I'm sure."

Jenx nodded. "The night McKondin harassed you at Vestige, Gribble was following him. Mindy, wearing her new 'gift' coat, went along for the ride. She'd been drinking shots. Gribble left her in the car with her bottle and took off on foot after McKondin. Gribble said he planned to show McKondin he had a knife and 'scare' him into leaving town."

"Oh yeah," I said. "That would work."

"The State Police figure the kid was so preoccupied talking to you on his cell phone that Gribble was able to follow him. Then you slowed McKondin down with your fancy footwork, and Gribble used his knife to finish him off. Or so he thought. When Gribble got back to the car, Mindy was dead—choked on her own vomit. Gribble must have panicked and dumped her body in your woods. Cassina's credit card fell out of her pocket."

I took a moment to digest Jenx's account. Then I said, "I know the rest of the story: The next morning, Gribble grabbed Chester from Bibi and started up the coast. A few hours after that, Bibi walked into my unlocked home and out again with Avery's twins."

Suddenly my door chimes rang. I jumped as if I'd just heard gunfire.

"Easy, Whiskey," Jenx said. "You're expecting company, remember?"

"Not this early!" I blurted. "I've got to boil water!"

Jenx gave me the kind of look usually reserved for the drunk and disorderly. She said, "How about you answer the door, and I'll get the water started?"

"You can do that?" I asked, incredulous. "*You* can boil water?"

"Answer the damn door."

I did. Nash Grant was standing there, smelling of citrus and spice and holding an oversized bouquet of yellow roses.

"Hi, Whiskey," he said in his buttery Biloxi voice. "Thanks so much for inviting me."

I summoned the presence of mind to step aside so that he could enter. Who cared if the man was an hour early when he smelled so good and brought a gift like that?

Before I could speak, Nash continued, "I want to thank you for something else, too. This whole Redemption Dinner theme has started me thinking. For the sake of the twins, I've decided that Avery and I should give our relationship another try. She agrees."

Redemption Dinner, my ass! That was Roy Vickers's label, not mine. I had been hoping to get laid at the end of the evening—by the very man who had just announced he was here to court my stepdaughter.

"Did you know that yellow roses are Avery's favorite?" Nash added. "They bring out the highlights in her hair."

"Not to mention the sallowness of her skin."

I'd found my voice, and it wasn't pretty.

"Of course, if you like, we can also use this as a centerpiece," Nash offered.

"No, really, I couldn't. Why don't you go on upstairs and present them to Avery? Then you can enjoy her *delightful* company for a whole hour . . . while I prepare dinner."

I knew I was wearing one of those pasted-on smiles because my face hurt. So did my heart, but that was a familiar sensation. Suddenly I missed Leo more than I had in weeks. As I watched Nash and his roses head upstairs toward Avery, my eyes brimmed with tears.

The door chimes rang again.

"Oh, for god's sake!" I moaned. "The invitation said seven-thirty!"

I flung open the front door. On my porch stood Chester, Roy Vickers, and Evelyn Huffenbach. Mrs. Huffenbach wasn't wearing fur, but she was wearing oven mitts and holding a covered roaster pan.

"I know we're an hour early, Whiskey," Roy began, "but we want to share our joy with you. You're looking upon the very picture of redemption!"

"That's nice, Roy," I said, "but all I wanted was spaghetti." *And some sex*. I didn't say the last part out loud even though I meant it.

"Can we come in?" Chester asked. "It's kind of cold out here, and my grandma's holding a turkey."

Of course I let them in although, technically, two out of the three were gate-crashers. I hadn't invited either Chester or Evelyn, but if they'd brought their own turkey, I supposed they were welcome. Hell, Nash had brought flowers for Avery, and I'd let him in.

"Whiskey, guess what? Roy's my grandpa!" Chester beamed up at me, the light of my foyer chandelier bouncing off his round glasses. "Grandma Evelyn told us."

"You knew?" I asked Mrs. Huffenbach.

"Oh, yes," she said. "Bibi told me Roy's name between contractions when she was giving birth. I think she thought she might die. We never spoke of it again, and I never told my late husband."

"Whiskey's a widow, too," Chester informed his grandma. "So you have something else in common, besides me and Grandpa Roy."

I looked from Chester to Evelyn and back to Chester. "Does your mother know . . . about Grandpa Roy?"

Chester nodded excitedly. "Grandma Evelyn just told her. She's with Noonan now. Getting a vibration infusion."

Jenx appeared with pot holders and took the roaster pan from Evelyn.

"When you're ready, Whiskey, I'd like to see you in the kitchen," the police chief said.

I trailed after her like a scolded child. She was boiling water.

"Did you use your . . . *magnetic powers* to do that?" I asked respectfully.

"I turned on the burner," Jenx said. "It's too early to cook your pasta, but this is to show you how it's done." She studied me. "I overheard your conversation. You found out the hard way about Nash and Avery."

"You already knew?" I gasped.

"The whole town knows they're giving it a second shot. Be happy for them. It won't work, but at least they will have made the effort—for the twins' sake."

I brightened. "You're right. I still have a chance with Nash!"

"Sure," Jenx said mildly. "But Magnet Springs is betting you'll end up with Jeb."

Abra and Prince Harry chose that moment to scramble in through the doggie door, their snowy paws sliding across my clean floor. They made a beeline to Jenx, who patted their shiny heads.

"Life's full of surprises, Whiskey," she remarked. "Keep learning new tricks."

I had never expected to care deeply about somebody else's kids. Yet Chester, Leah, and Leo were changing my life. And I didn't resent it . . . too much. Even Prince Harry had his charms.

"I'll keep learning," I told Jenx.

She said, "Spaghetti's a good place to start."

ABOUT THE AUTHOR

NINA WRIGHT is a professional actor turned playwright and novelist. When not at her keyboard, she leads entertaining work-shops in writing and the creative process for adults and kids. Nina recently completed the third Whiskey Mattimoe mystery, *Whiskey & Tonic*, and is now writing the sequel to her teen novel, *Home-free*, published by Flux. She also writes for middle-grade readers. Nina loves big dogs and beaches.

Contact her at

www.ninawright.net

http://whiskeymattimoe.blogspot.com/

http://ninawrightwriter.blogspot.com/

Read on for an excerpt from the next
Whiskey Mattimoe Mystery by Nina Wright

Whiskey & Tonic

COMING SOON FROM MIDNIGHT INK

ONE

"This isn't a tonic. It's toxic," I rasped, setting the glass down so hard that its contents splashed onto Mother Tucker's bar.

"Tonics aren't supposed to be tasty," Odette intoned. "They're supposed to cure what ails you."

"Who said anything ails me?"

My top salesperson gave me a look that could freeze lava. Then she took a sip of her *chocotini* and waved toward the bar crowd.

"Shall we take a poll? Ask whether anyone here thinks Whiskey Mattimoe needs a tonic?"

Talk about a set-up. Odette's mellifluous voice can compel complete strangers to do her bidding. I've decided that her velvety Tonga accent is the reason she sells more real estate than anyone else in west Michigan. That plus the fact that she pretends not to understand the word *no*.

"No," I said emphatically. "We don't need a poll."

"True. Your misery is obvious." Odette shoved the vile cocktail toward me. "It's a traditional African tonic. Drink up."

I eyed the sparkling contents suspiciously. "Your people drink this?"

"No. Your people drink this," she said.

"I don't have people in Africa."

Odette narrowed her eyes. "Of course you do. How else did so many of my people end up here?"

Embarrassed, I held up the glass and peered deep into it. "Okay. Why do 'my people' drink this in Africa?"

"For the malaria."

I put the glass down. "There's no malaria in Magnet Springs."

Odette sighed heavily. "Then what is your problem?"

Good question. It was officially spring. The days were getting longer, warmer, and sweeter smelling. Daffodils and crocuses were blooming. People were starting to smile again. Some were even falling in love. Or at least lust. Not with me, though. And therein lay my problem: I wasn't getting laid.

"Uh-oh," Odette murmured. "Are you wearing the camisole?"

Following her gaze, I immediately understood the question. Handsome Nash Grant, the lust of my life, was entering the bar. For my birthday, two weeks earlier, Odette had tried to boost my bland beige wardrobe by giving me a black silk and lace camisole. With it she had included these written instructions:

Wear at all times. Be prepared to peel off whatever you put on over it.

Remember: You can't go wrong in a black camisole.

Well, you can, but you'll thank me later.

In case I missed the point, she had added a simple equation:

Black Camisole = Sex Appeal
You need it.

Now, reflexively, I yanked my camel-colored mock-turtleneck over my head. I had it almost all the way off before I remembered that my sexy black camisole was in the laundry hamper at home . . . and I was wearing one of my oldest yellowish-white bras. In public. In front of Nash Grant.

Odette gasped in horror at the same instant I realized my gaffe. Fortunately, my head was inside my shirt. Even though the whole room could see me, I couldn't see anybody. Whiskey the Ostrich. Who says denial is a bad thing? When my exposed torso felt a chill, I began fumbling for my sleeves. I seemed to have lost one. The sweater rolled back down, but only my left arm slid into its rightful place. Still groping under the fabric with my right hand, I reluctantly opened one eye.

"Hot flash?" teased Nash Grant in his soft Mississippi accent.

"Not yet!" I replied indignantly. "I'm only thirty-four!"

He laughed. "That makes you officially the youngest grandma I know."

"*Step*-grandma," I corrected him gravely. "I'm young enough to be Avery's sister."

"Of course you are." Nash made a mock bow, the bar lights glinting off his thick, walnut-colored hair. If I hadn't been tangled in the straightjacket of my shirt, I might have swooned.

"Do you need a hand there, Whiskey?" he asked. "You seem to be missing one."

Before I could answer, Nash deftly reached under my sweater to connect my right arm with my right sleeve. He guided the entire limb safely home. A delicious tingle shot through me; I knew my face was flushed.

"Thanks," I mumbled.

"My pleasure. Any time." Our gazes locked just long enough for his coppery eyes to penetrate mine. I was sure he saw clear through to my brain waves, which were screaming, "I want you bad!"

Nash said a few things to Odette. Then he was gone, moving along the bar to shake hands and trade pleasantries with other patrons. He didn't help anyone else put a shirt on, however.

If only Nash weren't the father of my late husband's grandchildren. Bottom line: If only he weren't determined to make up with my late husband's daughter. Nash and Avery had produced twins as the result of a one-night stand. She expected me, Leo's widow, to finance her new family since her kids were Leo's heirs. But Nash was determined to do the right thing. On sabbatical from the University of Florida, where they'd met, he tracked Avery down. She and the twins were living with me; now Nash was courting her. Under my roof.

"Where's the camisole?" Odette hissed.

"Waiting to be washed. You should have bought me *two*."

"You can afford a second. I suggest you buy it tomorrow. And start wearing it in public! You need to replace the image of that hideous brassiere now burned into our retinas. . . ."

Walter St. Mary appeared on the other side of the bar. He glanced from my beverage to me. "You've hardly touched it! I thought the Leprechaun made you do it."

"The what?"

"The Leprechaun. Where I come from, that's what we call Irish whiskey and tonic. It's been known to make a few lasses take off their shirts." Walter winked.

"It didn't—I didn't—." I gave up.

Mother Tucker's proprietor checked his watch. "They're crowning Miss Blossom at 2:30. Isn't your office intern one of the contestants?"

"Faye Raffle," confirmed Odette. "She's going to win. I've got fifty dollars riding on it."

I turned to Odette in disgust. "You bet on a beauty pageant?"

"I bet on our office intern. If Faye wins, I'll donate the money to her college tuition fund. So will everyone else in the office."

"There was a pool? Why didn't I know about it?"

"Try reading your office bulletin board."

"Jonny's one of the judges," Walter said, referring to his partner in both business and real life. "Rico Anuncio was supposed to be on the panel, but he didn't return from his cruise in time. Jonny's nervous about making the right choice. He's never had mainstream taste in female beauty."

"I'm sure he'll do fine," I said as I handed Walter my credit card. "I'd trust his taste over Rico's any day."

Odette snorted in agreement. She and I disliked the flamboyant owner of the West Shore Gallery. The previous fall Rico had threatened us with a frivolous lawsuit, for which we weren't yet ready to forgive him. We'd enjoyed every day he was gone on his round-the-world cruise. My secret hope was that he'd fall in love with an exotic person or place and forget all about returning to our town. Odette would be more than happy to get him an astonishing price for his Magnet Springs home. Rumor had it that he was due back soon, however.

While Walter processed my plastic, I asked Odette, "Do you really think Faye can win? I hear Tammi LePadanni's daughter's drop-dead gorgeous."

Tammi LePadanni was a part-time agent in our office. In other words, a hobbyist. I kept her on staff for one reason only: She was a doctor's wife; ergo, she knew rich people.

Odette made a rude raspberry noise. "You're forgetting the Q-and-A portion of the competition. Tammi LePadanni's daughter couldn't speak a declarative statement at gunpoint."

"Really?"

"Really. You've got to hear her to believe it. Everything from her Angelina Jolie lips sounds like a question." Odette glanced at her diamond-studded wristwatch. "The fun starts in five minutes. Let's go!"

I hastily completed my credit card receipt to include the usual 25% tip for Walter. Since he never charged me full price for anything, I was always trying to say thanks.

"What's Tammi LePadanni's daughter's name?" I asked Odette. "Don't tell me it rhymes, too."

"Brandi LePadanni. Feel a kinship to the girl?"

"I don't drink my name, and I hope she doesn't drink hers," I quipped. "Especially since she's underage."

"And is Whiskey your real name?" Odette asked innocently.

"You know it isn't. Are you saying Brandi's a nickname, too?"

"Short for Brandolina. Awful, isn't it? Tammi's parents loved Marlon Brando."

"Then why not name her Marla? By the way, I've met Dr. LePadanni. He looks like late-stage Brando. Wonder where the daughter got her good looks. Mom's no beauty queen, and Dad's a real barker."

"Speaking of canines," Odette said, "what's the latest on yours?"

I cringed as I always did at the mention of Abra. The Afghan hound was my late husband's legacy and, second only to my real-estate business, my biggest headache. Aside from her penchant for stealing purses and other forbidden treats, Abra was high maintenance in the extreme. Just grooming her long blonde tresses required more time and patience than I was born with. Add to that her propensity for escape. And for consorting with criminals.

"Last I checked, Deely was installing a mesh cover over the kennel," I said. "And laying concrete along the fence line. Hopefully that will contain the bitch."

"Which one?"

I grinned. I'd hired Deely Smarr, fondly known as the Coast Guard nanny, to assist my shrewish stepdaughter and her infant twins, but the capable woman was also babysitting Abracadabra. She had the perfect background for the job: Military Damage Control. An expert at fixing boats, guns, and assorted life forms, Deely had only one flaw that I could see. She was a founding member of Fleggers—a.k.a. Four Legs Good—a radical animal rights advocacy based in Ann Arbor. Deely believed that animals, including Abra, were our equals. A terrifying premise. Nonetheless, she understood that the general public needed protection from my dog.

Odette and I were crossing Main Street toward Town Square where Miss Blossom was about to be crowned when we spotted my office manager Tina Breen. She was easy to spot because she was jumping up and down and waving her arms.

"Whiskey! Oh my god, Whiskey!" Tina shrieked in her dentist's drill voice. "Abra is loose again! She stole Miss Blossom's tiara!"

That was a big deal. In fact, it was a felony.

Magnet Springs has been a tourist town since before the Civil War. As a result, our long and convoluted history has spawned many an insane tradition, one of which is this: Miss Blossom is annually crowned with a tiara made of solid gold and emeralds, a bequest from the obscenely rich widowed mother of the first Miss Blossom. Legend has it that back in 1847, Mrs. Slocum Schuyler was so proud of her beauty queen daughter that she commissioned a tiara. Upon her death, Mrs. Schuyler bequeathed the tiara to the village of Magnet Springs expressly for the coronation of all subsequent Miss Blossoms. We've been obsessed with safeguarding the damn thing ever since.

"Look!" screeched Tina Breen, pointing across Town Square. Sure enough, there went my big amber dog, a glistening green crown gripped in her pearly whites.